SHEYANNE WARREN

THE MANIFESTED
Lie

TWO REALMS.
ONE UNFORGIVABLE LIE.

SHEYANNE WARREN

The Manifested Lie

First published by Forever Seven Press 2026

Copyright © 2026 by Sheyanne Warren

All rights reserved. No part of this publication may be reproduced, stored or transmitted in any form or by any means, electronic, mechanical, photocopying, recording, scanning, or otherwise without written permission from the publisher. It is illegal to copy this book, post it to a website, or distribute it by any other means without permission.

This novel is entirely a work of fiction. The names, characters and incidents portrayed in it are the work of the author's imagination. Any resemblance to actual persons, living or dead, events or localities is entirely coincidental.

Sheyanne Warren asserts the moral right to be identified as the author of this work.

Sheyanne Warren has no responsibility for the persistence or accuracy of URLs for external or third-party Internet Websites referred to in this publication and does not guarantee that any content on such Websites is, or will remain, accurate or appropriate.

This work may not be used to train artificial intelligence systems, machine learning models, large language models, or similar technologies, nor may it be used to generate derivative or synthetic content.

This novel contains mature themes that may be triggering for some readers, including but not limited to: violence, death, grief, trauma, betrayal, emotional manipulation, and morally complex situations. Reader discretion is advised.

First edition

ISBN: 979-8-9856989-5-4

Editing by Shelley Lopez

*This book was professionally typeset on Reedsy.
Find out more at reedsy.com*

Contents

Pronunciations	vi
Prologue	1

I Spellbound Shenanigans

Gargoyles, Gaffes, and Grand Beginnings | Selene	9
Trust, Flight, and Fateful Encounters | Selene	15
Portal Pandemonium | Selene	24
Falling From Grace |Selene	29
Portal Misadventures | Selene	37
Inheritance of Secrets | Selene	45
Open Sesame | Selene	51
Maps, Memories, and Misunderstandings | Selene	61
Trust, Betrayal, and Truth | Selene	70
Pressure, Power, and an Unwanted Jump Scare | Selene	82
Riddle in the Dark | Selene	93
Manifestation & Mistrust | Selene	100
The Truth at Last | Selene	109
The Seeker's Shadow | Selene	117
A Fate We Cannot Change| Leia	125
Training, Terror, and a Mild Existential Crisis | Selene	129
Odessa, Please Leave | Selene	140

II One Quest Down, I Hope No More To Go

Split Up, They Said. It'll Be Fine, They Said| Selene	149
Jungle Spirits and Emotional Damage| Astrid	157
Bound by Roots, Freed by Fire | Selene	161
Only One Lies	171
Not the only Bloodline | Selene	184
We Are Not Ready | Selene	193
I Feel Stupid | Astrid	199
I Regret Nothing | Selene	202
The Things She Didn't Say | Leia	208
Her Voice, Not Mine | Selene	212
Fire Donuts	220
Nothing Suspicious, Just Totally Normal Students | Selene	225
Mama Said Knock You Out | Selene	234
They didn't ask for the truth | Leia	240
The Bond Beneath | Selene	244
Not My King | Selene	251

III Oh, when it all (yeah), it all falls down (this the real one, baby)

Spiderweb of Lies | Selene	257
The Path Beneath | Selene	263
Where Shadows Remember | Selene	268
The Seeker's Game | Selene	274
The Second Gates Open | Selene	278
The Hollowed Bargain | Caspian	284
The Shattered Choice | Selene	290
The Fractured Hollow | Selene	294

Flood and Flame | Selene	299
The Cost of Power | Selene	306
After The Storm | Selene	313
Magic? Never Heard of Her | Selene	320
Note To The Readers	323
Discussion Leader's Guide	325
General Questions To Discuss	329
Faith-Based Questions To Discuss	334
About the Author	342
Also by Sheyanne Warren	344

Pronunciations

Selene Trueshadow - Se/l/ee/n

Astrid Wolflance - A/s/trid

Caspian - Cas/Pee/in

Zephyr Heray - Ze/f/r

Sunna Flatbash - Sun/nah

Killian - Kill/e/an

Ereriath - air-ER-ee-ath

Odreazah - oh-DREE-uh-zah

Prologue

My heart pounded in my chest as I dashed through the dense forest, leaves and branches whipping past me. My skin—a beautiful shade of rich, dark cocoa—glistened with a light sheen of sweat. My curly, voluminous hair bounced with each stride, a crown of wild beauty that framed my face like an untamed halo. Its ebony strands mirrored the dark shadows of the woods around me.

I heard the thunderous roar of the dragon behind me, its wings flapping with menacing fury. I knew I couldn't outrun it forever.

With every stride, I reached deep within myself, tapping into the well of energy that fueled my gift. I didn't dare look back, fearing that even a moment of distraction could be my downfall. Instead, I focused on the trees surrounding me, my mind connecting with the ancient roots hidden beneath the forest floor.

I felt a stinging heat slap my back—I screamed and stumbled. Tears sprang to my eyes as branches sliced through my legs. My eyes, the color of warm, melted chocolate, darted around me, scanning for any more signs of obstacles. I didn't dare take a breath. Quickly I got back on my feet. I shifted course, turning left from my original path and shooting forward.

"Move!" I commanded in my mind.

The roots responded, rising from the earth like guardians coming to life. They formed a tangled barricade behind me, hoping to slow down the relentless predator. But I knew it wouldn't be enough. The dragon let out a terrifying roar. The roots split and cracked behind me before its explosive force broke through my defense.

As I ran, I felt my power surge through me, seeking another source of energy to aid my escape. A swarm of fireflies danced up ahead, and I directed them with a thought, creating a dazzling, luminescent cloud of distraction. The dragon hesitated, momentarily captivated by the glowing spectacle, which allowed me to put some distance between us.

My athletic frame propelled me forward, muscles working in harmony. There was no room for aches and pains, so I shoved them down and kept going. With another thought, the fireflies attacked—swarming to hide my path from the dragon's sight.

I turned right and headed down a dirt path. Relief hit me so hard it made me stumble. But the dragon was fast, much faster than I'd given it credit for. Its scorching breath brushed against my back, and I could feel pinpoints of pain spreading across my body. I needed something more substantial to stop it.

Ahead, a massive boulder loomed, and desperation fueled my focus. "Move!" I commanded again, pushing with all my might. The boulder seemed to wiggle but didn't move. I whimpered. No, there was no room for that. Taking a deep breath, I pulled from all the power I had, slowing down slightly to draw from that energy too. "Move!" I shouted, this time out loud.

The ground rumbled when the boulder tore itself from the earth, soaring through the air and crashing down before the dragon. The boulder's impact sent me flying. I hit the ground hard—my bones grinding in unnatural ways—before I forced myself back into a sprint. The beast roared in fury, struggling to get past the obstruction.

PROLOGUE

I pushed myself harder, the strain of using my power beginning to take its toll. Panting, chest heaving, and my legs burning, but I couldn't stop. The Academy of Arcane Wonders was not far, and I knew I had to reach its safety.

Bursting into a small clearing, I saw a stream sparkling in the sunlight. With a last reserve of energy, I lifted the water into the air, forming a cascading wall to blind the dragon. The beast roared again, but with its eyes obscured, I gained the advantage. My feet barely touched the water's surface as I sprinted across, my power pulsing around me. The dragon's pursuit was relentless, its fiery breath only a short distance away. But I had to make it to the Academy—I had to survive.

Finally I had reached the safety of the Academy's wall. I learned against the brick and mortar, catching my breath, my heart still pounding from the chase, when I heard the thundering roar of the dragon drawing closer once more. Panic surged through me as I realized the dragon was not far behind and was not giving up easily. Just as I braced myself for another desperate attempt to fend off the beast, a familiar voice called out, "Leia, look out!"

I turned to see Kofi—my boyfriend and a master of pyromancy—racing toward me with determination blazing in his eyes. Without hesitation, he lifted his hands, and in a dazzling display of fiery prowess, conjured a pair of blazing swords. Twin flames danced along the blades as he dashed forward to join me in the battle against the relentless dragon.

"Stand back, Leia!" he commanded, positioning himself between me and the approaching menace. His eyes locked onto the dragon, and his fiery weapons seemed to respond to his every thought. Kofi's dark skin glistened under the rays of the moon. Every step he took was purposeful, his well-developed muscular frame mirroring the immense power within.

With a strong, chiseled jawline and expressive, deep-set eyes that mirrored the warmth of his soul, Kofi's face betrayed years of war and hardships. His eyes, the color of dark cocoa, demanded the attention of everyone. His coiled, textured hair framed his face like a crown of glory—worn with pride as a symbol of heritage. As the moon's rays danced on his hair, it created a halo of ethereal beauty around him.

As the dragon charged, Kofi met it head-on, wielding his blazing swords with precision. With every swipe and thrust, he sent arcs of searing heat slicing through the air, forcing the dragon to veer away and giving us a moment of respite. I watched in awe as Kofi danced with the dragon, his movements fluid and graceful despite the chaos. He was like a force of nature, commanding fire and steel to protect us. It was then I realized I wasn't alone in this battle; I had someone by my side—someone willing to risk everything for me.

Kofi's eyes met mine for a brief moment, and I saw a flicker of determination and reassurance. I knew I could trust him with my life. As the dragon lunged again, Kofi summoned a wall of fire between us and the beast, buying us a precious few seconds to catch our breath.

"We can't hold it off forever," he said, his voice steady in the chaos. "We need a plan."

I nodded, my mind racing with possibilities. "There's a nearby cliff. If we can lead the dragon there, maybe we can trap it."

Kofi's eyes lit up with excitement. "Good idea. We'll have to work together, Leia."

With renewed determination, Kofi's blazing swords and my powers worked in tandem. We drew the dragon's attention, leading it toward the cliff's edge. The ground trembled beneath its weight, and I could feel the heat of its breath on my skin as it closed in. As we reached the edge, Kofi unleashed a torrent of fire, engulfing the dragon's wings and momentarily hindering its ability to fly. Seizing the opportunity, I used my abilities to create a powerful gust of wind, pushing the dragon toward the precipice.

With a mighty roar, the dragon teetered on the brink before tumbling over the cliff and disappearing. Kofi and I stood there, breathing heavily, as the dragon's roars faded into the distance. My legs wobbled and I crumbled to the ground, the full extent of my injuries catching up to me as my adrenaline faded.

"We did it," Kofi exclaimed triumphantly as he moved to my side.

"Thank you, Kofi. I couldn't have done it without you."

He grinned, his eyes still gleaming with the intensity of battle. "Anytime, Leia. We make a good team, forever."

We travelled back into the forest, to the spot where I had steered the dragon away. Approaching a tree with its trunk hollowed out to the size of a watermelon, I stopped and smiled at Kofi. "

There she is," I said, and he stepped forward cautiously. He bent down, reached into the tree trunk, and pulled out our everything. Selene giggled and cooed at the sight of her father, and I felt a newfound relief and confidence. He cuddled her and then looked at me. "Come on, let's go."

The three of us headed back to the Academy and a surge of hope filled me. We were home and safe.

I

Spellbound Shenanigans

Gargoyles, Gaffes, and Grand Beginnings | Selene

The Academy of Arcane Wonders towered before me, an awe-inspiring sight nestled deep within an ancient forest. I had seen sketches of the place in old books, but nothing prepared me for the real thing. The enchanted vines wrapping around the towers shimmered as they caught the fading sunlight, their colors constantly shifting between shades of blue, green, and violet. It was like the entire structure was breathing magic.

Two massive stone golems flanked the entrance, their eyes glowing with a cold, ghostly light. Symbols carved into their bodies pulsed faintly as if warning anyone who might approach with ill intentions. I shuddered as their glowing eyes seemed to lock onto me. Were they sizing me up? Determining if I was worthy? A voice deep inside me whispered, *Keep moving.*

Taking a deep breath, I passed under the colossal archway. My eyes widened as the courtyard stretched out before me. It was like something out of a dream. At its center, an elaborate fountain sprayed water in delicate arcs, enchanted droplets glittering in the twilight. Statues of mythical creatures—griffins, phoenixes, and dragons—adorned the fountain's base, their features so lifelike I half-expected them to spring to life. The academy's towers spiraled toward the heavens, their peaks disappearing into misty clouds. Gargoyles perched at the edges of the rooftops, their stony faces twisted into various expressions. I felt their gazes on me as I walked by, a chill crawling down my spine.

Students bustled around the courtyard, their various hued robes denoting different areas of study. Some hurried between towering trees and colorful flowerbeds that seemed to bloom perpetually, while others sat in small groups, their heads bent together in animated discussion. The air thrummed with magic—a buzz of energy I could almost taste. I paused for a moment to take it all in, my heart racing.

"This place is insane," Astrid whispered beside me. I turned to see her staring wide-eyed, her short hair catching the last rays of sunlight. She grinned at me, her excitement contagious. "We're really here, Lee."

"Yeah," I breathed, still in awe. "We made it."

We passed through a series of arched corridors, the walls lined with animated paintings that told stories of the academy's legendary past. Figures in the portraits paused to observe us as we walked by. Soft, haunting music drifted through the air, though I couldn't tell where it was coming from.

It felt like the academy was alive—breathing, watching, waiting.

"I've never seen anything like this," Astrid murmured. She reached out to touch a wall, her fingers brushing a patch of ivy that shimmered like liquid stardust.

"Me neither," I admitted. The weight of expectation settled on my shoulders. This place was legendary, not just for its beauty but for its history. My parents had walked these very halls years ago, their names still whispered with reverence. Leia and Kofi Trueshadow—top of their class, renowned mages who had somehow managed to raise a child while mastering their crafts. Now, here I was, expected to follow in their footsteps.

No pressure.

We finally reached the dormitory, a sprawling building with ivy-covered walls and large, arched windows. Inside, the air was warm and welcoming, filled with the scent of aged wood and something floral I couldn't quite place. The common room was bustling with activity. Students laughed and chatted.

Astrid led the way up the creaky stairs, barely containing her excitement.

"Second floor, left side. It better not smell like potion fumes," she muttered.

Our room was tucked into a corner, with a slanted ceiling and dust motes dancing in a shaft of afternoon light. Two beds, two desks, and a window that framed the forest like a moving painting. It wasn't grand, but it felt like the kind of place where secrets might bloom.

I dropped my bag on the bed nearest the window, trying to ignore the thrum of magic beneath my skin. New room. New world. Same tangled nerves.

"This is it," I whispered.

"I can't believe we're actually here," Astrid said again, flopping onto her bed with a grin. "The Academy of Arcane Wonders! It's like a dream come true."

I grinned, but a part of me couldn't shake the nervous flutter in my stomach. I was excited, sure, but there was also a nagging fear that I didn't belong here. My powers hadn't manifested yet. What if they never did? What if I spent all my time here as an ordinary girl in a school full of magical prodigies?

My thoughts were interrupted by Astrid's voice. "Hey, have

you heard about the Elemental Exhibition tonight?" she asked, holding up a pamphlet that was laying on the desk. "It's a tradition here. The upper-year students showcase their magical abilities. Apparently, it's a huge deal."

I froze. The Elemental Exhibition. I had heard about it during orientation, and I knew exactly why Astrid was bringing it up. It was the perfect opportunity to see him—Zephyr.

The thought of him sent a shiver down my spine. I'd noticed him the moment I arrived at the academy. He stood out in a crowd, not just because of his features but because of the confident and regal way he carried himself. His dark, tightly curled hair framed a face that was both beautiful and intimidating, and his piercing green eyes...I'd never seen eyes like that before. They seemed to see right through you, like he knew all your secrets.

I'd overheard other students talking about him. His parents were renowned for their mastery of Ice Magic, and everyone was curious to see if Zephyr had inherited their abilities.

"Sounds interesting," I said, trying to sound casual.

Astrid gave me a knowing look. "Uh-huh. What's that tone?"

"What tone?" I asked, feigning innocence.

She narrowed her eyes. "Don't play dumb with me. I know you, Selene. You're up to something."

I rolled my eyes and stared at the floor, hiding my blush. "I have no idea what you're talking about."

"Sure you don't." Astrid's grin widened. "Come on, let's get ready. We don't want to miss the show."

As evening fell, we joined the students making their way to the Exhibition Hall, the air buzzing with anticipation. Inside, the hall was transformed into a magical arena. Floating lanterns cast a warm, golden glow over the crowd, and the stage at the center pulsed with energy.

The performances were nothing short of great. Water mages danced gracefully, manipulating streams of water in mesmerizing patterns. Fire flared and crackled as pyromancers showed off their control over the element. Earth mages summoned towering vines and stone constructs.

But my mind was elsewhere. I scanned the crowd, searching for Zephyr. When I finally spotted him, my heart skipped a beat. He stood near the edge of the hall, his dark robes accentuating his rich ebony skin. His green eyes seemed to catch the light, glowing faintly as he watched the performances. He exuded an air of quiet confidence, completely at ease in the chaotic energy of the exhibition.

Astrid followed my gaze and snorted. "Ah, there it is. That's the tone."

"Oh, hush," I muttered, my cheeks burning.

She elbowed me playfully. "You've got it bad," she teased.

I shook my head, trying to focus on the performances. But no matter how hard I tried, my eyes kept drifting back to Zephyr. There was something magnetic about him, something that drew me in.

As the performances continued, I felt a twinge of self-doubt. These students made magic look effortless, their abilities honed to perfection. Meanwhile, I was still waiting for my powers to manifest. Would I ever be able to stand on that stage and command magic with such ease?

"How am I supposed to do all that when I can't even manifest yet?" I whispered to Astrid.

She gave me a reassuring smile. "You'll get there. Everyone starts somewhere. Besides, you've got potential—I can feel it."

I wanted to believe her, but the doubt lingered. As the final act unfolded and the hall erupted in applause, I was determined. I was here for a reason. My journey was just beginning, and I was ready to face whatever challenges lay ahead.

After the exhibition, Astrid and I made our way back to the dormitory, our heads buzzing with excitement. But just when I thought the night was over, something unexpected happened.

Bump. Bump.

We froze, glancing at each other. The sound had come from the direction of my dresser—or rather, the armoire.

"Did you hear that?" I whispered.

"No," Astrid whispered back, her voice trembling slightly.

"Then why are you whispering?" I hissed.

Bump. Bump.

The sound came again, louder this time. My heart pounded in my chest.

"Okay, that's definitely not normal," I muttered.

"Maybe it's just...a magical glitch?" Astrid suggested, unconvinced.

We slowly approached the armoire, and Astrid nudged me forward. "You open it," she said.

"Why me?"

"Because you're the brave one," she snorted.

I rolled my eyes. "Fine. But if something jumps out at me, I'm blaming you."

With a deep breath, I reached for the handle. The moment my fingers brushed the wood, a sudden burst of light blinded me. I stumbled back, shielding my eyes.

When the light faded, everything had changed.

Trust, Flight, and Fateful Encounters | Selene

Something grabbed my arm and yanked me closer. My instincts screamed at me to pull back. Instead, I stared into the eyes of this new glorious creature, my body tense and ready. Astrid turned her gaze toward me, searching for answers I didn't have. Then she looked back at the newcomer with the blazing eyes.

"Who are you?" Astrid asked defiantly.

The beautiful creature's lips curved into a sly smile. "So many questions," she mused as she gestured toward a valley nestled between two colossal peaks that had replaced the Academy's dorm room. "This way," she said, her voice as light as the air itself. Then, to our shock, she rose gracefully, floating mid-air like it was the most natural thing in the world.

Astrid blinked at me and back at floating being. "Um... we can't fly," she called out, her words almost apologetic.

The floating woman paused, turning back with an exasperated expression. "All is possible in the Realm of Odreazah. If you wish to fly, it will be so."

Astrid snorted. "Yeah, no. We're normal people. Normal people can't fly."

Those glowing eyes narrowed as she descended. Her feet

barely made a sound as they touched the ground. "This will take twice as long," she muttered under her breath before turning on her heel. "Come."

Astrid glanced at me as we hesitantly followed. "So, we're just going to trust this weapon-wielding creature and follow her through a magical realm?" she whispered harshly.

"What other choice do we have?" I hissed back. "You want to tell her no?"

Astrid huffed but didn't argue. As we walked, I marveled at our surroundings. The landscape transformed with each step. Rolling green hills cushioned our feet, and vibrant gardens sprawled on either side of us. Flowers in impossible hues towered over us like sentinels, while others were so tiny they grew off the petals of larger blooms.

As we entered the valley, a subtle dimming of light caught my attention. The sun's rays weakened, as if reluctant to venture further. Astrid shivered. "Yup," she whispered. "We're walking straight to our deaths. Even the sun's too scared to stick around."

An ethereal voice echoed ahead. "There will be no harm to Selene and her comrades in this realm."

The air grew heavier as we moved deeper into the valley, like the very ground was holding its breath.

A cluster of shimmering stones lay across the path glowing with a soft lavender pulse. They looked like they'd been placed intentionally. A message, maybe. Or a warning.

"Wait," Astrid said, narrowing her eyes. "That's not natural."

"It's fine," I said, already stepping forward. "They're just enchanted markers. I read about them. They're used to guide travelers."

"Yeah, or trap them," Astrid hissed.

But I was already moving. The second my boot landed on one of the stones, the ground beneath us *sank*—not a pit, but something worse. The air shimmered, and then we were standing in *nothingness*.

The valley was gone.

The path, the sky, even our guide.

"SELENE!" Astrid's voice echoed beside me—but her hand wasn't in mine anymore.

Then I was falling.

Not fast. Not down. Just... *away*.

Until something jerked me back—like a tether yanking on my chest—and I gasped, blinking back into the valley again, coughing on air like I hadn't breathed in hours.

Our guide was there. And furious.

"You stepped into a phase trap," she snapped. "Had I not marked your signature, you'd still be falling between worlds."

Astrid grabbed my arm. "Are you *trying* to die?"

I couldn't even speak. My throat was dry. My pride, worse.

"I thought I was right," I whispered, too ashamed to meet her eyes.

The woman turned, cloak snapping. "You thought without knowing. And in Odreazah, that's how people vanish."

Her words echoed into a tense silence. Astrid and I exchanged a look, both of us too shaken to speak. I swallowed hard, my pride bruised more than anything else.

I turned slightly toward Astrid. "She heard us," I muttered.

"Great," Astrid sighed. "So, uhhh, Ma'am, where are we going?"

"My name is Nyx Warrior of Odreazah Service to the King and Queen," she said. "King Victor and Queen Grizél have been awaiting your return."

My face scrunched in disbelief. "My return? I'd remember if I'd been here before."

Astrid shook her head. "Yeah, and I'm pretty sure I'd know too."

Nyx slowed and turned, her piercing gaze locking onto mine. "You are certain you remember nothing?"

"Nothing," I said firmly.

Her expression hardened for a split second before she masked it. "You will understand soon enough."

Astrid elbowed me lightly, signaling for me to keep my mouth shut. "Don't get mad at me for not knowing stuff," I snapped, ignoring her.

Nyx glared at us. "You refused to fly, so we walk."

"We can't fly!" Astrid and I shouted in unison.

Nyx rolled her eyes. "Give me your hands," she ordered, holding out her palms.

Astrid and I exchanged hesitant glances.

"I swear on King Victor and Queen Grizél, I will cause you no harm," Nyx said with a sigh.

Astrid hesitated before grumbling under her breath. "We don't even know those people."

"What happened to not pissing off magical warrior women?" I reminded her. I reluctantly placed my hand in Nyx's.

The moment our hands touched, a strange sensation surged through my body. My feet lifted off the ground, and I let out a startled yelp. I felt weightless, like I'd just shed a hundred pounds. My arms flailed instinctively, trying to find balance.

"Child," Nyx said through gritted through her teeth. "Willing yourself forward is all it takes. This is not a balance beam."

Taking a deep breath, I focused. I willed myself forward, and my body shot upward like a rocket. An exhilarated giggle that escaped my lips. I soared higher and higher until Nyx's voice cut through the euphoria.

"Watch yourself, child! The higher you go, the less human oxygen there is to breathe."

I slowed my ascent and gently floated back toward the ground. Nyx turned to Astrid, her hand extended once more. "Are you ready now?"

Astrid swallowed hard and nodded. She cautiously took Nyx's hand. The moment her feet left the ground, her eyes went wide. "Holy shit," she gasped, giggling uncontrollably. "This is insane!"

"Let go of my hand," Nyx said flatly.

Astrid immediately began spinning in the air, shrieking. "Make it stop! I'm going to hurl!"

Nyx sighed and tapped Astrid's arm, stabilizing her. "Calm your mind. Control comes from within."

Astrid took several deep breaths, her body gradually coming to a stop. We followed Nyx through the air, marveling at the surreal landscape below. Astrid veered dangerously close to trees.

"Astrid, seriously. Chill," I urged.

Before us, a castle emerged from the horizon, taking my breath away. It was a masterpiece of alabaster walls, silver spires, and sparkling enchanted gardens. A shimmering moat surrounded the structure, guarded by water nymphs that glided gracefully through the waters.

"Oh my gods," I whispered in awe. "Is that where the King and Queen live?"

Nyx floated down elegantly. Astrid, not so much. She crashed to the ground with a graceless thud.

"There's legit a King and Queen?" Astrid muttered. "I thought you were joking."

"I do not lie," Nyx said with a tone that brooked no argument. "Follow me."

The massive oak doors of the castle opened as we approached.

"How did she do that?" Astrid whispered.

"Her presence was sensed," Nyx answered matter-of-factly.

Astrid glared at her. "Stop listening to me when I'm whispering!"

Nyx smirked. "If you know I hear all, why continue to whisper?"

Astrid huffed. We stepped into a grand hall where candlelight flickered along ancient stone walls. Tapestries told stories of both triumph and tragedy. Suits of armor stood like silent sentinels, their dark designs intimidating.

"Don't touch anything," I hissed when Astrid reached for a sword.

"Listen to Selene. She is wise," Nyx said with a grin.

Astrid scowled but obeyed. As we ascended a spiral staircase, the mystical atmosphere shifted. The top floor was stark and modern, with white walls and minimalist furnishings. A large fireplace crackled invitingly as two figures sat waiting.

"Ah, finally," a regal woman said, clapping her hands. "Victor, our guests have arrived."

Nyx bowed low. "King Victor and Queen Grizél of Odreazah, I present Selene of Leia and Kofi Trueshadow, and Astrid of Michael and Luna Wolfance."

The Queen's eyes sparkled. "What are your manifestations?"

Astrid perked up. "I control wind."

The Queen nodded before turning her gaze to me. I shifted uncomfortably under her scrutiny.

"I haven't manifested yet," I mumbled.

The King frowned. "None at all?"

"No," I admitted.

Queen Grizél smiled kindly and placed a comforting hand on my shoulder. "We can help with that."

Astrid's head snapped toward her. "You can? How?"

"With the help of our son, Caspian," the Queen said.

A voice echoed from the far end of the room. "You called, Mother?"

I turned and froze. Caspian's presence was magnetic, his mahogany eyes locking onto mine. I felt my heart race as he approached.

Astrid nudged me with a grin. "This just got interesting."

I stood there, still reeling from Nyx's demonstration and the whirlwind of surreal events that had carried us into this strange new realm. Caspian's magnetic presence suddenly filled the space between us. His eyes, deep and earnest, locked onto mine.

"Selene," he said softly, "are you ready to discover your power?"

I swallowed hard, my heart pounding in my ears. I had been so afraid of not manifesting, of never living up to the legacy of my Mom and Dad.

Before I could muster a response, he reached into the folds of his cloak and produced a sleek phone that glowed with subtle, iridescent magic. I blinked.

"This is for you," Caspian said, extending the phone into my trembling hand.

I turned the device over in my hands, marveling at its smooth surface and the way it hummed with an energy that resonated with something deep within me. I wondered if it was somehow linked to the magic I'd been desperate to manifest.

I looked up at him, my voice barely above a whisper. "Thank

you," I said, with a mixture of gratitude and hope.

Caspian smiled, that familiar gentle warmth in his eyes. "You're welcome, Selene. Remember, magic isn't just about casting spells—it's about discovering who you are, and sometimes, who you're meant to be."

As I clutched the phone, I felt a surge of determination. The weight of my legacy no longer felt like a burden; instead, it became a beacon, guiding me toward the promise of my own magic. With Caspian's encouragement echoing in my mind, I took a deep breath, ready to embrace the uncertain, exhilarating journey that lay ahead.

"Selene," The Queen said, her eyes reflecting the flicker of enchanted candlelight, "in this realm, time flows not as you know it but like a river that meanders through dreams. What seems like a fleeting moment to you may be an eternity for us, and hours can vanish like whispers on the wind. We knew your parents—Leia and Kofi—long before you arrived. They were extraordinary. Though I cannot share all the secrets of our past now, know that their legacy lives on in you."

Her mysterious words stirred something inside me—a mix of comfort and a burning curiosity about the life I was only beginning to understand.

Just then, the door creaked open and another young man traipsed in, a confident smile playing on his lips.

"I'm Killian, their Majesties favorite son," he introduced. He strode up to us and lightly grasped Astrid's hand, barely brushing his lips against the back of it.

Astrid's widened in delight—she practically drooled at the sight of him. Their brief exchange added a light-hearted counterpoint to the gravity of the moment, and I found myself smiling at the absurdity of it all.

Clutching the phone tighter, I felt the weight of destiny and the promise of magic intertwining within me.

Portal Pandemonium | Selene

We landed with a thud. I was still sprawled on the floor while Astrid quickly bounced to her feet, exclaiming, "They couldn't let us down easy?"

I barely had time to catch my breath as I watched the portal swirling, shrinking until—poof—it vanished into nothingness. "Did we just go through a portal to a magical realm, and meet a warrior, a king, a queen, and their prince sons?" I managed to squeak out.

A huge grin spread across Astrid's face as she screeched, "We have the best life, ever!" and began jumping up and down.

I forced a smile as I propped myself up. I patted my pockets until I found the phone Caspian had given me. Holding it up toward Astrid, I said, "And we have this."

Astrid lunged at me and snatched the phone away. I watched her intently as she started typing away on the screen, then giggled and held the device up so I could see. Squinting in confusion, I asked, "What?"—only to find the screen displaying a simple message thread: "Killian says hi." Astrid practically drooled over it.

Rolling my eyes, I reached for the phone. "We're definitely going to have to ask about getting you your own phone," I teased.

With a resigned sigh, I walked over to my bed and tucked the phone under my pillow.

Astrid sucked her teeth. "Wow, great hiding place, Lee. No one will ever find it there," she remarked. I opened my mouth to retort, then shut it again. "It'll be fine for now. Come on, we were going to go eat before we got swept into Odreazah."

"Yes, food. I'm down," Astrid agreed, glancing at the clock on the wall. "I should take my bag too. I have class in an hour." Following her gaze to the grand clock, I sighed and thought, *Me too. Manifest, here I come.*

Astrid and I made our way to the café. "This is way less busy than the last time we were in here," I commented loudly.

"Yeah, that's what happens when they don't make us all eat at the same time. Let's hurry—we don't have a lot of time," she replied.

We split up to grab our food, then regrouped by the beverage station. Astrid mixed three different things into her cup, prompting me to wrinkle my nose. "Eww, Addy, have you ever tasted that before? What if you don't like it?" I teased.

Astrid just grinned. "That's the fun part."

After gathering our trays, we moved to a table by the big windows. Just as we settled down, another girl set her tray on the table. Astrid and I exchanged amused glances. "Oh, umm," the girl said nervously, "I really want to sit by the window," as she gazed dreamily outside.

Astrid rolled her eyes, and I elbowed her playfully. "Wanna sit with us?" I asked. The girl's eyes lit up as she quickly replied, "Yes!" and joined our table.

"I'm Sunna. Sunna Flatbash," she introduced herself, and then I chimed in, "I'm Selene Trueshadow, Lee, and this is Astrid Wolflance, Addy" while I pointed to Astrid

"Hey Sunna. Are you a first-year?" Astrid asked.

"Yeah," Sunna replied with her mouth full of food, "and I know you," she said teasingly, pointing her fork at me. "You're the daughter of the great Leia and Kofi Trueshadow. Your parents are legends!"

I looked down, my cheeks burning

"Or are you like, a celebrity kid who doesn't understand your parents' fame?" the girl joked further. Before I could find a retort, Astrid jumped in, "She didn't think anyone would know them here—they went here a while ago."

"Yeah, but they are the first in Academy history to have a child within the realm, graduate the Academy, and even take their child to the Earth realm," she continued in one breath. I raised my eyebrows and opened my mouth, but nothing came out. Then Astrid asked, "Have you manifested yet?"

I watched her shoulders slump. "No," she sighed, "What about you two?"

"Aerokinesis here," Astrid said, raising her hand. "I haven't manifested yet either," I added.

"Which power do you think you'll have, your mother's or your father's?" Sunna asked more seriously. I shrugged, "I don't know. Which is more cool? Fire or—" Before I could finish, Astrid and Sunna chimed in at once, "Fire!"

Laughter erupted around the table. "So, my next class is about to start. I'm going to Manifest. What about y'all?" Sunna announced, pushing her glasses up with her index finger. Then she swung her bag around and pulled out her tablet, tapping a bit before looking up. "I have Professor Vinocia."

I reached into my pocket and pulled out my folded-up schedule, grinning as I looked at it. "Me too—thank God I'll know someone."

"I have Histories for first-years," Astrid added, holding her crumpled paper schedule.

We walked out, weaving through tables toward the café entrance.

As the hallway widened, we moved side by side, leaving the dormitory buildings behind. Outside, the sun touched every surface, making everything glisten and glow. Towering spires adorned with intricate magical runes reached toward the sky, casting long shadows across the cobblestone courtyard. I watched as some people rushed past while others lounged on the grass or at benches in the square.

We walked through the courtyard to the opposite side, where the roads to the instructional buildings started. All first-years go to the same buildings; we don't mix with other years until second year. The gardens, filled with vibrant, otherworldly flora, surrounded The Academy—their petals seemed to dance in the enchanted sunlight. A gentle breeze carried the scent of mystical herbs, and the distant melody of ethereal creatures added a whimsical touch. Stone gargoyles perched atop the entrance way appeared almost alive in the sunlight, their expressions subtly different from the first time I saw them.

Passing through giant copper doors, we were immediately met with chaos. Signs pointed everywhere: "Manifest this way," "Histories this way," "Weapons and Wonders this way," "Battle Tactics this way." I glanced at Astrid and said, "I guess this is where we part." She rolled her eyes. "Don't be dramatic—I'll see you in Battle Tactics fourth. We have that together."

"I have that too," Sunna squealed.

"There, it's settled," Astrid said as she waved, then walked over to a tall, thin boy who was yelling, "Histories this way!"

Sunna and I linked arms and walked toward a very pretty girl with long hair, holding a sign that read "Manifest this way." We approached her, and she smiled, "Manifest is down the hall. You can't miss it. It's the only door straight ahead; the others are on either the left or right side. Good luck on your first day!"

We turned and walked down the hall. We unlinked our arms to walk through the crowded corridor. I imagined a massive lecture hall like on TV—rows of seats rising up five levels with a little teacher's desk at the front—but this class was nothing like that. Instead, there were ten armchairs arranged in a semi-circle, with one chair directly opposite in the middle and a single stool in front.

Sunna glanced back at me and flashed a quick smile before composing herself and turning around. *Right, we're cool. Not eager first-years*, I thought.

Then, in what felt like slow motion, I sensed that the most terrible thing was about to happen...

Falling From Grace | Selene

The floor was rushing up at me faster than I could comprehend. I threw my hands out, hoping to catch myself. Instead of stopping my fall, the momentum only launched me down faster.

Then, bam—face first. My entire body hit the floor with a painful thud. My book bag flew forward and landed on my head for extra humiliation. Just great. Falling flat on my face in a new class, in front of new people, should've been the worst part. But no, the universe wasn't done laughing at me. The worst part?

Zephyr.

Zephyr Heray, standing over me, offering his hand.

"Damn, are you okay?" he asked, his voice deep and concerned.

My stomach dropped so hard it might've splattered on the tiles. I lay there for a moment, processing. His voice. His presence. And of course, me, sprawled out like roadkill. Lovely.

I adjusted to push myself up. My book bag flopped dramatically over my head, and I winced. I could only imagine how my curls looked right now—probably like a bird's nest on steroids. I peeked up to see Zephyr, his hand still outstretched.

His eyes met mine, warm and gentle. My face heated up

instantly. Sweat beads made their grand appearance, and I'm pretty sure they brought backup. My brain screamed, *Do not make this any worse.*

"Oh my God, Selene!" Sunna's voice screeched across the room, snapping me out of my trance.

I forced a smile and took Zephyr's hand. The contact was brief but electric.

"Thanks," I muttered as he helped me to my feet.

"No problem. Are you sure you're okay?" He gave me a once-over, his gaze traveling quickly from my head to my feet.

Okay, so he was probably just checking to make sure I wasn't injured, not checking me out. But still, Zephyr Heray just looked me up and down. My traitorous lips twitched upward.

Nope. Not now, Selene. Keep it together.

I bit the inside of my cheek to stop my grin. Way to go. First, fall on your face, and now you're standing here looking like an idiot who's about to giggle for no reason.

"Alright, everyone! I'm feeling jealous that the attention isn't on me. Come on, grab a seat," Professor Vinocia clapped his hands, reclaiming the room.

Zephyr motioned for me to go ahead. I walked toward the seats, hoping my face wasn't as red as it felt. There were only three chairs left. I plopped down on the farthest one, exhaling in relief. Sunna slid into the chair next to me. And, of course, Zephyr took the seat on the other side of her.

Pull yourself together, Selene.

I shot a brief glare at Sunna. Why was I annoyed? He let her walk ahead of him, just like he did for me. He was being polite, like a gentleman. Nothing special.

"Welcome to Manifest!" Professor Vinocia exclaimed, pointing at the chalkboard behind him. The chalk moved on its own, writing his name in large, elegant letters.

"I am Professor Vinocia. That's Vin–o–see–a, and my affinity is Telekinesis," he said, clapping his hands with each syllable for emphasis. He sat down, crossing one leg over the other.

"Let's get introductions going, huh? Then we'll jump right in."

He gestured to the student on the far end of the semi-circle. One by one, the class introduced themselves, stating their names and their parents' affinities. When it was Zephyr's turn, I sat up straighter without thinking.

"I'm Zephyr. Both of my parents have Cryokinetic Regeneration," he said.

A girl a few chairs down frowned. "What's that?"

"It means they can manipulate ice" he explained simply.

Professor Vinocia tilted his head. "Interesting. Both your parents have the same affinity?"

Zephyr looked down at his hands. "Yeah. Their marriage was arranged. My mom's mother made sure she married someone with the same ability."

"So, it's a pretty good chance you'll manifest Cryokinetic Regeneration, too?" Professor Vinocia asked.

Zephyr shrugged. "My dad says your parents' affinities don't necessarily determine yours."

"Ah, that's true...kind of." The professor paused, glancing around the room. "Affinities are like DNA. You inherit traits from both parents. Sometimes, though, a dormant gene can activate if both parents' genetic codes align in a certain way. There are always exceptions to the rule."

"So, I might still get CR?" Zephyr asked.

Professor Vinocia nodded. "It's likely, yes."

Profressor Vinocia's eyes scanned over Sunna. She smiled

brightly while she introduced herself.

Then his eyes shifted to me quickly like he couldn't wait for Sunna to shut up. My heart pounded in my chest.

"Ms. Trueshadow. Introduce yourself to the class."

"See? I told you you were a legend," Sunna whispered excitedly. I glanced at her, catching her bright-eyed grin. Great. Now I really felt like I was on display.

Taking a deep breath. "Um, I'm Selene Trueshadow. My mother is Telekinetic, and my father is a Pyromancer."

Professor Vinocia smiled warmly. "Ah, Leia Trueshadow. One of the best pupils I've had. I remember when you were just in diapers."

"Diapers?" A girl—Odessa, I think—sneered from the end of the row.

"I was born here at the Academy," I explained, addressing the entire class.

Odessa's sneer deepened. "Your parents had you while they were here? What were they, like, fourteen?"

My eyes narrowed, and I glared at her. "No. They were older than that, and I'm sure my birth isn't the class's main concern."

"Oh, excuse me for finding it curious," Odessa muttered, rolling her eyes.

Professor Vinocia cleared his throat. "Hey, hey! None of that. We've got a lot of work to do today, so let's stay focused."

He clapped his hands together. "Open your devices and check your dashboards. I've uploaded the syllabus."

"Syllabus?" someone muttered. "I thought this was just about helping us manifest and then leaving."

I powered on my clunky old laptop. Beside me, Sunna snickered.

"What are you going to do with that dinosaur?" she whispered.

I shot her a glare. "Hey, it works."

"You need a tablet. How do you even use a planner or take notes in class?"

I frowned. "You take notes on that thing?" I pointed to the sleek device on her lap.

"Girl, yes. It's my life. All my notebooks, planners, everything's on here. You need to upgrade."

Professor Vinocia clapped his hands again. I ducked my head into my screen, pretending I hadn't just gotten distracted. Already caught not paying attention. Great.

"As I was saying, Manifest is not a year long class. We're not just staring at objects and willing them to move. This is about understanding what's blocking your affinity. Who can tell me why some people can't manifest?"

The room went silent. Slowly, I raised my hand.

"Ah, Ms. Trueshadow. Go ahead."

"Selene, please," I corrected softly. "Um, I always thought it was random. Like, some people just didn't have it. But now...it seems like there's something preventing it from happening?"

"Exactly. Go on."

I hesitated, then continued. "Is it...like a prerequisite? Something blocking us that has to be removed first?"

Another student chimed in. "It's like we have something others don't. Something stopping us from manifesting naturally."

Odessa snorted quietly. "Or maybe some of us aren't strong enough."

I glared at her. "Or maybe some of us just don't have a chip on our shoulder."

Professor Vinocia raised his hands. "Precisely," he said, cutting off any further exchange. "In fact, it's tied to ancient history."

"What's the connection?" Zephyr asked, leaning forward slightly.

"The originators. Four figures chosen by the gods to protect this realm," Professor Vinocia explained. "They were given immense power, but one of them, Hakim, grew jealous of Wyny, the eldest and most trusted."

I scribbled notes as fast as I could. "Jealousy led to blocking powers?"

"Yes," Professor Vinocia replied, pacing slowly in front of the class. "Hakim envied the trust and responsibilities bestowed upon Wyny. He felt overshadowed by his brother's role and the reverence others had for him. So, in a desperate act of vengeance, he cursed Wyny's bloodline, ensuring that many of his descendants would struggle to access their affinities."

A few students exchanged uneasy glances.

"Wait," Sunna interrupted, raising her hand slightly. "So, some of us might be descendants of these cursed families?"

Professor Vinocia nodded. "Correct. And it's our goal to unlock those hidden affinities. The good news is that we have tools and techniques to reverse the block. That's why you're here."

I drummed my fingers against the keyboard. "So...how do we figure out who's descended from which originator?"

"Good question, Selene," the professor said, his eyes gleaming with approval. "Each of you will go through a series of exercises designed to awaken your latent abilities. Over time, patterns will emerge, giving us clues about your lineage."

"Patterns?" Zephyr echoed, folding his arms. "Like what?"

"Similar traits, specific responses to certain challenges," Professor Vinocia explained. "For example, someone with ties to

Wyny's family might exhibit an affinity for earth-based magic or defensive tactics. However, remember that affinities can manifest differently depending on generational changes."

Odessa leaned back in her chair and rolled her eyes. "Sounds like a lot of guesswork."

"Perhaps," the professor replied calmly, "but guesswork informed by centuries of study and experience. Now, if you're done being skeptical, Odessa, perhaps we can move forward?"

The class chuckled. Odessa huffed but stayed silent.

Professor Vinocia walked back to the chalkboard. "Each of you will also be assigned chapters to read from *The Chronicles of Origin.* This text details the history of the originators and the early conflicts between the realms. It's essential reading."

He turned to the board, and chalk scribbled across it again, outlining our assignments.

"Chapters one through ten by tomorrow," he announced as the chalk wrote on the board "Be prepared to discuss the significance of the four originators' powers and the role they played in shaping the modern magical world."

I groaned inwardly. Ten chapters in one night? Was he serious?

Sunna leaned over and whispered, "Guess we know what we're doing tonight."

"Yeah," I muttered. "Homework party."

Zephyr grinned from across Sunna. "Need someone to save you a seat in the study hall?"

My heart skipped a beat. "Uh, no...I mean, maybe. We'll see."

Sunna snickered, and I shot her a warning glance.

Professor Vinocia clapped his hands again. "Alright, class dismissed. Remember—this journey isn't just about learning magic. It's about understanding who you are and where you come from. Now go."

Chairs scraped against the floor as everyone began packing up. I stuffed my laptop into my bag and stood, trying to avoid eye contact with Zephyr as we all shuffled out of the room.

As we exited, Sunna looped her arm through mine. "So... how long have you had that crush on Zephyr?" she teased.

"Shut up," I hissed, my face heating again.

She laughed. "You're so obvious. Come on, let's meet Astrid and figure out where to start with this insane reading assignment."

I sighed, adjusting the strap on my book bag. This whole manifestation journey was already shaping up to be more complicated—and distracting—than I'd expected.

Portal Misadventures | Selene

After 4th hour classes, the four of us—Zephyr, Sunna, Addy, and I—walked back to the dorm building together. The sun hung lower in the sky, casting long shadows across the cobblestones as students rushed past us. I tried to think of any excuse to avoid what I knew was coming.

"We all have History and Weapons homework to do. You guys want to meet up and work on that together?" Zephyr asked.

I bit the inside of my lip, trying to think of a way to suggest just Sunna and Astrid come by without making it weird. Before I could form a single word, Astrid jumped in, grinning like the Cheshire Cat.

"Sure," she blurted out. "We can meet up at dinner and then come back to our room after that. Sounds good?"

Sunna and Zephyr nodded. My jaw tightened as I turned to glare at Astrid, who refused to meet my eyes. She just kept smiling innocently ahead, as if she hadn't just sabotaged my escape plan.

When we reached the dorms, Zephyr veered off toward the boys' wing. The girls and I took the elevator. Sunna got off on the 1st floor with a cheerful wave, leaving Astrid and me alone. The second the doors slid shut, I whirled on her.

"Astrid, what do you think you're doing?"

She blinked at me innocently. "What do you mean?"

"Don't play dumb," I hissed as the elevator chimed and the golden doors opened to reveal our floor. We stepped out, the patterns on the doors fading behind us as we walked down the hall.

The dorm layout was one of the few things I liked here—only eight rooms per hall, making it feel less cramped. Ours was at the very end of the second floor. I stomped ahead.

"Why would you say it's okay for Zephyr to come to our room to study?" I demanded as we reached our door.

Astrid shrugged. "We all have homework. And honestly, it's kind of a miracle that your Manifest assignments match up with our History homework. What did you want me to do? Say, 'Oh, sorry Zephyr, Lee has a crush on you and loses all brain function when you're around, so maybe just Sunna should come'?"

She gave me a pointed look as the door scanned her hand, unlocking with a click. The green light faded, and we stepped inside. The mix of old-world charm and advanced tech in this place annoyed me—magic sensors in the doors, but phones straight out of the Stone Age.

I sighed and dropped my bag near the entrance. "You didn't have to say it like that."

Astrid smirked. "Sounds dumb, huh?"

"Obviously," I muttered, walking over to the closet.

"Where are you going?" she called.

"I'm changing. Sweatpants are calling my name," I replied.

She guffawed. "You sound like a ten-year-old about to play outside."

"Whatever," I shot back, pulling a hoodie over my head.

By the time I came out, Astrid was standing by the armoire with a mischievous glint in her eyes. "Time to go to Odreazah.

You said Caspian told you how to make sure we end up where we want, right?"

"Yes," I said, glaring at her. "Give me a second."

"You know we only have an hour until dinner, right? You're going to make us late."

I folded my arms. "Time works differently there, remember?"

Astrid cocked a hip, hands on her waist. "Is this about dinner, or are you stalling because of Zephyr?"

Astrid's lips twitched. "Can we just move on to the portal thing?"

I sighed, walking over to the armoire. "Caspian said I just have to visualize where I want to go.

"Good. Let's go then." Astrid gestured toward the armoire like she was presenting a game show prize.

I opened the doors and closed my eyes, picturing the castle. The grand spires, the polished stone walls... I took a deep breath.

"Did it work?" Astrid whispered beside me.

I cracked one eye open. "It would've if you hadn't interrupted."

"Hey, just checking," she said with a shrug.

Rolling my eyes, I took a step forward and entered the portal. A rush of wind yanked me inside like a vacuum. Astrid's scream echoed as we were flung through the magical tunnel.

We landed hard on a tiled floor. I stayed upright, but Astrid hit the ground with a loud thud.

"We really need to work on that landing," she groaned, rubbing her head.

I glanced down at her and crossed my arms. "Why do you always land like that? I'm always fine."

"You probably pushed me because you were scared," she shot back, narrowing her eyes.

I laughed. "So now I screamed and pushed you? Sure."

"Whatever," she muttered, getting to her feet.

"I think I heard screaming," a deep voice said suddenly.

We jumped, and Astrid actually yelped. Caspian stood in front of us, bare-chested and dripping wet, a towel wrapped around his waist. I blinked rapidly, my brain short-circuiting.

"Holy shit," Astrid whispered, grinning like a maniac. "You brought us to his bathroom?"

"I—what—no!" I stammered. My gaze snapped between her and Caspian. "You said to think about where I wanted to be!"

"And you wanted to be here?" Astrid teased, giggling.

"No!" I hissed, smacking her arm.

"There's somewhere else you can wait," Caspian said, chuckling softly. He pointed toward a doorway. "That's my room. Go ahead. I'll be there in a second."

I grabbed Astrid's arm and dragged her out of the bathroom. She couldn't stop laughing.

"You totally thought about his bathroom," she said between giggles.

"Did not," I muttered, but the argument died in my throat when we stepped into his room.

Velvet curtains draped over large windows, and a sleek, charcoal-colored bed stood at the center. Bookshelves lined one wall, filled with ancient tomes and modern titles. The entire room felt...magical.

"Oh. My. Gods," I whispered, turning in awe.

"How old is he?" Astrid asked, still gawking.

"I'm the same age as you," Caspian said, entering fully dressed in tailored pants and a cream shirt. "You think I'm old?"

Astrid gestured to the room. "Based on this? Yes."

Caspian frowned. "What's wrong with my room?"

"It's beautiful," I said softly.

Our eyes met, and for a moment, everything else faded. Butterflies somersaulted in my stomach. I flexed my hand unconsciously, the memory of his touch lingering.

"So," I said, breaking the silence. "You're supposed to be helping me get unblocked."

"Right," he agreed. "Let's find my parents."

* * *

As Caspian and I stepped into the room, the stark contrast to the rest of the castle was noticeable. The walls were plain white, devoid of the ornate embellishments I'd seen elsewhere. No portraits, no enchanted lights—just simple walls enclosing a spacious area. The only furniture was a large black leather couch, two sleek swivel chairs, and a low glass table in the center. It was minimal, almost too modern for such an ancient castle.

King Victor and Queen Grizél sat comfortably on the couch, their presence filling the space despite the simplicity of the room. I took a few hesitant steps forward and cleared my throat. "King Victor, Queen Grizél, hello. How are you?"

Queen Grizél immediately stood and waved me off with a smile. "Oh, dear, drop all the formalities. Grizél and Victor will do just fine."

"Are you sure?" I asked, unsure if I was breaking some ancient royal protocol.

"Of course," she replied warmly, pulling me into a gentle hug that caught me off guard.

Victor chuckled. "Glad you arrived safely this time. Your portal brought you right to the castle?"

I froze. "This time?" My eyes widened in horror as the memory of stumbling into Caspian's bathroom resurfaced. I opened my mouth to respond, but Caspian cut in with a teasing grin.

"She didn't get it perfect," he said, clearly enjoying my embarrassment. "But at least she wasn't halfway across the realm."

Queen Grizél gave me a knowing wink. "I'm sure you landed exactly where you wanted."

My face heated, and I gasped sharply—only to end up coughing from inhaling too much air too quickly. I covered my mouth and tried to regain my composure while I explained how Caspian took me on a tour. I wanted as far away from Caspian's bathroom as possible so we talked about how beautiful the garden was instead.

"What's wrong, Lee?" Astrid asked, her brow furrowing. "Why are you choking?"

"Come sit," King Victor said, gesturing to the couch.

Astrid and Killian moved toward the table in the center of the room. Killian hopped onto it casually, while Caspian crossed the room and sat on the opposite end. I opted to sit between the king and queen, feeling much safer there than near Caspian.

Queen Grizél turned to Astrid with a smile. "How was fencing, my dear?"

Astrid's face lit up. "You knew about that? Did you see me out there?" She puffed out her chest with pride. "I'm a natural. Totally kicked Killian's butt," she added, jabbing him with her elbow. King Victor cleared his throat and Astrid's cheeks heated and she played with her fingers.

"I let you win," Killian retorted, bypassing his fathers warning.

"Mm hmm, sure. Whatever makes you feel better," Astrid teased.

Queen Grizél slapped King Victor's shoulder narrowing her gaze at him.

Victor chuckled softly, steering the conversation away from Caspian's antics. "How have your classes been? What are they teaching you at The Academy?"

Astrid jumped in before I could answer. "I'm in History for first years, and Lee's in Manifest. But we somehow ended up with the same homework."

"Speaking of time," I interjected, "how does it work here? We were supposed to meet our friends for dinner in an hour. How will we know when that time's up?"

"The difference in time between realms is complicated to explain, but don't worry—we'll make sure you're reminded."

As if on cue, a maid entered the room and curtsied respectfully. "Your Majesties?"

She glanced at me and Astrid with a polite smile. "Ms. Trueshadow, Ms.—"

Astrid scrunched up her face. "Please, just Addy and Lee. No 'Misses,' please."

I nodded in agreement. "Exactly."

Grizél turned to the maid. "Please ensure they are reminded at 6:30 p.m. Academy time."

The maid bowed. "Yes, Queen," she said before exiting gracefully.

"Well, that's handled," Grizél announced with a clap of her hands. "Now, tell us more about your classes."

"In Manifest, we learned that some of us are descendants of an originator whose children had their abilities blocked," I explained. "We touched on the gods and goddesses who granted the originators their powers but didn't go too deep into it."

"Hakim cursed Wyny's children," Astrid chimed in. "He was jealous of how much responsibility and trust the gods placed in Wyny. That's why Wyny's descendants had their abilities blocked."

I nodded. "Right. We talked about how some of Wyny's children eventually unblocked themselves, but it took him a long time to free the others."

Victor leaned forward, his expression serious. "Yes, and now we need to figure out which of Wyny's children you descend from."

"Why does that matter?" I asked, narrowing my eyes.

Both Victor and Grizél hesitated. The room grew noticeably quieter.

Astrid crossed her arms and raised an eyebrow. "Well, that's not suspicious at all," she said sarcastically, glancing between the king and queen.

I turned to Caspian, hoping he'd shed some light on the situation. He shrugged. "I know they're eager to help you unlock your abilities. I don't know all the details though."

"Okay, but how do you even know me?" I pressed. "You've never explained that."

He looked at me with a soft, almost apologetic expression and shrugged again. Before I could demand a proper answer, Astrid piped up.

"Hello? Don't get all quiet on us now. Spill."

Grizél sighed and exchanged a glance with Victor. Finally, she spoke. "You know we knew your parents, right? Well, it's time we told you the full story of how we came to know them."

Inheritance of Secrets | Selene

Queen Grizél glanced at King Victor, a worried crease forming between her brows. They were hiding something.

"Any day now," I muttered, crossing my arms and tapping my foot.

Grizél sighed deeply and finally began, her voice low but steady. "Alright. Your parents—Kofi and Leia—we, well...we know them very well."

"How?" I cut in, my gaze narrowing.

Grizél exchanged another brief look with Victor before answering. "Victor and I were professors at the Academy. We both taught fourth-year classes. By the time Kofi and Leia reached us, they already had quite the reputation."

"Reputation?" I asked skeptically, and Astrid chimed in, "Which classes?"

Grizél's eyes crinkled in amusement. "One question at a time. Let me tell the full story first. Then you can ask anything."

She inhaled slowly, her posture straightening as though she were about to give a lecture. "Victor taught battle tactics. He was the most decorated warrior of his era. He had just retired with the highest honors and had climbed to the very top of the power hierarchy."

Astrid's eyes widened, her mouth opening before she slapped a hand over it, muffling a gasp.

"Yes, Astrid," Grizél said with a knowing smile, "he was a ranked Anvil."

Anvil. The word conjured images of unstoppable warriors wielding magic and steel in perfect harmony.

"I," Grizél continued, "taught history. We focused exclusively on fourth-year students because Victor was still occasionally called into battle. Wherever he went, I went. The Academy required students at that level to be highly capable, able to manage on their own in our absence."

Her voice softened. "Our first encounter with Kofi and Leia was…chaotic. They had already gained notoriety for their skills, which didn't sit well with many of their peers. Kofi was a prodigy in pyromancy, unparalleled in his generation. And Leia…"

She paused, as if searching for the right words. "Leia was extraordinary. Her telekinetic abilities weren't limited to objects—she could manipulate elements like wind and earth. It was a power unseen for centuries. For that reason, it had to be kept secret. Only a select few knew the truth: Victor, myself, the headmaster, and her parents."

"Wait," I interjected, "you're telling me my mom's power was that rare, and no one could know?"

Grizél nodded solemnly. "Yes. The headmaster recognized her potential and sent both Kofi and Leia on private missions. They often missed classes but still excelled, which only fueled resentment among other students. Add to that Kofi's reputation as the Academy's most eligible bachelor, and, well…let's just say there was no shortage of tension."

Astrid's eyes sparkled. "Hold up. They were on secret missions? Like, actual covert operations?"

I shot her a warning look. "Addy, seriously?"

"What? You're skipping the juicy details!" she argued. "I want to know—what kind of missions? How did the headmaster find out about their powers? Did Leia's parents tell him?"

Grizél's expression didn't waver. "Leia's parents were non-magical. They never manifested any abilities despite going through the full four years at the Academy. They were worried Leia might inherit the same fate and sought our help. We used an ancient spell to encourage her magic. It was unusually potent because Victor and I cast it together, which isn't typically required."

"And that's why my mom was so powerful?" I asked.

"That's our best guess," Victor said. "The headmaster, however, had his own motives. He had enemies across various realms and couldn't leave the Academy due to his responsibilities. He used Kofi and Leia to deal with those threats."

"But it wasn't just defense," Grizél added, her tone darkening. "He sought to conquer this realm. When your parents discovered the truth, they changed sides."

I blinked, trying to absorb her words. "So...my parents were soldiers in some kind of realm war?"

Grizél nodded. "During our final battle, we discovered Leia had a daughter and was hiding her, you. Knowing they couldn't stay here, we sent them back to the Academy through a portal hidden in the Forrest outside of The Academy walls. Unfortunately, a dragon followed them through."

Astrid gasped. "A dragon? Are you serious?"

"Dead serious," Victor said grimly. "We couldn't follow them; we had to protect our realm."

I swallowed hard, my thoughts spinning. "So, you think I inherited some kind of block from my grandparents?"

"That's the most likely explanation," Grizél said gently.

Astrid crossed her arms. "Then why can't you just finish the spell now?"

Grizél shook her head. "It's risky to perform the spell without knowing whether the magic is present. If too much power is released—"

"Boom!" Killian interrupted, miming an explosion with exaggerated hand gestures.

Astrid snorted. "Okay, but you two are ancient, super-powerful magic users. You're telling me you can't handle this?"

"Yeah," I added, my voice sharp. "It sounds more like a won't than a can't."

Victor sighed and motioned for me to stand in the center of the room. "Fine. Let's see what happens."

I hesitated, but curiosity pushed me forward. Grizél and Victor positioned themselves on either side of me. Their presence was reassuring and unnerving as they began chanting:

"Rapha, haelen, ga-hailjan."

Their words vibrated through the air, resonating with an ancient, untamed power. A warm, golden light wrapped around me, tendrils of magic weaving through my skin, into my very soul. It was as if I were being stitched into the fabric of something far greater than myself.

For a moment, I felt infinite—a conduit for raw, celestial energy. But just as quickly as it came, the magic fizzled out. The light vanished, leaving an empty void in its wake.

"I guess it didn't work," I murmured, my voice hollow.

Before anyone could respond, the room plunged into darkness. A fierce wind roared around me, lifting me off the ground. My heart raced as I twisted and flailed in the vortex.

"Addy!" I screamed. "Is this you?"

"Hell no!" she yelled back. "Are you okay? I can't get to you!"

The wind howled louder, encasing me in a whirlwind of raw magic. I gasped as a whisper echoed in my mind.

Quiet, my child.

A wave of calm washed over me, soothing my frantic thoughts. My limbs went slack as I took a deep breath, letting the tension drain from my body. I repeated the process, slowly centering myself.

Ahhh, that's it, the voice murmured again.

I closed my eyes, waiting for something extraordinary to happen. Instead, gravity reclaimed me, and I crashed onto the floor with a painful thud.

"Lee!" Astrid cried, rushing to my side.

Caspian knelt beside me, his warm hands steadying me as I stumbled to my feet.

I looked over at Grizél and Victor, who stood behind Nyx, their expressions unreadable. My throat tightened, and tears blurred my vision.

"I guess it didn't work," I whispered, my voice cracking.

Grizél approached and knelt before me, gently taking my hands in hers. "Don't lose hope, Selene," she said softly. "We'll find a way. You are not alone in this."

A maid entered, breaking the moment. "Your Majesties, the time you requested has come."

I took a deep breath, straightening. "It's time for us to go," I said, glancing at Astrid.

Astrid whispered something to Killian before turning back to me. Grizél raised her hand, swirling it in the air. A shimmering portal materialized, its edges crackling with soft, golden energy.

"Please, come back soon," Grizél said.

I gave a small nod, wiping my face. Without looking back, I stepped into the portal, leaving behind more questions than answers.

Open Sesame | Selene

The moment Astrid shut the armoire door, there was a sharp knock. She frowned and glanced back.

"We really need to tell them to give us some wiggle room," Astrid muttered, making her way toward the door.

I sighed, grabbing my bag from where I'd dropped it earlier. "Or," I said, slinging the strap over my shoulder, "we could figure out how to do it ourselves instead of always relying on them."

Astrid paused with her hand on the doorknob, a mischievous grin spreading across her face. She looked over her shoulder at me and winked. "Sounds like we need a private lesson with two certain brothers."

I felt heat creep up my neck and quickly pressed my lips together to stop a smile from forming. Before I could respond, there was another knock. This time, Astrid whipped the door open.

"Finally," Sunna huffed dramatically, pushing past Astrid.

Astrid grabbed her bag from beside the door and flopped onto her bed. Zephyr followed Sunna inside, quietly closing the door behind him. Sunna shot Astrid a look—one of those conspiratorial ones they always shared like they were in on a secret. I narrowed my eyes. What were they plotting?

A sudden *thump* snapped me out of my thoughts. Zephyr's bag landed on my bed. My bed. I blinked at it in shock.

"You guys ready to eat?" Zephyr asked casually, like he hadn't just commandeered my personal space.

Sunna and Astrid jumped to their feet. "Yes!" Astrid practically shouted. "Fencing works up an appetite."

"Fencing?" Sunna frowned, giving Astrid a sideways look. "Girl, what are you even talking about?"

"Oh, uh, nothing," Astrid said quickly, leading the way out the door.

Zephyr leaned in close to my ear, his voice dropping low. "Which line are you going to?"

I barely registered his words because his warm breath brushed against my ear, sending goosebumps skittering up my arms. I swallowed hard. "Uhh...probably the salad line," I mumbled.

He made a face. "Salad line? Ew. No greens for me." His playful grin softened the words. "I'm hitting the exotic line. Come with me."

He gave me an almost puppy-dog look, and before I knew it, I was nodding. We walked together to the exotic line, and I grabbed a tray, trying to focus on anything other than how close he was beside me. As I reached for the plastic silverware, a spicy, savory aroma wafted through the air, making my nose wrinkle.

The main dish was chicken covered in a thick red sauce. The man behind the counter smiled and extended his hand.

"Your tray, my lady," he said with a playful bow.

I smiled back and lifted the tray. He carefully placed a piece of chicken on it, then ladled the sauce generously over the top before passing it back to me.

I stared at the chicken, unsure whether to be intrigued or

horrified. Zephyr's laughter brought my gaze back to him.

"They call it berry heat sauce," he explained. "Trust me, it's good."

We moved further down the line, adding sides here and there. By the time we reached the end, I noticed Zephyr's tray was suspiciously void of anything green.

"No vegetables?" I teased, giving him a playful nudge.

"Hey, I thought this was a no-judgment zone," he shot back, raising an eyebrow.

"Uh, yeah...I never said that," I retorted.

Zephyr chuckled and scanned the cafeteria. "So, where'd Addy and Sunna go?"

"Ah, so we're done with the vegetable conversation?" I teased, but I looked around as well. "They're probably near the windows. Sunna likes sitting there."

We made our way toward the back of the café, where sunlight streamed in from massive floor-to-ceiling windows. Sure enough, Astrid and Sunna were waiting for us in a booth. I rolled my eyes when I saw they'd both taken the same side, leaving the opposite side open—for me and Zephyr, of course.

"No salad?" Astrid asked as I slid into the booth.

"She eats salad a lot?" Zephyr asked, sitting beside me. "I convinced her to try something new."

Astrid grinned. "I've only seen Lee eat something other than salad like...three times. Ever."

My mouth dropped open. "I eat chicken, Addy."

"Yeah, in your salad. If it doesn't belong in a salad, you're not touching it."

Sunna snorted. "Is that true, Selene?"

"Like this one time..." Astrid's eyes sparkled as she launched into story mode. "Remember when we went to the zoo with your dad and mine? The drive-through one?"

I groaned and buried my face in my hands. Oh no. Not *that* story.

"This should be good," Sunna said, her curiosity piqued.

"Okay, so we're at the zoo, and Lee—" Astrid started giggling. "She wouldn't even roll down her window to feed the animals. Like, she was terrified."

"They were sticking their necks in the car!" I interjected. "Invading my personal space. You fed enough for both of us."

"But the best part," Astrid continued, her grin widening, "was when we went to eat afterward. My dad got us kids meals, but there was no salad for Lee. And she lost it. Full-blown tantrum."

"How old were you guys?" Zephyr asked.

I peeked out from behind my fingers. "We were ten," I mumbled.

"Oh, sorry, what was that?" Astrid cupped a hand around her ear. "Didn't catch it."

I lowered my hands and shot her a glare. "We were ten," I repeated firmly.

Zephyr's jaw dropped. "Ten? I thought you were, like, three."

Astrid laughed. "Nope. She was ten and bawling her eyes out over not getting a salad."

Zephyr turned to me, pretending to hold an invisible microphone. "Selene Trueshadow, your response?"

"Yeah, Selene," Sunna chimed in. "What did the French fries ever do to you?"

Laughter erupted around the table, and despite myself, I couldn't help but join in. I shook my head, biting my lip to stop the giggles.

"I just prefer salad," I said with a small shrug.

"Well," Zephyr said, giving me a teasing grin, "looks like

you're breaking that habit. How's the chicken and berry heat?"

I glanced down at my plate, surprised to see I'd eaten most of it already. "It's actually… really good."

Astrid waggled her eyebrows. "See? You *can* eat something other than salad."

"Okay, I think it's time to go study," I said, standing quickly to escape further embarrassment.

The others laughed, but thankfully, they didn't protest. One meal without salad wasn't going to kill me, but I had a feeling I'd never live down this story.

* * *

"Okay, Sunna, how do you have your tablet set up?" I asked, trying to shift focus back to something productive. I was too aware of how close Zephyr was. We were stretched out on my bed, our books sprawled on either side of us, pushing us closer in the center. His presence was magnetic, and it took everything in me not to fidget under the weight of it.

"Pass it over here," Sunna responded, crawling off Astrid's bed.

She moved to the floor, propping herself on her hands and knees near the space between the beds. Her feet hooked onto the edge of the mattress like an anchor. I shimmied closer to meet her halfway, reaching out to pass her the tablet.

"I'm just going to set up your digital notebooks for each class," Sunna said, fingers already flying across the screen.

Zephyr shook his head dramatically. "I don't know how you

all do this. I'm sticking with my paper and pencil."

"Come on, Zephyr," Sunna teased, peeking up at him. "Everything's advancing so fast. You've got to keep up."

"I will not," he said with mock defiance, shaking his head again.

"If I have to eat chicken outside of a salad," I interjected, raising an eyebrow, "you can try switching to a tablet. Even Astrid's getting one. Her parents approved it today."

"Exactly!" Astrid piped in, leaning forward eagerly. "I'm picking mine up tomorrow morning before class. You don't want to be the odd one out, do you?"

Zephyr crossed his arms. "None of the guys on my floor have one," he defended.

Sunna sucked her teeth. "Maybe it's just you rugby players."

I blinked in surprise. "You're on the rugby team? Wow."

"Why do you say it like that?" he asked, his brow furrowing slightly. "We played rugby all the time at home."

I shrugged, feeling a little sheepish. "We were around more football players than rugby. I just don't know much about it. But it's cool."

The corner of his mouth quirked into a smile. He leaned in, his shoulder brushing against mine. "You should come to practice sometime."

My cheeks warmed instantly. "Sure," I murmured, trying to sound casual despite the sudden fluttering in my chest.

"What are you two whispering about?" Astrid's voice broke the moment.

Zephyr leaned back abruptly, clearing his throat. Sunna and Astrid exchanged knowing glances, snickering like conspirators.

"Alright, alright," Sunna said through her laughter. "Let's get to studying."

"Thank the Gods," I muttered under my breath, grateful for the distraction.

"Lee," Sunna began, "your history class is purple-coded, right? Do you guys want to read the chapters together or separately?"

"There's no point in us being here if we're going to work separately," Astrid reasoned.

"Agreed," I said. "If we rotate the reading, I can take notes while listening. It'll be faster than stopping and starting to write everything down. Can we all do a few pages each?"

Everyone nodded, and we dove into the homework. The assignment was hefty—ten chapters on the Originators and the Gods, followed by a one-page paper for Manifest class. We started by reviewing what we already knew.

Wyny, the most powerful of the Originators, was created by Nodreus, the God of Moving Realms. His geokinetic combat abilities allowed him to manipulate the earth in battle. Then there was Hakim, born of Cene, the God of Time. He wielded aerokinetic transportation, moving objects and people at lightning speed. His envy of Wyny's favored position with the Gods drove much of the conflict. Kamal, the third Originator, was gifted by Xynake, the God of Justice. His mind-reading powers made him a critical strategist. Finally, Sevon, the only female Originator, was empowered by Ohnir, the Goddess of all living creatures. Sevon had the ability to transform ordinary animals into magical beings, creating legends like the phoenix and the dragon.

Time blurred as we worked through the chapters. Hours passed, our notes growing in piles around us. The room was filled with the quiet sounds of pages turning, pens scratching on paper, and the occasional groan of frustration.

Finally, Zephyr sprawled across the bed dramatically, his arm and leg draping over me. "And I am done," he groaned. "If this is what all our classes are going to be like, we need to start earlier. This was just one class. I still have battle tactics and weapons to do."

"We all have weapons class together," I reminded him. "We can knock that out tonight. But Astrid and I have different battle tactics teachers."

"Same here," Sunna added. "Addy and I are in the same tactics class."

"Alright, so let's finish the weapons assignment," Astrid said, clapping her hands. "Then we can split up for tactics. Lee and I can work together, and you guys can pair up."

"Sounds good," Astrid agreed. "But what's the weapons assignment?"

"Research," Sunna answered, scrolling through her tablet. "We just need a timeline of weapons approved by the Justice and War Department over the past century."

"See? That won't take long," Astrid chimed in. "Let's get it done."

An hour later, we were packed and ready to head out. Astrid grinned from her bed. "Bye, you guys," she said in a singsong voice.

I rolled my eyes but couldn't suppress a smile. Sunna and Astrid's teasing might have been relentless, but there was something comforting about the easy camaraderie of all of us studying together. As Zephyr and I stepped out into the hall, I felt the warmth of belonging wrap around me like a cloak. Tonight, for once, it felt like everything was falling into place.

* * *

Zephyr insisted on walking me back after our homework session—though we both knew the moment was stretching beyond just "walking."

The hallway was quieter than usual, lit by the soft flicker of mage-lanterns that pulsed in sync with the runes etched along the ceiling. His presence beside me was effortless.

"You have four roommates?" I asked, raising a brow as we passed the northern wing. "Isn't the max two per room?"

"Per bedroom, yeah," he said with a grin. "Our suite's a little different. One of the perks of being on the rugby team."

"Figures." I sighed dramatically. "If Addy and I could summon extra space through sheer will, we would."

He paused in front of a carved column. "There's something I want to show you."

"If this is your secret stash of snacks, I swear—"

He didn't answer. Just pressed his hand to the wall.

A sigil lit up—faint and golden—then the seam of a door appeared.

"What—how did you know this was here?" I asked.

"Stumbled on it," he said. "Literally. The first time I leaned on it too hard and—well, just... be careful going in—"

I tripped.

Not a graceful stumble. Not a cute wobble. A full-body, magical slapstick face-first tumble into the room.

Except—Zephyr caught me.

I crashed into his chest with a very undignified *oomph*, grabbing his arm to stop myself from dragging us both down.

"Graceful," he said, smirking.

"Shut up," I muttered, still very much plastered to him.

"You okay?"

"Physically? Yes. Emotionally? I'll never recover."

He chuckled and helped me up, not letting go quite as quickly as he probably should have.

And then I saw the room.

Ancient scrolls, enchanted weapons, and a single glass case in the center—covered in a velvet cloth.

The sharp crack echoed in the small chamber, followed immediately by Zephyr's groan.

His eyes widened. "Oh, crap."

"What?" I asked, following his gaze.

His hands trembled slightly, and as he lifted them, I saw frost creeping up his fingertips, spreading rapidly like ink in water. The air around us dropped several degrees in an instant, and Zephyr clenched his fists as if trying to suppress whatever was happening.

"I think—" he took a shaky breath. "I think I'm manifesting."

A low crackling noise filled the chamber. A thin layer of ice spread outward from where Zephyr's hands then surrounded him, creating some sort of Armour.

"Zephyr," I said carefully, reaching out. "Can you control it?"

"I - I don't know how yet." Panic flickered in his usually steady eyes, and for the first time, I saw something that scared me—uncertainty.

He lifted his hands quickly, too quickly when a wind gust flew at me, knocking me back.

"You have two," I said in awe, as I got up from the ground, again.

Maps, Memories, and Misunderstandings | Selene

His fingers tightened around mine helping me up from the ground. Then, just as suddenly as it had appeared, his armour dissipated, leaving only the lingering sensation of something shifting in the air.

Zephyr let out a breath, running a hand through his curls. "Well...that was something."

"Yeah. It really was." My heart did a weird somersault. I quickly looked anywhere but at him, feeling a blush creep up my neck. His teasing shouldn't have affected me this much, but here I was, completely flustered. My gaze darted around the room, taking in our surroundings for the first time.

"Oh my gods," I whispered, standing up slowly. "What is this place?"

The wall we had fallen through was gone. In its place was a solid slab of gray concrete, smooth except for an intricate map etched across its surface. I stepped closer to focus on the details. The map wasn't just any map—it depicted the major realms: Odreazah, Arcane Wonders, Earth, and a realm I had never heard of before—Ereriath. Pinpoints marked several locations, and beside one of them was the word "Gods."

I stepped toward the center of the room, where the pedestal sat, pulsing faintly with light.

Zephyr moved beside me, but I raised my hand to stop him.

I pressed my palm to the pedestal. A shock of energy pulsed up my arm—familiar, ancient, and unmistakably mine.

"Ereriath?" I murmured, tracing the unfamiliar name with my finger. "I thought the gods lived in Odreazah. I mean, I know there are multiple sets of gods, but our gods...I've never heard of this place."

I didn't hear Zephyr approach, but I felt the warmth of his presence as he leaned in over my shoulder. His head brushed my ear, and a shiver ran down my spine.

"Aren't there more realms than just these?" he asked, his breath tickling my skin. "Why would this map only show these?"

"Good question," I muttered, still studying the map. I was hyper-aware of how close he was, the heat radiating between us.

He reached down and grabbed my hand. "Check this out."

His hand was warm and steady, fitting perfectly around mine. The contact sent a strange sense of calm through me, like an anchor in a sea of confusion. Together, we crossed the dimly lit room, the faint glow of crystals embedded in the walls illuminating our path.

"This feels like something out of a spy movie," I said as we approached a cracked wooden table covered in scrolls, maps, and ancient artifacts. Rich velvet drapes in deep blues and greens framed the room's edges, giving it an oddly regal atmosphere despite the cold concrete walls.

Zephyr released my hand to reach for one of the scrolls. The absence of his touch left me oddly disappointed, but I quickly shook the feeling off. *Get it together, Selene.*

He unfurled the scroll, spreading it across the table. I gasped.

"What?" Zephyr asked, glancing at me with curiosity.

"That's...my dad's handwriting," I whispered, barely able to believe it. My fingers traced the familiar strokes on the parchment. Memories of the journals he'd left me surfaced in my mind. "I have one of his journals in my room. It's full of spells and notes from when he was a student here. This...this is his work." My mind raced as my words escaped me in a rush. "It has to be. The King and Queen told me my parents were sent on secret missions when they were students. This looks like some sort of mission archive."

"Missions?" Zephyr echoed, clearly trying to wrap his head around it all. "Damn, Selene. That's...intense."

He stepped closer again, his gaze softening as he placed a comforting hand on my shoulder. "Hey. You can talk to me. Whatever this is—a Queen and King?" he questioned.

I swallowed hard, meeting his eyes. They sparkled like emeralds, drawing me in. Could I really trust him? Or was it just my stupid, fluttery feelings clouding my judgment?

Taking a deep breath, I decided on a half-truth. "My parents... they were sent on dangerous assignments by the headmaster. Secret stuff. They thought they were fighting for our gods, but they were deceived."

Zephyr's eyes widened in surprise. "Wow. And this place...?"

"I think this is where they planned those missions," I explained, gesturing at the scrolls and maps.

He leaned against the table beside me, processing everything. "So, Odessa was right," he finally said.

My expression darkened instantly. "Odessa? That girl from class?"

"Yeah," he said cautiously. "She's been going on about how

your parents had special privileges here."

Anger flared in my chest. "Special privileges?" I spat. "They were used. Manipulated. They risked their lives and fought for years to protect this realm. Nothing was handed to them!"

"Hey, I didn't mean to upset you," Zephyr said gently. "I don't believe her. I know you're not like that."

I crossed my arms, fuming. "People should stop judging me based on rumors. They don't know a damn thing about me or my parents."

Zephyr gave me a concerned look but didn't push further. After a moment, he nodded toward the wall. "We should figure out how to get out of here. It's getting late."

"Agreed," I muttered, stomping over to the wall and pressing random spots. To my surprise, it slid open with a low rumble. I turned to see Zephyr stepping on a hidden switch.

"Looks like this was the way out," he said softly.

"Thanks," I murmured, stepping through the opening without another word. I needed space. Time to cool off.

By the time I reached my room, Sunna practically tackled me at the door. "Selene! Oh my Gods, I've been waiting for you!"

"Where's Zephyr?" she asked, looking around.

"He went back to his room," I replied, trudging inside.

Sunna's grin widened. "Guess what? My powers manifested! I'm a hydromancer!"

Her excitement was contagious, lifting my mood slightly. "That's amazing! Hydromancy—wait, isn't that the one where you can do things with water?"

"Exactly!" Sunna beamed.

"Zephyr did too. He can make armor of ice and has wind too," I said dryly.

"He has two?" Astrid asked.

We celebrated for a while, but I couldn't shake the lingering tension from earlier. After a long, hot shower, I finally crawled into bed. The room was dark and quiet, except for the soft glow of the nightlight by the bathroom.

"You wanna talk about what happened with Zephyr?" Astrid's voice broke the silence.

I sighed, staring at the ceiling. "Might as well," I said, beginning to recount the strange events of the night.

I should've let it go.

* * *

But later that night, I couldn't sleep. Something about what Zephyr said stuck with me—Odessa's comments. Is she picking on me or is this really what everyone thinks?

So I left the dorms and went for a walk.

I didn't expect to see her.

Odessa stood just outside the west wing of the library, her hand pressed to a locked archive case. Her lips moved like she was whispering a spell—but when I stepped into view, she snapped upright like a blade.

"Trueshadow," she said, voice flat.

"Bit late for academic excellence," I replied.

"Don't pretend you're the only one who gets curious," she snapped, stepping away from the case.

I glanced at the glowing seal. "You know that's Headmaster's access only, right?"

"I wasn't touching anything."

"No," I said, stepping closer. "Just lurking. In the dark. With your hand on a banned relic vault."

Her jaw tightened. "You don't know what you're talking

about."

"Don't I?"

She turned to leave, muttering, "Not everyone who asks questions is the enemy, Selene."

Maybe not.

But sometimes the enemy wears a familiar face.

* * *

The morning air was crisp, but I couldn't muster any warmth in my mood. I slung my book bag over my shoulder and prepared to leave the dorm, determined to keep my thoughts to myself. I wasn't in the mood for idle chatter, and honestly, I just didn't feel like explaining anything to anyone today.

"So, we're going to ignore each other now?" Astrid's voice cut through the silence as she sat on her bed, arms crossed in that all-too-familiar dramatic way.

I paused, gripping the strap of my bag a little tighter. "I'm not ignoring you, Astrid. I just don't have anything to say," I replied curtly, my tone edged with sourness.

Astrid sighed. "Selene, you need to communicate. You can't just shut down every time someone says something you don't like."

I exhaled sharply, biting back the retort that I knew would come. "I'm not shutting down. It's perfectly fine for me not to talk. I just don't feel like it," I said, then turned and left the room before she could press any further.

Breakfast was equally awkward. Astrid stole glances at me while eating her oatmeal, and I could almost read her thoughts: "Selene's being difficult, again." But it wasn't about her—I had my own reasons for keeping to myself. No one understood the pressures I carried. My parents didn't get special treatment; they had to work twice as hard, juggling their responsibilities while taking care of me during the headmaster's endless missions. No one saw that side of the story, and it left me with a bitter taste.

I gathered my tray and marched over to the garbage, catching Astrid's eye-roll as I dumped it. I didn't care; I was in no mood for pretense. I headed toward Manifest class.

Inside the classroom, the familiar scent of parchment and old wood greeted me as students began filing in. Professor Vinocia was at the front, his presence as commanding and energetic as ever. I slumped into my usual seat, trying to blend into the background while my mind churned with thoughts I wasn't ready to share.

"Ah, Ms. Trueshadow," he greeted me. "How are you doing? Have you completed your reading?"

"Yes, sir," I mumbled, keeping my eyes on my down.

"Good. Why don't you tell me how the first battle began and its relevance to our history?"

I blinked, feeling caught off guard. "Uh...the battle started when the Gods..."

"Nope," he cut me off with a sharp clap of his hands. "We're going back *way* before the gods. The very first battle. That was in the reading."

I floundered, searching my mind for an answer, but thankfully, the rest of the class began trickling in. I exhaled and sank further into my seat.

Zephyr entered last, his gaze locking onto mine the moment he stepped inside. "Hey," he greeted softly as he slid into the seat next to me.

"Hey," I mumbled back, barely looking at him.

"We need to talk about last night," he said, leaning closer.

Before I could respond, Professor Vinocia clapped again. "Alright, let's dive right in! We're going to discuss the first battle."

From across the room, Odessa's voice cut through the air like a knife. "Why don't you ask Selene? I'm sure she can just ask her parents for all the answers."

The heat in my chest flared, but I forced myself to stay calm. I rolled my eyes and looked at the professor. "I was thinking about the battle of the Gods, but since you said it wasn't that one…" I trailed off, keeping my voice even.

Professor Vinocia gave Odessa a sharp glare. "Odessa, your green is seeping out. Keep it in check, please."

She huffed, crossing her arms and muttering under her breath. I ignored her, focusing instead on the professor as he resumed the lesson.

Throughout the class, Zephyr kept sending me messages that popped up on my tablet screen.

I'm sorry.
I didn't mean to upset you.
I know they worked hard.
I just have questions and handled it wrong.

I didn't respond. I kept my eyes on the professor, refusing to give Zephyr the satisfaction of an answer.

When class ended, I shot out of my seat, eager to escape. But Zephyr caught my arm before I could make it to the door.

"Selene, please," he said, his voice full of quiet urgency.

"Trouble in paradise?" Odessa sneered as she approached.

"Mind your business," I snapped, spinning to face her. "You'd be better off getting your own stuff together instead of worrying about me."

"Nobody's worried about you," she shot back, crossing her arms.

"Could've fooled me," I retorted. "You've got my name in your mouth enough. You're in this class just like the rest of us, struggling to manifest. Maybe you should focus on that instead of spreading rumors."

I jerked my arm free from Zephyr's grip and stormed out of the classroom. Behind me, I heard Odessa mutter, "The nerve."

Zephyr didn't respond, but I could imagine the exhaustion on his face as he walked away from her. I didn't need to hear the rest. I had more important things to focus on than petty jealousy and rumors.

Trust, Betrayal, and Truth | Selene

I clenched my eyes shut, willing myself to see it—the towering spires, the grand archways, the golden glow of its welcoming halls. The castle had always been clear in my mind, a beacon in the darkness. But now, in my panic and exhaustion, my vision blurred. Instead, I saw something else entirely.

The instant I stepped into the armoire, I knew something was wrong. The magic twisted, the familiar pull warping into something jagged and unruly. When I opened my eyes, I wasn't greeted by the castle's warm embrace or the steady presence of Caspian.

I was in a swamp.

Thick, gnarled trees loomed above, their twisted branches clawing at the sky like skeletal fingers. The air was dense, suffocating, heavy with the stench of decay. My heart plummeted. First Caspian's bathroom, now this? I would never get this right.

Defeat seeped into my limbs. I glanced down—my jeans were ruined, soaked in the mucky, knee-deep water that clung to me like a second skin. A shudder crawled down my spine as something unseen slithered past my leg. No. Absolutely not.

I forced myself forward, even as exhaustion gnawed at my bones. Each step was a battle, the thick mud clinging to my legs, as if the swamp itself was reluctant to let me go. Every rustling leaf, every distant croak set my nerves on edge. Shadows twisted among the trees, and the weight of unseen eyes pressed against my back.

Then I heard it.

A low, desperate hissing.

I froze.

Slowly, I turned, my breath catching as my gaze locked onto a massive snake writhing in a shallow pool of boiling water. Steam rose in thick, ghostly tendrils, its scales sizzling under the searing heat. It thrashed wildly, its enormous body coiling and uncoiling, desperate to escape.

I couldn't move. Couldn't breathe. My pulse pounded in my ears as fear wrapped its icy fingers around my throat..

Then it turned.

And it saw me.

The snake lurched forward, its massive body propelling through the water with terrifying speed.

Oh my Gods.

Panic shot through me like a lightning strike. I stumbled back, my arms flying up in a useless attempt at protection. My boot caught on something beneath the water, and I went down hard. Mud splattered across my face, filling my mouth with the taste of earth and rot.

The hissing intensified, an agonized screech splitting through the thick air.

I squinted through the muck dripping from my face and my breath hitched.

The snake was convulsing, but not from the boiling pool. Steam poured from its scales in furious waves, the heat intensifying, blistering. Its body writhed, desperate, its pain escalating beyond what it had been moments before.

Something inside me twisted, an unfamiliar heat blooming beneath my skin, pulsing through my veins like fire.

Did I do that?

The snake let out one final, earsplitting screech before slithering away, disappearing beneath the murky surface.

I sat there, gasping, trembling, my hands pressed against the sodden earth as I tried to ground myself. My skin was hot—too hot. My breath came in shallow bursts, my limbs heavy and sluggish, like I had just run for miles.

No. Not the water.

Me.

I pushed myself upright, my movements shaky. The warmth inside me still smoldered, coiling beneath my ribs, refusing to fade. My mind raced back to the Manifest class discussions, to the way I felt in the presence of the Queen and King. Pyromancy was my father's affinity.

Could this be the first sign of mine?

"Not the time to figure that out," I muttered, forcing my legs to move again.

I pressed forward, dragging myself through the sludge until the trees began to thin. Golden sunlight pierced through the canopy, spilling onto the ground in soft patches. The shift was almost jarring—like stepping from one world into another.

Then, at last, I saw it.

The meadow.

The dark, suffocating presence of the swamp shrank away behind me as I stumbled into the clearing. The scent of damp earth and rot faded, replaced by wildflowers and fresh air. A stone archway stood at the edge of the field, draped in vines, its silhouette framing the distant spires of a castle.

Relief crashed over me so hard I nearly collapsed.

"Finally," I breathed.

My legs ached with every step as I trudged toward the archway. My mind swam with exhaustion, with confusion, with the terrifying realization of what had just happened. But I pushed forward, one step at a time.

Then a voice called my name.

"Selene?"

Caspian stood at the castle gates. His eyes widened as he took in the state of me. "What happened to you?"

I stared down at my hands, still trembling from the heat I'd summoned in the swamp.

It wasn't real, I told myself. *It couldn't be.*

That wasn't manifestation. It was panic. Fear. A reflex. Like a cornered animal biting back. Nut it didn't make sense. It had to be more than a reflex. I scorched a beast back into the wild, boiled water without lifting a finger.

I shook my head. I didn't *choose* to do it. It just happened. I couldn't even control it.

I groaned, gesturing to my mud-splattered clothes. "Your realm decided to give me a warm welcome. Literally."

Caspian frowned, his gaze flickered as he reached for my arm. His fingers hovered for a second before he hesitated. "Let's get you cleaned up," he said instead, wrinkling his nose slightly. "You smell like you fought a swamp demon."

"Feels like it too," I muttered.

As we walked, his presence steadied me. The warmth inside me hadn't faded it was contained. For now, I wasn't alone.

I stole a glance at him. "Caspian...have you ever heard of a realm called Ereriath?"

He stopped, confused. "Ereriath? No, I haven't. Why?"

I shook my head, pressing my lips together. "I saw it on a map in the Academy. It had something to do with the Gods...but I don't understand it yet."

Caspian's expression darkened slightly. "We'll figure it out," he said, his voice softer than before. Then, with a teasing tilt of his head, he added, "But first, you need a bath."

Despite everything, I snorted. "I hate you."

He grinned, nudging me toward the castle. "You love me."

And, for the first time since stepping through the armoire, I laughed.

The hot water rained down from the ceiling, pounding against my skin in the best way possible. A deep, satisfied groan slipped out before I could stop it. No—*not just one.* I groaned again. And again. At this point, I didn't even care. After everything I'd been through, I *deserved* this.

Caspian had actually asked the maid what a *shower cap* was, like it was some mythical artifact. *"A cap...for the shower? Why would you need that?"* As if I was about to let my hair get soaked under this waterfall of a shower. Absolutely not.

I had scrubbed off the swamp water a while ago, but I wasn't ready to step out of my personal slice of heaven just yet. The heat loosened the knots in my shoulders, chased away the lingering chill from the murky water, and for the first time since stepping into this realm, I actually felt *comfortable.*

Then—*knock, knock.*

"All good?" Caspian's voice carried through the door.

I stiffened, blinking at the tile. Had I really been in here that long? *Oh my gods.* I was in here *so* long he thought I might've drowned.

"Uh—yeah! Sorry! Coming out now!" I called back, my voice a little too rushed.

I sighed and reluctantly turned off the water, instantly missing the warmth. Peeling off the shower cap, I let my hair fall over my shoulders, running my fingers through it.

Then I froze.

What was I supposed to wear?

My clothes were a *disaster*—muddy, torn, and probably still smelling like swamp water. My eyes darted around the bathroom, heart hammering, until they landed on a neat stack of folded clothes sitting on the toilet seat.

Wait...

Had I really been in here long enough for someone to *wash and dry* my clothes?

Or—*duh, Selene*—they probably just used magic.

I groaned, rubbing a hand down my face. Of course they did. *Everything* was laced with magic. I should've expected it.

Still, the thought of the staff—or worse, Caspian—seeing my mud-covered, ruined outfit made me want to melt into the floor.

I pushed open the bathroom door, and there was Caspian—sprawled across an enormous armchair like he owned the world. One leg dangled lazily over the armrest, the other stretched out, his phone held loosely in his hand. He looked *ridiculous*—and yet, somehow, still managed to look effortlessly cool.

He glanced up as I stepped out, a slow smile spreading across his face.

Those damned dimples.

"Better?" he asked, his voice smooth, easy.

I rolled my eyes, crossing the plush carpet toward the oversize bed. "Yeah, I smell normal now," I muttered, flopping onto the edge with an exhausted sigh.

Caspian shifted, setting his phone down as he swung both feet to the floor. He leaned forward, resting his elbows on his knees, his expression suddenly more serious. "So... what exactly happened?"

I sighed, dragging a hand down my face. "I stepped through the armoire and landed in the middle of a swamp, and—"

"The *swamp*?" he barked, straightening abruptly.

I blinked at his sudden shift in tone.

"Selene, the swamp is over three kilometers away," he said, his brows knitting together. "You *walked* all the way here?"

I exhaled sharply, already feeling tired all over again. "*Yes.* That, plus the snake, plus my *maybe magic*—I literally almost died."

Caspian didn't respond. He just stared at me, his jaw tight, his expression unreadable.

I frowned. "Uh, say something?"

He hesitated, then stood abruptly. "We need to find my parents."

Before I could react, he grabbed my arm and *dragged* me through the castle.

I stumbled after him, barely keeping up as he yanked me from one grand hallway to the next. My head was spinning—one moment, we were passing through regal rooms filled with gilded mirrors and priceless antiques, and the next, we were in stark, modern spaces with whitewashed walls and sleek furniture. The contrast was jarring.

Finally, we reached a door, and Caspian knocked—three sharp raps, quick and impatient.

The door opened to yet another white-walled room, but this one was *huge*. At the front, two upholstered chairs flanked a sleek glass table, and two wooden side tables stood nearby, each topped with a softly glowing lamp.

And then—there they were.

King Victor and Queen Grizél.

Wearing *robes*.

Not regal, elegant, embroidered-with-magic robes. No. *Fluffy* robes. The kind with giant hoods, the kind people wore when they had *absolutely* no intention of leaving their rooms.

The Queen smiled warmly, completely unbothered by our abrupt entrance. "Ahh, Selene. How are you, dear?"

She reached out, pulling me into a gentle hug before I could even answer.

"Selene has something to tell you," Caspian cut in, his voice urgent. He turned to me. "Go ahead. Start from the beginning."

Queen Grizél placed a comforting hand on my shoulder, guiding me toward one of the chairs before perching gracefully on the armrest.

I inhaled deeply, steadying myself.

And then I told them everything.

I recounted my chaotic entrance through the armoire. The swamp. The way I had to *walk* all the way back here. How I had been *covered* in filth.

Caspian shifted beside me. "*The snake,*" he prompted.

I swallowed hard. Right. *The snake.*

I met their expectant gazes, fingers curling into my lap. My heartbeat picked up, because suddenly, I wasn't just retelling a story anymore.

I was admitting—to the King and Queen—that something inside me had *changed*.

"This has gotten dangerous," King Victor said. "An unstable pyromancer is a danger to everyone."

Caspian tensed, arms crossed as he shifted his weight from one foot to the other. I could tell he didn't like the way his father was handling this, but he hadn't spoken up yet.

I, on the other hand, had many things to say, and unfortunately, none of them would help my case. Instead of spitting out some very justified sarcasm, I forced myself to breathe. I needed answers more than I needed to get the last word in.

"An unstable pyromancer is a danger to everyone."

What was I supposed to say to that? "Oh, cool. I'll just sit in a corner and try not to spontaneously combust, then."

Queen Grizél, thankfully, did *not* seem to share King Victor's doom-and-gloom assessment. Her eyes practically *sparkled* as she turned to me.

"Selene, this is *wonderful* news," she said, placing both hands on mine. "You've finally awakened!"

Awakened. Right. Because nothing says *beautiful magical coming-of-age moment* like accidentally boiling a giant swamp snake alive.

"Yeah," I muttered. "I'm *so* excited to add 'unintentional wildlife endangerment' to my skill set."

Caspian snorted but disguised it as a cough. King Victor, however, was *not* amused. His lips pressed into a thin line as he leaned back in his chair, arms folded.

"This isn't a joke, Selene."

I blinked at him. "You think *I'm* joking? Trust me, if I had *any* control over this, I'd have skipped the part where I nearly died in a swamp. I didn't *ask* for this."

His gaze sharpened. "No one asks for power. It manifests when it's ready. The question is—are *you* ready?"

Was I? Because it sure didn't *feel* like it.

The room went silent for a moment, thick with tension. That was when Caspian finally spoke up.

"Isn't that what The Academy is for? I mean. I finally manifested. Maybe. Because I can't make it happen again."

"You don't have time for how slow the Academy is!" King Victor bellowed.

"Why not," I asked while Caspian said.

"I think she needs training," he said, his voice steady, though I could tell by the way his fingers tapped against his arm that he was choosing his words carefully. "Before we even talk about containing or nurturing anything, she needs to learn how to control it."

Queen Grizél beamed. "I agree. and that will happen at The Academy and with our help."

"There is something y'all are not telling me." I said, glaring at King Victor.

He sighed through his nose like a man who was regretting his entire existence. "Fine," he said.

"Come on dad," Caspian said. "Remember that one time you threw your advisor into a pond when he said you didn't have enough 'natural leadership'? That was unstable, was it not?"

I choked on a laugh. "Wait—you *what*?"

King Victor pinched the bridge of his nose. "That is not relevant."

"Oh, I think it's very relevant," I said, grinning. "If I'm gonna be unstable, I at least want to do it with some flair."

Caspian smirked. "That's the spirit."

King Victor exhaled through his teeth, then turned back to the Queen. "Okay, we will work at the pace of The Academy while she also comes here for our guidance."

Grizél nodded, glancing between us. "Then there's something else we must consider. Selene, we know your father was a pyromancer. But…magic doesn't always pass down in a straight line."

I frowned. "What do you mean?"

She smiled softly, though there was something unreadable in her eyes. "I think it's time we talk about your mother."

Caspian stiffened beside me.

I sat up straighter. "Okay? We talk about my mother all the time. She's Leia Trueshadow, Academy legend, telekinetic prodigy, probably could've ruled the world if she felt like it. What's new?"

Queen Grizél hesitated. "The records of your mother's power..." She paused, as if searching for the right words. "They were... *incomplete.*"

I blinked. "Incomplete how? She was literally *the* telekinetic of her generation."

"Yes," the Queen said. "But there were rumors—whispers that her abilities extended beyond telekinesis."

A chill crept down my spine. "Like what?"

Grizél glanced at King Victor, who was watching me very carefully.

"You have her records at the Academy, don't you?" Caspian asked.

Queen Grizél folded her hands in her lap. "What's *on* paper only tells part of the story. Your mother was not just an extraordinary talent—she was different."

A tight knot of unease twisted in my stomach.

"I don't understand," I admitted.

Grizél's gaze softened. "Selene, we need to explore your magic to see exactly what you can do. Whether it's just your father or a mixture of both."

Caspian frowned. "Are you saying—"

"She may have inherited something *else*, too."

My pulse quickened.

"We need to test this," Caspian said abruptly. "Tonight."

"Whoa, whoa, tonight?" I threw my hands up. "I just found out I might be double the disaster I thought I was five minutes ago. Can I get, like, a day to process?"

"No," King Victor said simply.

I shot Caspian a look. "Your dad has zero chill."

Caspian just smirked. "Welcome to my life."

Queen Grizél, at least, looked somewhat sympathetic. "I understand this is overwhelming, Selene. But the sooner we know what's inside you, the sooner we can help you control it."

I groaned dramatically, flopping back into my chair. "Fine. But if I explode, I told you *so*."

Caspian grinned, nudging my foot with his. "Don't worry, I'll dodge."

King Victor rolled his eyes. "Enough. The sooner we start, the better."

Queen Grizél stood, smoothing out her robe. "Come, Selene. Let's find out what you really are."

Caspian held out a hand to me. "Ready?"

I sighed, taking it as he pulled me to my feet. "Absolutely *not*."

"Perfect," he said.

Pressure, Power, and an Unwanted Jump Scare | Selene

The training hall was massive, its high ceilings disappearing into the dim glow of floating lanterns. The walls were lined with old banners and ancient weapons—relics of warriors, probably with actual magic at their fingertips instead of the frustrating nothing I had right now.

Caspian stood a few feet away, arms crossed, watching me like I was some puzzle he couldn't quite solve. A chalk-drawn sigil glowed faintly beneath my feet, meant to help channel my magic. So far, it was doing absolutely nothing.

I exhaled sharply and flexed my fingers, willing *something*—heat, fire, even a spark—to appear. Nothing happened. Again.

Caspian sighed. "Selene—"

"Don't," I warned, shaking out my arms. "I *swear*, if you tell me to 'just relax' one more time, I will physically fight you."

He held up his hands in mock surrender. "I was not going to say that."

I narrowed my eyes at him.

He smirked. "I *was* going to say, 'clearly, relaxing isn't working.'"

"Oh, wow," I deadpanned. "So helpful. Thank you."

Caspian chuckled, stepping closer. "Look, you said you felt something in the swamp, right? A pull, a burn—whatever? Try to remember that moment. Close your eyes if you have to."

I groaned but did as he said, squeezing my eyes shut.

The swamp.

I forced myself to relive that moment—the boiling water, the snake thrashing, the air shimmering with heat. My heart had been pounding. My breath uneven. I had felt—

Nothing.

Absolutely nothing.

I groaned, dragging my hands down my face. "This is ridiculous. I feel normal. Maybe I imagined it. Maybe it was a swamp fever dream, and you all got excited for no reason."

Caspian tilted his head. "Selene—"

"I knew it," I cut in. "I'm not magic. I'm just a very tired girl who wants to go back to bed and never think about swamps again."

Caspian opened his mouth, probably to tell me to try one more time, but then—

A voice right behind my ear:

"Boo."

I screamed.

And then everything exploded.

A wave of heat burst from my body, sending sparks flying in every direction. The training mats curled at the edges, steam rising from the sigil beneath my feet. The torches flared wildly, burning hotter, their golden glow shifting to a strange blue-white.

Caspian cursed, stumbling back. I spun around, heart still lodged somewhere in my throat.

Killian stood there, grinning like he hadn't just scared the literal magic out of me.

"Oh, come on," I wheezed. "What is wrong with you?"

Killian laughed, dodging as Caspian chucked a stray training baton at him. "Relax, Trueshadow. I was *helping*."

I jabbed a finger toward the still-smoking sigil. "Oh, *helping*? So *this*—" I waved dramatically at the barely-contained disaster "—was your *plan*?"

Killian shrugged. "Hey, it worked."

Caspian was still staring at me.

"What?" I asked, suddenly feeling very self-conscious.

"You didn't just flare," he murmured. "That was—controlled."

I blinked. "Controlled? That felt the opposite of controlled."

Killian nudged a still-glowing training mat with his boot. "I dunno. You burned everything but us."

Caspian nodded slowly. "That means you had some level of awareness. Even if it wasn't intentional."

I groaned, pressing my hands to my temples. "So…you're telling me I can only do magic if I'm scared?"

Killian smirked. "Then we just need to keep terrifying you."

I scowled. "No."

Caspian clapped his hands together. "Alright, new plan—we figure out how to trigger it without Killian making you scream like a child."

Killian pouted. "But that was fun."

I glared at him. "For you."

Suddenly, the doors slammed open.

"LEE!"

I barely had time to react before Astrid stormed into the room, eyes blazing. Her bag was slung over her shoulder like she'd sprinted across the castle.

Oh, no.

"Why am I," she said, breathing hard as she stabbed a finger in my direction, "getting a message that you almost got eaten by a snake?!"

I shot a look at Killian, who grinned, holding up Caspian's secret phone like a traitor.

"You *told her*?!" I shrieked.

Killian shrugged. "Of course I did. It was hilarious."

Astrid seethed. "You left me behind!"

I held up my hands. "Okay, technically, I didn't mean to go on a solo swamp adventure—"

"Oh, technically?" she snapped.

Caspian leaned against the wall, looking way too amused by this.

"You knew I wanted to come with you," Astrid fumed. "You knew I had class, and you went anyway."

"Okay, okay, let's not turn this into a thing—"

"Oh, it's a thing, Selene," she said, crossing her arms. "Because not only did you go without me, but you also almost got eaten by a snake and then just—casually manifested? And I had to find out through a text?"

Killian snorted. "Well, when you put it like that—"

Astrid whirled on him. "*You*—shut up."

Killian held up his hands. "Noted."

I sighed, rubbing my temples. "Addy, I swear, I did *not* plan to almost die. It was a complete accident."

She huffed, then eyed the scorch marks on the floor. "And what—this? This was an accident, too?"

"She got scared," Killian supplied helpfully.

Astrid's gaze snapped back to me, unimpressed. "You needed to be scared to do magic?"

"I'm working on it," I groaned.

Astrid sighed, shaking her head. "You are *so* lucky I like you. But I still need an apology."

I went up and hugged her "Sorry." She stiffed like she didn't want me touching her.

Caspian smirked. "We've all just accepted that Selene is a walking disaster."

"Rude," I muttered.

Killian grinned. "But true."

Astrid rolled her eyes and dropped her bag on the floor. "Alright. Move over. If you're gonna be figuring this out, I'm not missing it."

I blinked. "Wait—so you're no*t* mad anymore?"

"Oh, I'm *still mad*," she said, tying up her hair. "But I'm not stupid. If you're going to be some big bad fire-wielding mage, you need supervision. And I know these two aren't qualified."

Caspian sighed. "That's not fair."

Killian grinned. "I accept no responsibility."

I groaned. "I hate all of you."

Astrid smirked. "Then let's get started."

I was finally making progress. Astrid had rolled up her sleeves and declared herself my "superior instructor" (her words, not mine).

Honestly?

She was *way* better at this than Caspian and Killian combined.

"Alright," Astrid said, her hands on her hips as she studied me. "Let's do this properly."

I huffed, brushing soot off my shirt. "I am doing it properly."

"No, you're trying," she corrected. "But we need to figure out exactly what triggers your magic. Fear works, but obviously, we can't keep using that."

"I disagree," Killian chimed in, lounging against the far wall like this was the most entertaining thing he'd seen all week.

Astrid ignored him completely.

"Caspian," she called without looking back. "Go sit down."

Caspian raised an eyebrow. "Excuse me?"

"You heard me," she said. "Sit. You too, Killian."

Killian smirked. "Why?"

"Because Selene and I don't need you," Astrid said matter-of-factly, cracking her knuckles. "Your teaching method consists of saying '*just focus*' and '*relax*' like that's actually helpful. It's not."

Caspian sighed, clearly trying not to look offended. "Fine," he muttered, moving toward one of the benches.

Killian grinned and followed, making a very dramatic show of lounging across the entire thing. "Don't mess up, Trueshadow," he called.

Astrid turned back to me and clapped her hands together. "Alright, ignore them. Let's figure this out."

I exhaled, rolling my shoulders. "Great. What's the plan?"

She studied me for a moment. "Okay, so we know fear makes your magic react. But what about other emotions? Anger? Frustration?"

I blinked. "Oh, I have plenty of those."

Astrid smirked. "Perfect."

We started small. She had me recall moments of pure rage—every time Odessa opened her mouth, every time I got paired with someone useless for a group project.

For the first time ever, I felt *something*.

Not an explosion. Not an uncontrolled burst. But a warmth, curling like embers in my chest.

Astrid grinned. "You feel that?"

I nodded, breathing through it. "Yeah."

"Good. Now, instead of letting it flare, hold onto it."

Easier said than done. The heat wanted out, but I forced myself to control it, to mold it into something steady instead of chaotic.

The sigil beneath my feet shimmered faintly, the lines glowing gold.

Astrid's eyes widened. "That's it."

A flicker of heat passed through my palms, and for the first time, I actually felt my magic—not out of fear, not out of panic, but because I wanted to use it.

And then—

The entire thing fizzled.

I groaned, pressing my hands to my forehead. "UGH. It was right there."

Astrid smacked my arm. "Don't get discouraged! That was so close."

I opened my hands slowly, palms still warm.

This time, the flame didn't lash out blindly. It curled in my palm, steady and strong—like it was waiting for me to notice it had always been mine.

I shaped it—not the other way around.

This...this was real.

Not like the swamp. This was me—choosing. Controlling.

For the first time, I wasn't afraid of the fire.

I was becoming it.

"I know, but—"

"Stop overthinking it," she said, shaking me lightly. "You held onto it for a few seconds. That means you *can* do it. We just need to make sure it sticks."

Caspian cleared his throat from the bench. "She did well."

Astrid and I turned to him.

"Excuse me," she said. "We're working."

Caspian rolled his eyes. "I'm agreeing with you. She did well. But she's exhausted. We should stop here."

I opened my mouth to argue but then my legs wobbled.

Maybe I was tired.

Astrid sighed. "Fine. Next time *we* are in charge."

Killian grinned. "Oh no, I love this. Please continue to boss Caspian around. It's refreshing."

Caspian shot him a glare before looking at me. "You feel okay?"

I nodded. "Yeah. Just...drained."

Queen Grizél had warned me about this—how using magic for the first time could take a lot out of someone.

Caspian stood, stretching. "Then we should get you back to your realm before people start asking where you two are."

I groaned. "Ugh. Do we have to?"

"Yes," he said.

I turned to Astrid. "I say we stay here forever."

Astrid snorted. "Tempting, but we have class."

Killian stood. "Alright, let's go before she sets something on fire again."

I glared at him. "I will find a way to light you up first."

He winked. "Can't wait."

Astrid rolled her eyes. "Come on."

Caspian led the way. The swirling light of the portal shimmered, stretching into existence. I stepped through first, Astrid right behind me.

The moment my feet hit solid ground again, I flopped onto my bed with a groan.

"I am never moving again."

Astrid collapsed onto her bed. "Agreed."

I stared at my tablet, fingers hovering over the screen. The argument with Zephyr still rattled through my head, looping like a spell gone wrong. I hated feeling like I had to justify my parents' sacrifices, like their legacy was up for debate.

A soft chime broke through my thoughts. I glanced at the screen.

Zephyr: *Are you mad at me??*

Zephyr: *I didn't mean to say anything bad about your parents. I just wanted to understand.*

Zephyr: *Please talk to me.*

I sighed, flopping back onto my bed.

Ignoring him would be easier, but...this was Zephyr. He wasn't like the others. And no matter how annoyed I was, I didn't want to fight with him.

Before I could overthink it, I typed back.

Me: *I don't want to fight.*

Zephyr: *Me either. Can I see you?*

Me: *Yeah.*

A pause.

Zephyr: *Meet me in the courtyard?*

I let out a breath and pushed myself up. If I didn't go now, I might talk myself out of it.

The courtyard was quieter than usual, the floating lanterns bobbing gently in the air, their golden light casting shifting patterns on the cobblestones. The runes woven into the stone pathways pulsed faintly beneath my feet, their energy reacting to the presence of students even when the grounds were empty.

Zephyr stood near a low wall, hands in his pockets, his gaze on the enchanted lily pond in the center of the courtyard. The water shimmered under the light of the twin moons, the enchanted koi beneath its surface glowing in shades of indigo and gold as they swam in lazy circles.

"Hey," he said softly, turning toward me as I approached.

"Hey," I echoed, wrapping my arms around myself as the crisp evening air sent a shiver down my spine.

We stood there for a moment, the weight of our earlier fight settling between us. Then, Zephyr let out a heavy breath and ran a hand over the back of his neck.

"I messed up, didn't I?"

"A little," I admitted, glancing down at the ancient stone beneath us. The swirling patterns etched into its surface were remnants of old spells, magic so deeply embedded in the Academy's history that no one dared remove them.

He let out a soft chuckle, but there was no amusement in it. "I wasn't trying to discredit your parents. I was just...trying to understand. Why you've had such a hard time manifesting. Why everything about you feels so...different."

"I know," I murmured. "It's just—" I let out a slow breath, my gaze flickering up to the floating lanterns. "People have been talking about my parents my entire life. Either they think I have everything handed to me, or they assume I should be just like them. It's exhausting."

Zephyr was quiet for a moment, then nodded. "I get that." He hesitated before adding, "But you don't have to prove anything to me, Selene. I already think you're incredible."

My breath hitched.

I turned to look at him, caught off guard. His green eyes, sharp as emeralds, softened slightly under the glow of the lanterns. The runes along the courtyard walls pulsed in rhythm with the natural magic around us, but at that moment, I could only focus on the warmth in his gaze.

He cleared his throat and shifted, glancing away for a second.

"So...you want to go back to the room?"

I blinked. "Wait, the room?"

"The hidden one. The one behind the wall."

My stomach did a weird flip. The room. The one we'd fallen into. The one with maps of forgotten realms and documents written in my father's handwriting. It felt like it had been waiting for us.

"You want to go back?" I whispered as if saying it too loudly would make the walls hear me.

"Yeah," he said simply. "I don't think we found that place by accident. And I don't think we should ignore it, either."

I chewed on the inside of my cheek, glancing toward the darkened halls of the Academy behind us. Half of me wanted to pretend we'd never stumbled upon that room, but the other half? It burned with curiosity.

"The entrance might not even open again," I pointed out.

"Only one way to find out."

I let out a slow exhale, then finally nodded. "Alright. Let's go."

His grin was instant, but there was something else beneath it—relief, maybe?

Zephyr reached for my hand again, and this time, I didn't pull away.

"Come on, Lee," he said, leading me toward the Academy doors. "Let's see what secrets that room has been keeping."

Riddle in the Dark | Selene

Sneaking through the Academy at night was a terrible idea.

Not because it was dangerous—he enchanted gargoyles stationed at every archway had a nasty habit of watching students a little too closely—but because the castle itself had a mind of its own. Hallways shifted, doors disappeared, and sometimes, if you weren't careful, you'd take a wrong turn and end up in a completely different part of the Academy.

And yet, here I was, creeping down the west wing corridors with Zephyr at my side, trying to retrace our steps to the hidden room behind the walls.

"We're lost," I whispered.

Zephyr shot me an amused look. "We're not lost. We just—haven't found it yet."

I rolled my eyes. "That's literally the same thing."

"I swear it was near this section," Zephyr murmured, running his fingers along the wall.

I shuddered and rubbed my arms. "What if the entrance is gone?"

Zephyr hesitated, then shook his head. "No. Magic like that doesn't just disappear. There's always a way back in."

The first time we'd stumbled into the secret room, it had been an accident—a misstep, a shift in the wall, and suddenly we were falling into a hidden space beneath the Academy. But now, intentionally trying to find it again, was proving way harder than expected.

I bit my lip, my mind cycling through possibilities. Maybe it wasn't just a wall. Maybe it had to be triggered the same way as before.

I stopped walking and turned to Zephyr. "Remember how I tripped over your foot last time?"

His lips quirked. "Hard to forget."

I ignored the way my face heated at the memory. "What if it's not just about stepping on the right spot—what if we have to be off balance? Like, falling?"

Zephyr arched a brow. "So, what? You want me to trip you again?"

I shot him a flat look. "I was thinking more like... I could lean on the wall and see if it shifts."

He crossed his arms, pretending to think it over. "Or—hear me out—I trip you, and we see if the magic recognizes it."

I groaned. "Zephyr."

He chuckled but stepped back, gesturing for me to proceed.

I braced myself and leaned into the stone. Nothing. I pressed harder. Still nothing.

Frustrated, I pushed with my full weight—and the floor vanished beneath me.

I yelped as I fell through the wall, tumbling into darkness.

A second later, Zephyr crashed down beside me.

"Well," Zephyr groaned, rolling onto his back. "Guess you were right."

I pushed myself up, blinking in the dim light. We were back—the secret room spread out before us, its dusty shelves and forgotten artifacts waiting in eerie silence.

This place felt...untouched. Like a pocket of history sealed away, waiting for someone to uncover its secrets. Runes lined the walls, their symbols shifting slightly under the flickering candlelight. Scrolls and papers were scattered across the wooden table at the center of the room, and along the far wall, the massive map still stretched from floor to ceiling.

I exhaled slowly. "It's still here."

Zephyr pushed himself up beside me, his gaze sweeping over the space. "Yeah...and I still don't think we found this place by accident."

I swallowed and made my way toward the desk, my fingers trailing over the worn leather covers of the books stacked haphazardly across it. The scent of aged parchment and ink filled the air, the kind of smell that felt like history.

And then—I saw it.

My father's handwriting.

I barely breathed as I pulled the old, cracked journal from the pile, my fingers trembling slightly. I knew this script—the slanted, deliberate strokes, the way the letters curled at the ends.

"Zephyr," I whispered. "This was his."

Zephyr was at my side in an instant, peering over my shoulder as I carefully flipped through the pages. Notes, diagrams, even sketches of sigils I didn't recognize. But then—

I stopped.

A single passage stood out, the ink slightly darker, as if he'd pressed harder when writing it. It wasn't a spell, or instructions, or anything I immediately understood.

It was a riddle.

"Four doors, four keys, four paths untaken.
A hidden truth in shadows shaken.

One who seeks but does not see,
Will find the lock, but not the key."

My heart pounded. "What does that mean?"

Zephyr took the book, reading the passage again. "Four doors. Four keys. Sounds like some kind of puzzle."

I shook my head slowly. "I don't know. But if my father wrote this…" I trailed off, my thoughts colliding in a storm of possibilities.

It wasn't like something happened to my parents. They were at home. I could just call and ask.

My shoulders slumped. I just knew they wouldn't tell me. they'd say stay focused on work and manifesting your magic.

This journal—this room—was something they'd never spoken about. They had never once mentioned hidden chambers, ancient riddles, or anything remotely close to this.

If I asked, they'd just say it wasn't my time yet.

My stomach tightened.

They'd been keeping secrets from me my whole life. Maybe to protect me. Maybe because they didn't trust me to know the full truth.

But this—this was my father's handwriting, his words.

And for the first time, he couldn't keep them from me.

Zephyr exhaled. "I think this is a warning."

Zephyr and I crouched over the old wooden desk like two thieves in a heist—if thieves were mostly just flipping through really old, really dusty papers and occasionally sneezing.

"I think I just inhaled a century's worth of dust," I muttered, waving a hand in front of my face.

Zephyr snorted. "Yeah, well, I think this entire room is a health hazard. I'm pretty sure I just saw a spider the size of my hand."

I stiffened. "You—what?"

"Never mind, let's keep going," he said.

"No, no, back up. Was it near me?" I was already on the verge of abandoning this entire mission. Discovering Academy secrets? Yes. Being near spiders? Absolutely not.

Zephyr grinned. "Wouldn't you like to know?"

I glared at him and aggressively flipped a page in the old journal. Cursed. All men are cursed.

The room felt heavier the deeper we dug. The shelves were full of things no student should have access to—confidential mission logs, war reports, and old spell books with warnings scrawled across their covers. This wasn't just a forgotten archive. This was a buried secret.

"Alright," Zephyr said, holding up a tattered document. "You ready for some Grade A sketchiness?"

"I was born ready."

He smirked. "Says here that your parents weren't just on random 'missions.' The Academy assigned students to strategic takeovers."

I blinked. "Like...military takeovers?"

"Yeah." He tossed the document in front of me, rubbing his temple. "And the headmaster made it sound like these were diplomatic assignments. Helping with 'realm stability' and 'peacekeeping' efforts."

I scanned the paper. My parents' names were listed over and over again. Leia Trueshadow. Kofi Trueshadow.

But then, another name caught my attention.

Headmaster Marcellus.

There was a note scribbled in the margins next to his name.

"Ensure Trueshadow pair remain unaware of full directive. Eyes must stay on target—do not disclose true objective."

I gripped the edges of the page. "They didn't just use my parents for their power, they lied to them. Sent them on these 'missions' while keeping the real goals a secret."

Zephyr whistled. "Yeah. That tracks. And it looks like they weren't the only ones." He gestured to a stack of reports. "Dozens of students. Sent off on what they thought were peacekeeping missions. Turns out, the headmaster was just playing chess with real people."

I let out a slow breath, my thoughts tangling together.

This had to be the secret my parents had discovered—the one they had barely escaped from.

And suddenly, as if my brain was actively trying to make this situation more complicated, I thought of Caspian.

Because of course I did.

I grimaced. Why was I thinking about him right now?

"Selene?"

I snapped back to reality. Zephyr was staring at me.

"What? No. I'm fine," I blurted. "Completely focused. Love reading about government betrayals. Not thinking about anything else at all."

Zephyr squinted. "I didn't ask if you were thinking about something else. Why do you look guilty?" he pressed.

"I don't look guilty," I said, probably looking very guilty. "Let's move on."

Zephyr, to his credit, let it go. But not before giving me a long, suspicious glance like he was filing this moment away for later interrogation.

Focus, Selene.

I flipped through more pages, my pulse still slightly unstable for reasons that had nothing to do with Caspian and everything to do with the fact that my parents had been used as unwitting weapons by the Academy.

Then, I found it.

The last entry in my father's journal.

The handwriting was more rushed than the others, like he'd been writing in a hurry.

"We have to run. Leia and I—we can't stay. We found something. We were never supposed to. He's coming for us. The Headmaster is lying.

The keys are hidden in plain sight.

The truth is buried beneath the Academy.

What he wants—what he's always wanted—is locked away."

"The truth is buried beneath the Academy," I murmured.

Zephyr leaned in. "What truth?"

"I don't know," I admitted. "But my father was afraid of something. And whatever it was, he thought the headmaster would come after him for it."

Zephyr tapped the page. "The keys are hidden in plain sight. That sounds like something we can figure out."

Manifestation & Mistrust | Selene

The Academy had always breathed magic, but today, something different thrummed beneath my skin—anticipation. I settled into my usual chair, running a hand over the armrest, tracing the spiraling symbols carved into its surface.

Professor Vinocia clapped his hands, instantly silencing the murmuring students.

"Alright, class! Today's lesson will be particularly special," he announced. "We've spent some time, unlocking potential, and experimenting with your affinities.

Now, I expect progress." A hush fell over the room. I could feel the weight of a dozen gazes flicker toward me, each one wondering the same thing. Had Selene Trueshadow finally manifested? I straightened in my seat.

Today was the day I spoke my truth. Today, I wasn't going to sit in silence while rumors twisted around me like vines. Before Vinocia could continue, I lifted my chin and spoke.

"I had...a moment," I said quietly. "But it wasn't real. I didn't control it."

Vinocia studied me for a moment. "That's common in blood-blocked lineages. A surge isn't manifestation—it's a symptom of pressure. When you manifest, you'll feel the difference.

Control is the marker."

"So we're all just ticking magical time bombs?" Someone muttered behind me.

Zephyr cleared his throat. "Well, I'm definitely ticking. There's been...some activity."

Vinocia's gaze snapped to him. "Activity?"

He rubbed the back of his neck, looking at me briefly. "Yeah, uh. Ice stuff. Wind, too."

A few students laughed like he was making a joke, but I didn't. I remembered the secret room—the gust that knocked me off my feet, the frost climbing his arms.

"You have two affinities," I said under my breath.

Vinocia didn't laugh. He narrowed her eyes, the corners of his mouth tightening.

"Manifesting two affinities. If you're serious, Mr. Heray... we'll need to speak privately after class."

Zephyr gave a tight shrug. "Wasn't planning on making it a group project."

Odessa leaned forward, a slow smirk unfurling on her lips. "What extra help did the princess get to manifest?"

The venom in her voice was sharp, coiled tight with something that wasn't just doubt—something closer to disdain. I met her gaze with unwavering calm, even as the heat in my chest began to rise.

"I didn't get extra help," I said through my teeth.

I mean I did, kind of, but she's saying it like it's a bad thing.

My pyromancy was random like everyone else's. A ripple of shock swept through the class. The floating lanterns above us flickered violently. I could see the calculation flashing behind Vinocia's eyes as he studied me, but he said nothing.

Odessa scoffed. "What are we supposed to believe? That

you've been stuck this whole time and mommy and daddy didn't jump in to save you. Please, we all know you got help."

A sharp chill ran down my spine, but I didn't flinch. "Help?" I repeated, my voice steady, even as a storm raged inside me. How did she know. It was not an unfair advantage. It was me just using my resources.

Odessa leaned back in her chair, crossing her arms. "Oh, I don't know. Maybe your parents had someone unlock your powers because they were embarrassed to have a Trueshadow without magic."

My nails dug into my palms. The heat rising beneath my skin threatened to spill over, but I forced myself to breathe. Odessa had been waiting for this—to pick, to prod, to make me react.

Vinocia finally interjected. "That is quite the accusation, Odessa," he said smoothly, though his sharp gaze flicked toward her with warning. "Unless you have evidence that Selene is receiving an outside help, I suggest you choose your words wisely."

Odessa, for once, had the decency to remain quiet, though the smirk never left her lips. Vinocia turned to me.

"Selene, when did this manifestation occur? And how?" The memory of the swamp returned with startling clarity—the thick humid air around me, the coiling snake hidden beneath the reeds, the moment its scales had begun to bubble as the water boiled with unnatural heat.

My breath caught at the recollection, but I swallowed it down before it could surface in my expression. "I was alone," I said carefully. "It just...happened. One moment I felt nothing, and the next, everything was burning." Whispers rippled across the room like a pebble skimming across a pond. Pyromancy was powerful, volatile. Manifesting without warning, without a triggering event, was rare.

Vinocia stroked his chin thoughtfully. "Fascinating. That level of elemental reaction suggests a high degree of raw potential." He turned to the class, addressing them as a whole. "Manifestations occur when something within us is forced to wake up. A moment of danger, extreme emotion, or necessity. Selene's case, while uncommon, is not unheard of."

Odessa scoffed again. "Still sounds convenient. The Trueshadow name just happens to spark magic out of nowhere?"

Vinocia ignored her, "Power doesn't always follow a straight path. If we think back to the Originators—the ones blessed by the gods—we see that elemental power was not merely an inheritance but a calling. Nodreus, the God of Moving Realms, gifted Wyny geokinetic might. Cene, the God of Time, bestowed aerokinesis upon Hakim. But rarely did their direct descendants manifest those same gifts exactly as before. Instead, abilities evolved, shifted, adapted over time."

A student raised a hand. "So, like, someone from Wyny's bloodline might have inherited some kind of earth magic, but not necessarily the same form of it?"

Vinocia nodded. "Exactly. The gods wove potential into their champions, but magic is a living thing. It does not stay stagnant. It changes based on the wielder, the time, the need. And sometimes, it resurfaces in ways even history cannot predict."

I stiffened. The map on the wall, the riddle in my father's handwriting—all of it suggested something long-buried, something evolving over time. If magic could shift, if affinities could be rewritten through generations, then perhaps my own manifestation wasn't as straightforward as I had assumed.

"Selene," Vinocia continued, his tone careful, measured. "Did anything else happen during your manifestation? Anything unusual beyond the pyromantic response?"

My lips parted, but I hesitated. The room. The symbols. The way the energy in my veins had resonated with something ancient beneath the Academy. But if I spoke of it now, I would be inviting questions I wasn't ready to answer.

"Not that I recall," I lied.

Vinocia held my gaze for a long moment before nodding. "Very well. Then we will monitor your progress. I suggest you start keeping a record—any surges, any shifts in sensation. Pyromancy is an affinity of destruction, but also of transformation."

His words rang in my head. Destruction and transformation.

I swallowed hard, nodding. "Understood, sir."

* * *

The Battle Hall was one of the largest training spaces in the Academy, its high ceilings supported by thick stone columns etched with symbols of legendary warriors.

The walls were lined with racks of weapons—wooden swords, enchanted staffs, and reinforced shields—each meant to prepare students for combat in a world where power alone wasn't enough.

Professor Darion, a battle-worn instructor with a jagged scar along his jaw, stood at the front of the class. He surveyed us like he was evaluating our worth.

"Combat is not just about power," he began, voice deep and steady. "It is about discipline, adaptability, and understanding the history of those who fought before us. Many of you believe your magic is enough. That it makes you untouchable."

His sharp gaze cut across the room. "That belief will get you killed." Silence blanketed the space.

Even Astrid, who had a habit of whispering snarky comments, kept her mouth shut. Professor Darion turned to a massive mural behind him, a detailed depiction of four figures engaged in battle, each wielding a different style. "These are the Four Pillars of Combat: The Guardian, the Duelist, the Elementalist, and the Shadow. Every warrior falls into one of these categories—or, if they are skilled enough, a mix of them."

He pointed to the first figure—a heavily armored fighter, shield raised. "The Guardian. Strength, endurance, and control. They weather every storm and strike when the enemy is exhausted. Who can give me an example of a Guardian in history?"

Zephyr raised a hand. "General Eryx. He led the defense of the Southern Gates, holding off an entire army for three days with only a handful of warriors."

Darion nodded. "Good. The Guardian survives the battle so their allies can win the war."

He moved to the next figure, a fighter with two curved blades, stance low. "The Duelist. Speed and precision. They look for weak spots and strike before their enemy can react. Who?"

Sunna answered, "Zyra the Swift. She could disarm an opponent in three moves."

"Correct." Darion stepped to the third, a mage engulfed in swirling fire and lightning. "The Elementalist."

Astrid smirked. "Raw power. They use the battlefield itself as a weapon."

Darion inclined his head. "Indeed. Elementalists reshape the fight to their advantage. But their downfall is over-reliance on magic, leaving them vulnerable when caught off guard." He took a step toward the final figure, a hooded warrior blending into the darkness. "And last, the Shadow."

I swallowed as his hand hovered over the mural. "Stealth. Deception. Winning before the battle even begins."

Darion's lips curved slightly. "Correct. Shadows slip through unseen, striking when the enemy least expects it. They do not need strength or brute force; they use their enemy's weakness against them."

He turned back to the class. "Throughout history, great warriors have blurred the lines between these categories. A Guardian may learn precision from a Duelist, an Elementalist may study the discipline of a Shadow. Those who adapt survive."

A student raised a hand. "Which is the strongest?"

Darion's gaze sharpened. "None. And all. A fighter is only as strong as their ability to recognize their own weaknesses."

The words sank into me. My own combat instincts had always been more reactionary than planned. What did that make me?

Darion clapped his hands. "Enough theory. Now, we put it to practice."

The training mats were rolled out, weapons distributed. We stood in pairs, ready to put our knowledge to the test.

Zephyr was paired with Elias, a towering brute of a student who looked like he was built to withstand an earthquake.

Sunna found herself opposite a wiry girl who moved like a dancer, daggers in hand. Astrid cracked her knuckles, grinning as we faced each other. "Let's see what you've got, Lee."

Professor Darion's voice rang out. "No magic. Just skill. Fight as if your life depends on it."

Astrid lunged first. I barely dodged, pivoting on my heel.

She was fast. Too fast.

I didn't need to weather the storm like a Guardian. I needed to be faster. I adjusted my stance, lowering my center of gravity, shifting on the balls of my feet.

Astrid threw a sharp jab, but I sidestepped, twisting my body at the last second.

She overcommitted, and I saw my opening. I struck before she could recover, sweeping my leg beneath hers. She stumbled but rolled away before I could pin her. She came back at me with a sharp jab, forcing me to pivot.

Every move she made, I studied.

We circled each other, trading blows—punches that barely missed, dodges that left us both gasping. My heart pounded. Astrid grinned like she was enjoying this a little too much. Then she changed her approach, going low again—but this time, I was ready. I twisted, using her own momentum against her, knocking her onto her back.

I pressed my forearm against her shoulder, pinning her just long enough to prove a point. She let out a breathless laugh.

"Okay, that was good." I grinned, offering a hand.

"Again?" Darion watched us all with a calculating look.

After class, the students dispersed, some staying behind to discuss techniques while others left in pairs or small groups. I wiped the sweat from my brow and turned toward the corridor, eager to get some air. Astrid said she would meet me in the room, she was going to shower and head to the library with Sunna. Zephyr went off with his rugby friends. I wanted to shower and get in my bed.

A nap sounded great before my pounds of homework.

I had to remember to call my parents too. They've been calling, and I've been putting them off.

Before I could make it down the hallway, a familiar, unwelcome voice cut through the noise.

"Trueshadow." I stopped, shoulders tensing.

Odessa stood near the training hall entrance, arms crossed, a smirk curling on her lips. "What do you want?" I said, exhausted from her games.

She took a slow step closer. "Just wondering how long you're going to keep up the act."

"What act?" I clenched my fists.

"Oh, come on," she drawled. "You suddenly manifest, just when people start doubting you? And let me guess, you can do all four fighting styles? How convenient." Heat crawled up my neck.

"No, I am duelist, Odessa. I didn't pick the style, it picked me."

"That's cute. But let's be real—magic or not, you don't belong here." She laughed, shaking her head.

"Care to explain?" I said fists balled up at my sides. The anger that had been simmering all day reached a boil. My breath came faster, my fingers tingling with heat. "Say that again."

Odessa stepped even closer, smug. "The Trueshadow reign is over—" The words never finished.

A blast of heat surged from my palms before I could stop it, fire roaring between us like an unleashed beast.

The hallway lit up in orange and gold, the heat pushing Odessa back as her eyes went wide with shock. I gasped, jerking my hands back, heart pounding. The fire faded as quickly as it had appeared, leaving behind only the scorched stone of the Academy walls. Silence stretched between us. Odessa checked over herself for injuries. "Well," she murmured. "Looks like you finally figured out how to fight."

Then she turned and walked away, leaving me standing there, breathless, hands still shaking.

The Truth at Last | Selene

The shadows in the Academy stretched unnaturally long as I moved through the corridors, my breath coming in short, shallow bursts. I felt like one of those girls in horror movies—the ones who were supposed to be silent but somehow managed to breathe too loudly, giving themselves away. Fantastic. Next thing I knew, I'd trip over absolutely nothing and die embarrassingly.

Zephyr was close behind me, his warmth pressing against my back.

"You sure about this?" he whispered, his voice barely more than a breath.

I wasn't. But I couldn't admit that.

I glanced at him. His green eyes, usually bright with mischief, were shadowed with something quieter. He'd been different since we found the hidden chamber, since the map of Ereriath changed everything. No more teasing. No more easy grins. Now, he watched me like I was something fragile—something dangerous.

The riddle tied to the map gnawed at me. From everything we'd learned in class, I had a sinking feeling it had to do with the war. But when I asked the professors, their gazes flickered away, evasive. Which, you know, was always reassuring.

A voice, low and almost melodic, slithered through the corridor. "Trueshadow...it's time."

Zephyr tensed beside me. The air turned sharp, charged with something unseen. Without another word, we shoved against the hidden door. This time, finally, we got it right. The wall groaned, shifting inward, and we stepped into the secret chamber.

I didn't know what we were looking for. We split up, rifling through ancient tomes, dust-covered maps, and relics still humming with forgotten magic. My fingers brushed over a leather-bound book, but before I could open it, a gust of cold air swept through the hall.

My skin prickled.

I turned just in time to see a figure materializing from the darkness.

Queen Grizél.

Only...it wasn't her. Not really.

Her normally warm brown eyes were voids of inky blackness, her expression eerily blank—like a puppet whose strings had been cut.

"What the hell?" Zephyr muttered, stepping in front of me.

I grabbed his wrist before he could move any closer, my pulse roaring in my ears. "It's Queen Griz—ahh...someone I know."

Great save, Selene. Very convincing.

Grizél—or whatever wore her face—cocked her head. "You were never meant to survive this long, child. Your parents were supposed to end the cycle. And yet, here you are."

Ice-cold dread curled through me. "What cycle?" My voice was steady, but a tremor lurked beneath it. This wasn't her. She had never spoken to me like this. Never sounded so...cold.

"The war never ended. It simply...changed its players."

Before I could react, a surge of unseen force slammed into me, sending me crashing to the ground. My vision blurred, Zephyr's curse barely reaching me as he scrambled to his feet.

And then—

Flames burst from my fingertips.

The heat pulsed beneath my skin, alive, wild, and untamed. Foreign, yet familiar—like it had always been inside me, waiting for the right moment to break free.

Zephyr let out a sharp breath, and I turned just in time to see ice shimmer over his torso. Armor—jagged and crystalline—encased his chest and shoulders, gleaming under the flickering torchlight.

"That's...cool," I murmured, mesmerized. "And a little unfair. I nearly set myself on fire, and you get an instant ice vest?"

"Selene!" Zephyr's voice snapped me back.

A shadow lunged from the darkness.

Before it could reach me, a wall of shimmering blue energy erupted between us, sending the figure staggering backward. I squinted against the sudden light, barely making out the silhouette standing near the trapdoor, magic crackling at his fingertips.

Caspian.

I blinked, disoriented. "How did you—"

He stepped forward, eyes burning with intensity, his hands still raised. "We need to go. Now."

"No kidding," Zephyr muttered, eyeing him warily.

I didn't move. Fire was still flickering along my arms. I could feel myself teetering on the brink—between control and chaos. If I let go...

I'd destroy everything.

Smoke curled around us, the heat dissipating as I clenched

my fists, forcing the flames back. As the haze cleared, Caspian's gaze flickered to me, concern softening his face. He reached out, his fingers brushing my cheek.

"Are you alright?"

His touch was cool against my overheated skin, sending a shiver down my spine. I looked up at him, breath catching at the way his stormy eyes locked onto mine. I should have pulled away, but I didn't.

Behind me, Zephyr shifted, his stance rigid. "She's fine," he muttered, stepping between us, back straightening like a shield. "And you are?"

Caspian's jaw tightened. He flicked his gaze toward the darkened hall. "We need to move."

The air between them crackled with something unspoken—challenge, maybe. Or jealousy. I didn't have time to figure out which.

Caspian turned toward the trapdoor.

"How did you get here?" I asked.

"We'll talk in your room," he said, holding out a hand for me to lead the way.

I stepped through. Behind me, Zephyr and Caspian hesitated before Zephyr bowed dramatically, smirking. "After you."

Caspian rolled his eyes and stepped through.

As soon as we reached my room, I called Astrid. She needed to be here.

"Addy's on her way," I announced, glancing between the two of them. "Caspian, this is Zephyr. Zephyr, Caspian. Can we skip the whole awkward thing?"

I didn't say anything about what happened in the chamber. About how her eyes had turned black.

About how she knew my name before I said it.

About how I *believed it was her*.

I'd been wrong—and if Caspian hadn't shown up when he did...I might not be standing here.

But how do you explain that to your friends, when they're waiting to laugh at awkward tension and decode magical maps?

Caspian arched a brow. "Is he your boyfriend?"

"Who's asking?" Zephyr challenged.

I groaned. "I do not have a boyfriend."

Never—not once—had I considered what would happen if Zephyr and Caspian were in the same room. Why would I? A guy from another realm and a guy from this one were never supposed to cross paths.

And yet, here we were.

The door burst open.

"I have Sunna!" Astrid announced, slightly breathless. "Is that okay?"

I shrugged. "The more, the merrier."

Sunna shut the door behind her, pressing a hand over her heart in a dramatic pledge. "Whatever it is, I swear to complete secrecy. I would never divulge anythi—" Her eyes locked on Caspian. "Uh... who are you?"

He smiled. "Caspian."

"Caspian who?" she asked suspiciously.

Astrid, stepping in beside her, crossed her arms. "Where's Killian?"

I raised a hand. "One thing at a time. Let's get everyone caught up."

And then, finally, I told them everything.

"Alright," I said, forcing a smile. "Let's start with the obvious." I gestured toward Caspian, who stood near the door like some brooding royal fresh out of an over complicated prophecy. "This is Caspian. He's not from here."

Zephyr narrowed his eyes. "Yeah, I gathered that much."

Caspian smirked.

Before Zephyr could say something potentially aggressive, I pushed forward. "He's from another realm—Odreazah."

Silence.

Sunna blinked. "I'm sorry. What?"

I sighed. "I know it sounds insane, but it's real. Odreazah exists. And Caspian is proof."

Zephyr let out a short, humorless laugh. "Okay, how exactly does this guy just *show up* out of nowhere? Did he take a wrong turn at inter dimensional Starbucks?"

I hesitated, glancing at Caspian, who—infuriatingly—looked completely unbothered.

"There are ways between the realms that you are unfamiliar with," he said smoothly.

Sunna squinted at him. "Wow. That was vague and unhelpful. You'd make a *great* politician."

Caspian just smiled.

I turned to Astrid and Sunna, dropping the next bombshell. "There's more." My voice lowered slightly. "Addy, I didn't tell you everything before."

Astrid's brows lifted, but she didn't say anything.

Sunna, however, sighed dramatically. "Oh, of *course* not. Because why would we ever be upfront about important, potentially life-threatening secrets?"

I ignored her.

"Zephyr and I found a hidden chamber," I said. "Inside the walls of the Academy. A secret room filled with maps, old books, and relics that shouldn't exist."

Sunna shot forward in her seat. "Wait, hold on—inside the

Academy? Like, actually *inside* the walls?"

"Yes."

She threw up her hands. "So you're telling me we have an entire semester of 'Advanced Theories in Magical Ethics,' but *nobody* thought to mention the underground library of forbidden knowledge?"

"Not the point," I said, pulling out the folded map and laying it on the desk.

Astrid leaned in. "This...this changed, didn't it?"

I nodded. "Yeah. The first time I touched it, the map revealed locations that aren't on any official record. And then we found a riddle—one that's somehow tied to Ereriath."

Astrid groaned, throwing her head back. "So let me get this straight. You and Zephyr have been *sneaking around*, finding *secret rooms*, *discovering lost history*, and only *now* you're telling me?"

I winced. "I'm really sorry?"

Astrid huffed and turned to Caspian like she had just identified the true villain in this situation. "And you knew too? Caspian knew *too*?"

Caspian lifted his hands. "No. I sensed she was in danger and came to help."

I turned on him. "Oh, right—let's not pretend I forgot your mother tried to kill me. We still need to talk about that."

Astrid did a double take. "I'm sorry, the QUEEN did WHAT?!"

"What Queen," Zephyr said. While Sunna said "I'm sorry, Queen?" at the same time.

"That was *not* my mother," Caspian argued.

Sunna let out a long, suffering sigh, rubbing a hand down her face. "Alright. So, secret rooms, shifting maps, and now a guy from another realm." She exhaled. "Yeah. No. That's totally normal. Nothing alarming here at all."

Caspian smirked. "Glad to see you're catching up."

Sunna shot him a glare. "I don't like you."

Astrid tapped a finger on the desk. "Okay. So what's the next step? If this map and the chamber are connected to Ereriath, then what does that mean for us?"

I exhaled. "It means...we need to go there."

Sunna *choked* on air. "I'm sorry—WHAT?!"

Astrid, already resigned to my terrible life choices, just sighed. "Of course we do."

Zephyr crossed his arms tighter. "Absolutely not."

Caspian met my gaze. "We need to talk to my mother first. And you're not going by yourself."

Astrid, suddenly perking up, clapped her hands together excitedly. "SQUAD QUEST!"

Zephyr groaned. "Selene, we don't have enough information."

Astrid smiled, "That's the whole point of a quest."

And just like that, things got even more complicated.

The Seeker's Shadow | Selene

The King and Queen lied to me.

As I stood in the living area, my mind reeled. The truth had been there all along, buried beneath carefully crafted deceptions.

They told me my parents had to be sent back during the war. They never told me they were the targets. That they were being hunted. And now, somehow, I am the target.

A cold pit formed in my stomach as I turned toward the Queen, my voice barely above a whisper.

"You should have told me."

Queen Grizél's face remained unreadable, her polished mask of royalty firmly in place. "We needed to protect you."

I let out a sharp, bitter laugh. "By keeping me in the dark? By lying to me about my parents? About the war?"

Caspian shifted beside me, his expression tight. He'd known—he had to have known—but even he looked shaken by the weight of the revelation.

King Victor stepped forward, his voice measured. "Selene—"

"Don't."

My magic flared beneath my skin, crackling at my fingertips. If I let go, the whole room might burn. But I didn't care.

"This child speaking to me as if I am not the King of the realm," he spat. His jaw clenched. "You don't understand."

"No," I snapped, whirling on him. "I do. You knew my parents weren't just soldiers. They were pawns. You used them, sent them to fight battles they didn't even know they were fighting. And now, I'm one too."

I turned to the Queen, my chest heaving.

"And you—" My voice caught. "You came and tried to kill me."

Victor hesitated. "That wasn't Grizél."

"What do you mean it wasn't her?" I asked, my voice sharp.

Victor's gaze flicked toward Caspian.

Caspian stepped forward slowly, tension in every movement. "It wasn't the Queen, Selene. It was an illusion—a mimic, maybe even the Seeker himself. He...copies people."

My breath caught. "So he made me think she turned on me?"

"He wanted to shake you," Caspian said. "Make you question what's real. And it worked—for a moment."

I looked toward the Queen. Her face was unreadable, but her eyes held regret.

"I would never hurt you," she said quietly. "Not in any form."

"You knew." The words fell from my lips like a curse, my throat tight with betrayal. "You knew."

"The thing that took my form was trying to gain your trust," Grizél said carefully, watching me as though I might shatter. "It never wanted you to see its true self. But I assure you, Selene, it was not me."

Astrid crossed her arms, her sharp gaze cutting through the room. "And remind me again how you 'sensed' Lee was in danger?"

Caspian opened his mouth, then hesitated.

Killian exhaled heavily. "There's...a spell. A link. It lets us sense when you're scared, sad, that sort of thing."

I felt the ground shift beneath me. "And you did that to me?"

"To both of you," Killian clarified, not even bothering to sugarcoat it.

My gaze snapped to Caspian. "Why didn't you just tell us?"

Astrid's sharp voice cut in. "So...you're just constantly tuned in to our emotions? Like—right now? Are you feeling this?"

Queen Grizél straightened. "I asked them to do it. We all want to make sure you're safe."

"Because you knew someone wanted me dead," I bit out, "and yet, you never thought to mention it?" My heart pounded in my chest. "Why? Why now? Why me? My parents are still alive—so what makes me the target?"

No one answered.

My stomach twisted as my gaze landed back on Caspian. "And why," I hissed, "is everyone answering for you?"

He swallowed hard. "I was afraid you wouldn't agree to it."

My magic flared dangerously. "So you decided for me?"

"I knew it was a good idea," he defended, his voice quiet. "At least until your powers came in."

"No." I stepped forward, shaking my head. "All of this comes down to the fact that every single one of you knew I was in danger and chose to keep it from me."

Silence.

I clenched my fists so tightly my nails dug into my palms. "Does my parents know?"

Nothing. No denial. Just silence.

I let out a sharp, frustrated groan and threw my hands up. "Unbelievable."

I turned to Queen Grizél, my voice steady despite the storm raging inside me.

"Tell me everything."

Her gaze flickered.

"Selene—"

"No more half-truths. No more lies. I want the whole story. From the beginning." My voice was sharp. "Why did my parents have to leave? What really happened in the war? And who was after them?"

Grizél exhaled slowly, her posture shifting as if bracing herself for what she was about to say. She turned to King Victor, who gave her a slow, almost imperceptible nod.

She looked back at me, and for the first time today, her royal mask cracked.

"Alright," she said softly. "I will tell you everything."

She turned toward the window, gazing out as if looking into the past. Then she began.

"The war was never about territory or power, as the history books say. It wasn't even about the gods."

She turned back to me, her eyes dark and solemn. "It was about magic. Specifically, your parents' magic."

I stiffened. "What?"

She nodded. "Leia and Kofi weren't just powerful, Selene. They were...an anomaly. No two mages had ever been born with such potent, complementary abilities. Fire and mind. Destruction and control. Someone—someone ancient, someone dangerous—wanted that power. And they would have done anything to get it."

A chill crept down my spine. "Who?"

Grizél's lips pressed into a thin line. "We don't know their true name. Only their title."

I swallowed. "What is it?"

Her voice dropped to a whisper. "The Seeker."

The name slithered through the air like a shadow, curling around me, sinking into my skin.

I glanced at Caspian, who had gone rigid beside me, his fists clenched at his sides.

"The Seeker..." I repeated. "What did they want with my parents?"

Grizél's throat bobbed as she swallowed. "To control them. To use them as weapons."

She walked toward the center of the room, her voice gaining strength. "The Seeker has spent centuries searching for magic that cannot be replicated. Your mother's telekinesis wasn't just rare, it was something more. She could move things—bend them, shape them—but she could also tap into the unseen forces that connected magic itself. And your father...Kofi wasn't just a pyromancer. He was a creator."

I frowned. "A creator?"

Victor finally spoke. "He could make fire exist where there was none. Fire mages pull from existing sources, shape what's already there. But Kofi could summon flames from the void. From nothing."

My breath caught. I'd always known my father was strong, but this was different.

Grizél continued, "The Seeker wanted them both. Fire to destroy, mind to control. With them under his influence, he could have reshaped the balance of power across all realms. We believe he was planning to bind them with magic, forcing them to his will."

My stomach twisted. "And you knew this? You knew someone wanted to enslave them?"

Grizél's expression darkened. "We didn't know at first. But with the headmaster sending them out on different missions and when the war began, the truth became clear."

I folded my arms. "Then why didn't you tell them?"

"Because we didn't have proof," Victor said. "And if they knew, they would have fought back. They would have stayed. They would have died."

I clenched my jaw. "So you sent them away."

Grizél nodded. "At the final hour, we had no choice. The Seeker's forces were closing in. They were winning."

Her voice grew heavier. "Leia and Kofi had already fought in countless battles, believing they were defending the realms. But in truth, every war, every battle, was a distraction. A way to force them to weaken them, to make them easier to take."

Caspian stepped forward. "So you tricked them," he said quietly. "You told them it was for their safety, but you really sent them away to hide them."

Grizél's shoulders stiffened. "Yes."

"And now?" I looked at her, my pulse hammering. "If The Seeker wanted my parents, what do they want with me?"

Grizél hesitated, and that hesitation sent ice through my veins.

"You don't know," I whispered.

Victor's voice was grave. "We have theories. But no, Selene. We don't know why they want you. Only that they do."

Silence settled over the room, thick and suffocating.

My thoughts raced, piecing together the fragments of truth. My parents had been hunted. Used. Lied to. The war wasn't about gods or realms—it was about them. And now, somehow, it was about me.

I swallowed hard. "Do my parents know?"

This time, there was no hesitation.

"No."

I let out a breath I didn't know I was holding.

Good.

Because if they didn't know...they wouldn't come for me.

And if they didn't come for me, they wouldn't die for me.

I took a slow, steadying breath and lifted my chin. "So we really have to go to Ereriath"

Victor frowned. "Selene, you don't understand—"

"No, I do," I interrupted. "There is something there that will help. My father's journal said it. We have no choice but to go. With or without you." I turned and looked at Killian and Caspian.

A flicker of something passed through Grizél's gaze—fear, pride, maybe both.

Caspian took a step forward, his voice low. "No, we do it together."

I nodded, my magic simmering beneath my skin, no longer a question of 'if' but 'when'.

The night air in Odreazah was crisp, the sky stretching endlessly above them—a place untouched by time. But no matter how unreal it seemed, they couldn't stay.

I stood in front of the portal.

Astrid rubbed her arms. "I can't believe we're leaving because of...homework."

I sighed. "I know. But we can't just disappear from the Academy. If we start skipping classes, people are going to notice. And I don't think lying to a bunch of professors who can read minds and manipulate time is a great idea."

Caspian stood a few feet away, his arms crossed, expression unreadable. "You'll be back soon, then?"

I met his gaze. "First chance we get."

Killian smirked. "Well, try not to get detention or anything. Kind of hard to go on a world-saving quest when you're stuck scrubbing cauldrons."

Astrid rolled her eyes. "You underestimate how often we get away with things."

Caspian stepped closer, lowering his voice. "Be careful, Selene."

I stiffened slightly, before turning to the portal.

When my feet hit the wooden floor, I stumbled forward, falling on the edge of the bed.

Astrid stumbled through a second later, muttering, "I swear, one of these days, I'm gonna land on my feet."

I barely heard her.

The weight of what I'd learned was still settling over me, heavy and suffocating.

My parents… the war… The Seeker.

I clenched my fists.

We would go back soon.

And when we did, it wouldn't be to ask questions.

It would be to start the fight.

A Fate We Cannot Change| Leia

The moment the portal sealed shut, silence fell over Odreazah like a shroud.

The golden glow of the gateway flickered once before vanishing completely, leaving behind nothing but the echo of its power.

Selene was gone.

Across the room, Queen Grizél stood motionless, her fingers curling into the folds of her robes. Her gaze was locked on the empty space where the portal had been, her shoulders drawn tight.

Her voice was calm, but it left no room for argument. "Caspian, Killian—leave us."

Caspian hesitated, his stormy gaze lingering on the space where Selene had disappeared. His jaw tightened, but he didn't challenge her. Killian, for once, had nothing clever to say. With a respectful nod, they turned and stepped out of the chamber.

The heavy doors shut behind them with a deep boom.

The silence that followed was suffocating.

Kofi shifted beside me, his jaw tight, his fists clenched at his sides. Across from us, Victor stood near the fireplace, arms crossed, watching, waiting.

"So." Grizél finally spoke, rubbing her temple. "It's come to this."

Kofi's voice was low, edged with frustration. "She doesn't know."

Queen Grizél's gaze snapped to him. "And whose fault is that? You still haven't told her," she continued, stepping forward. "After all this time?"

I swallowed, but Kofi was the one to respond. "Sixteen years," he muttered.

"Since the day she was born," Queen Grizél confirmed.

Kofi dragged a hand down his face. "Since the day The Seeker failed to take us."

Grizél's voice was quiet, but her words cut me. "Then he will come for her."

Victor's golden-brown eyes flickered in the dim light. "The Seeker took your power?"

Kofi laughed harshly. "No." His head shook once. "The Seeker didn't take it." His eyes burned. "The gods did."

Victor's posture stiffened, but Grizél spoke. "Your power was so dangerous. So unpredictable. The Seeker wanted to use it to break the laws of magic. The only way to keep balance was to—"

"To bind us," I finished.

Victor's expression didn't change, but the silence after my words was thick.

"And Selene?" he asked finally.

Kofi clenched his fists. "She's can be stronger than we ever were."

Grizél's eyes flicked to mine, searching, assessing.

"If The Seeker finds her..." I exhaled sharply, shaking my head.

"We all know what will happen," she murmured.

Kofi turned to the fireplace, his back to us, fingers digging into the mantel. "She can't do this alone."

"She thinks she has to," I whispered. "She hasn't even called us. She didn't tell us she was leaving."

"She's struggling to find who she can trust," Grizél admitted. "She feels betrayed."

Kofi's head snapped toward her. "We are her parents. She has not been here long enough to distrust us."

"She's realizing you haven't told her the entire truth," Victor countered.

Grizél cut in before he could argue again "Her power has started to manifest."

Kofi turned fully, brows drawn low. "She takes after me?"

Grizél gave a small nod. "So far."

Victor folded his arms. "Caspian and Astrid have been helping her strengthen it."

A strange weight settled in my chest. "What do you mean, so far?"

"We believe she has both of your gifts."

"No one can know," Kofi cursed, voice flat. "If The Seeker finds out—not only does she have one of our gifts, but both—" He shut his eyes, shaking his head. "I will not stand by and let my child walk into danger."

I crossed my arms. "And what do we do, Kofi? We have no power. We can't even portal without assistance."

Victor watched us carefully. "Caspian and Killian are with them. She won't be alone."

Kofi exhaled through his nose, turning back toward the fire.

"She has your journals," Grizél reminded him. "You heard her. There are things she needs to discover. We won't be able to stop her."

Kofi shook his head. "That's not enough." His voice was

barely controlled. "If her powers are manifesting, we need to be there."

"We cannot interfere," King Victor said evenly. "Not yet."

Queen Grizél's lips thinned. "Not unless we want to draw attention to her before The Seeker even realizes what she is."

Kofi turned toward me, his expression unreadable. "Leia—"

"If we go after her, we risk exposing her," I said. "But if we wait, we may be too late."

The room fell into silence.

For the first time since Selene had left—since the past had come clawing back to life—none of us had the right answer.

We had spent years keeping secrets.

Now, those secrets were unraveling.

And the only one who didn't know the truth was the one who needed it the most.

Training, Terror, and a Mild Existential Crisis | Selene

The training grounds smelled like sweat, burned grass, and bad decisions. The sun had dipped below the horizon, leaving the sky a dark, inky blue, but we were still here—training like our lives depended on it. Because, apparently, they did.

"You hesitated," Zephyr said, his voice all calm and instructor-like, but his judgy emerald eyes said failure.

I clenched my fists, still on the ground, irritated. "I didn't hesitate."

Zephyr lifted a brow. "Then why are you on your ass?"

From the sidelines, Astrid let out a dramatic snort, arms crossed like she was the official referee of my humiliation. "Come on, Z. Let her breathe before you start giving a full performance review."

I pushed myself up, dusting off my dignity along with the dirt on my training gear. Losing sucked. Losing in front of Zephyr and Astrid? Even worse.

"Again," I said, rolling my shoulders.

The second I was steady, Zephyr moved—fast. Too fast. A rush of wind wrapped around him, blurring him as he lunged. The air itself became his weapon, slicing toward me in an arc of invisible force.

Instinct took over. My hands lifted before my brain could even process what was happening.

Flames erupted.

Heat met wind in a violent clash, sparks flying, the force sending us skidding back. I barely managed to hold my ground. Zephyr, of course, landed perfectly—like the universe had custom-built him for combat and grace.

He exhaled sharply, watching me with an unreadable expression. "Better," he admitted. "But you're still too reactive."

I wiped sweat from my forehead, my curls sticking uncomfortably to my face. "I've been practicing controlling my emotions."

Zephyr tilted his head, like he was seeing something he wasn't sure about. Then, finally, he nodded. "You're doing well."

I let out a breathless laugh. "You're still kicking my ass."

His lips twitched, almost smiling. Almost. "We're training. And when we get out there, if anything happens..." His voice dipped. "I got you."

Astrid strolled over, flipping her hair like she hadn't just watched me get completely manhandled by the wind. "We all do," she added, cracking her knuckles. Then she dropped into a fighting stance. "Now, my turn."

I groaned. "Of course it is."

A gust of wind hit me like a wrecking ball. My feet left the ground, and I was sailing backward like a ragdoll.

I landed hard. Again.

Astrid, meanwhile, was still standing, perfectly fine, her hands swirling through the air, creating a controlled wind tunnel.

Zephyr's ice armor slid into place effortlessly, covering him in a thin, crystalline sheen of frost, making him look like some kind of winter war god.

A deep, agonizingly disappointed sigh cut through the air.

Astrid froze. "WHAT THE ACTUAL—" She spun around, eyes wide. "WHERE DID YOU—HOW DID YOU—ARE WE IN TROUBLE?"

Standing at the edge of the training field, arms crossed like she'd rather be anywhere else but here, was Nyx.

And nothing ruins an evening like an unreasonably powerful, mildly terrifying warrior appearing out of thin air.

I swallowed. Oh no.

"You are unfocused," Nyx said, in that completely emotionless, I-could-kill-you-with-my-pinky tone.

I blinked at her. "I—You—Excuse me?"

"You hesitate," she repeated, stepping forward.

I sat up straighter. "Okay, not this again—"

"You land on your ass."

Astrid muttered, "Okay, she's got a point there."

I glared at her. "Not helping."

Zephyr—who should have been on my side, might I add—murmured, "She's not wrong."

Astrid, however, was still not over the fact that Nyx had just materialized out of nowhere.

She turned to Zephyr. "No, seriously—how did she get here?"

Nyx exhaled sharply, like dealing with us was physically painful.

"I was sent by King Victor and Queen Grizél," she said, stepping forward like a storm cloud. "They believe your training lacks...discipline."

Astrid stiffened. "Okay, but why are you suddenly appearing like some combat grim reaper?"

Nyx ignored her. "The King and Queen have instructed me to

oversee your combat readiness."

Zephyr just nodded. "So, you're someone from the other realm okay." He looked at me. "Any other people I should know about?" he asked as his armor dissolved.

Astrid grabbed my arm. "No, Lee, this does not 'make sense.' This means we are about to die. Via terrifying, overpowered military-lady." she said ignoring Zephyr.

Nyx stared at her.

Astrid swallowed. "Unless…you're here to help in a gentle, supportive, encouraging way?"

Nyx tilted her head. "Does it look like I do gentle?"

Silence.

Astrid turned back to me. "We're dead."

Nyx clapped her hands once, the sharpest, most military-level threatening sound I had ever heard in my life. "Up. Now."

I scrambled to my feet so fast I almost tripped again.

Astrid made a weird strangled sound that was either a laugh or an internal scream.

Nyx gestured toward the training mat. "Selene, you will spar with me first."

I choked.

Zephyr smirked and took a step back like he was front-row seating for my impending doom.

Astrid gasped. "Oh my gods, Lee, you're about to die."

I slowly stepped onto the mat, my body already regretting every choice I'd made in life.

Nyx lifted a single hand. A single hand.

Astrid whispered in horror, "She's not even using two hands, Lee."

I turned my head just enough to glare.

And then—before I could even mentally prepare—Nyx moved.

There was no time to think.

No time to react.

One moment, she was standing. The next—

I was flying through the air.

Again.

I hit the ground hard—again.

At this point, my body and the dirt had a deeply personal relationship. The ground, it seemed, had fully accepted me as its own.

Astrid let out an incredulous gasp from the sidelines. "Did she just flip you with one hand?"

Zephyr, standing beside her, arms crossed like he was analyzing a chessboard instead of my slow demise, nodded. "Yeah. That was definitely one hand."

I groaned and pushed myself up, spitting. "I hate both of you."

Nyx—who hadn't so much as broken a sweat—sighed in disappointment. "You're slow."

I wiped my face with the back of my sleeve, scowling. "I am trying."

"Trying isn't enough." Nyx's voice was so flat, so devastatingly unimpressed, I think a piece of my soul withered. "Again."

I gritted my teeth. Fine. I was done letting her launch me like a ragdoll.

I dropped into my stance, muscles already aching, and forced myself to focus.

Nyx shifted forward, her speed unnervingly controlled. This time, instead of trying to block her attack head-on, I twisted at the last second, letting her momentum carry her past me.

It worked.

For approximately 0.5 seconds.

Then she adjusted mid-step, caught my wrist, and flipped me

anyway.

I hit the ground so fast, I actually saw stars.

Astrid let out a choked laugh. "Lee, I swear, she's defying physics."

Zephyr just shook his head. "She's adapting faster than we are."

Nyx finally let out a slow exhale, stepping back. "You're starting to read movement," she admitted, which I think was the closest thing to a compliment I was ever going to get from her. "But you rely too much on reaction. You must anticipate."

Astrid straightened. "Okay, but, like…if one of us can't beat you alone, what about all three of us?"

Nyx tilted her head. "You believe you will fare better together?"

"Well, we can't do worse."

I pushed myself up, ignoring the full-body regret pulsing through me, and looked at Zephyr. "You in?"

Zephyr rolled his shoulders, ice crackling faintly along his skin. "We might as well see how much we suck as a group."

"Then come." She raised one hand, gesturing for us to make our move. "Together."

Astrid went first, rushing in like a storm, wind surging behind her.

Zephyr followed, ice spreading under his feet in slick, strategic patterns to cut off Nyx's movement.

I circled, waiting for an opening.

Nyx moved like a shadow, effortlessly weaving between us.

Astrid launched a blast of wind—Nyx sidestepped like she had all the time in the world.

She spun toward me, so fast I barely had half a second to react.

Fire burst from my palms, blocking the attack—

Only for Nyx to use my flames to her advantage, twisting mid-air and slamming a kick into my ribs.

I flew back, gasping, barely keeping my balance.

Zephyr tried to grab her arm—she caught his wrist and flipped him like he weighed nothing.

Astrid shot forward with a gust of wind—Nyx let the wind carry her, flipping over Astrid's head before slamming her to the ground with one brutal strike.

All three of us landed in the dirt, groaning in unison.

Nyx exhaled slowly, staring down at us like we were a trio of particularly disappointing recruits.

"That was marginally better," she said.

Astrid rolled onto her back, wheezing. "Did she did she just say we were better?"

Zephyr pushed himself up, glancing at the ice still clinging to his skin. "I think so."

I sat up, still trying to force air back into my lungs. "We still got our asses kicked."

Astrid groaned. "Yeah, but we lost better this time."

Nyx studied us for a long moment. "You are learning."

I blinked. "Wait...was that another compliment?"

Astrid sat up, grinning. "Lee, she's warming up to us."

Nyx's face was unmoving. "I am not."

Zephyr snorted. "That was fast."

Nyx ignored him, stepping back. "Your coordination is sloppy. You predict each other's moves, but you do not trust them. You hesitate. You second-guess. If you cannot function as a unit, you will be overpowered individually."

I rubbed my temples. "So basically...train more?"

Nyx nodded once. "Much more."

Astrid sighed, flopping onto her back again. "Okay, but maybe not right now."

Zephyr rolled his shoulders, wincing slightly. "Yeah. I think we met our survival quota for today."

I exhaled, letting my body relax.

Nyx just watched us. Then, after a long pause, she finally said, "Rest. Tomorrow, we start again."

Astrid muttered under her breath, "Tomorrow? I just started believing in life again." We went to our separate locker rooms to change.

The walk back to the dorms was supposed to be a break—a moment to catch my breath, maybe convince myself that my body wasn't actively trying to stage a rebellion against me after Nyx had tossed me around like a training dummy.

But, of course, the universe had other plans.

The moment we stepped into the main courtyard, I saw her.

Odessa.

Leaning casually against one of the enchanted fountain statues, tossing her sleek, silver-blond hair over one shoulder like she was the main character of an over dramatic novel.

And right in front of her, looking way too polite for my liking, was Zephyr.

I slowed down immediately. Astrid followed my gaze and made a low, knowing noise.

"Ohhh no," she whispered, biting back a grin. "It's happening."

I ignored her and kept walking, but at a deliberately slower pace so I could, you know, listen.

For educational purposes.

"—you were incredible today," Odessa cooed. "Honestly, it's unfair how naturally gifted you are."

Ugh.

I could hear the flutter of her lashes.

Zephyr, ever the gentleman, gave a short chuckle, rubbing the back of his neck. "I wouldn't say that."

Odessa tilted her head, stepping closer. "Oh, come on, Zephyr. You're being modest."

Astrid side-eyed me hard.

I clenched my jaw. I was not irritated.

Not at all.

Perfectly fine.

Completely normal.

Then Odessa did the worst thing possible. She touched his arm. Astrid sucked in a sharp breath, clearly holding back laughter. Okay. Maybe I was a little irritated.

I strode up before I even made the conscious decision to do so, cutting right between them like I had urgent business that required Zephyr's immediate attention.

"Hey," I said, much louder than necessary.

Zephyr blinked. "Uh—"

"Oh, am I interrupting?" I asked, tilting my head slightly.

Odessa's lips twitched into a smirk. Oh, she knew exactly what she was doing.

"Not at all," she purred. "Zephyr and I were just talking about training. You know, the kind of advanced techniques you only pick up when you've had years of refinement."

I ignored the very obvious dig at my clearly less refined combat skills and forced a very neutral, very unbothered smile.

"That's great," I said flatly. "Zephyr, didn't we have something important to do?"

Zephyr, completely unaware of the slow murder happening in my brain, blinked again. "We do?"

I elbowed him lightly. "Yes. We. Do."

"Oh," he said, catching on. "Right. That thing."

Odessa gave me one last amused glance, then let out an exaggerated sigh. "I suppose I'll see you later, Zephyr."

She walked away gracefully, like she had just won some silent competition.

I turned to Zephyr, arms crossed. "Really?"

He stared at me blankly. "What?"

I scoffed. "Odessa was obviously flirting with you."

Zephyr, to my absolute frustration, just shrugged. "So?"

"So?" I repeated. "So, do you like her?"

Astrid was fully invested at this point, arms crossed, eyes practically gleaming.

Zephyr just sighed, like this conversation was exhausting. "Why do you care?"

"Excuse me?" I spluttered. He gave me a very smug look. "Do you want to talk about Caspian?"

My mouth snapped shut.

Astrid actually wheezed.

"I—That is not the same." I recovered quickly.

Zephyr smirked. "Isn't it?"

I hated him. So much.

Astrid was barely holding it together. "Okay, children," she said, slapping me on the back. Too hard, might I add. "You can figure out your feelings later. Right now, we have homework."

I groaned, all irritation shifting into exhaustion. "Oh, gods. Right. The homework."

"Sunna's waiting for us in the study lounge," Astrid added. "We should shower first, though."

"Definitely," Zephyr said, grateful for the subject change.

I rolled my shoulders, still aching from training. "Okay, meet up in an hour?"

Astrid nodded. "Deal." Zephyr shot me one last smug look before heading toward the boys' dorms.

Astrid, still grinning, leaned in.

"You're totally jealous."

I groaned and shoved her toward our dorm.

Odessa, Please Leave | Selene

The library was packed, a sea of students hunched over ancient tomes and glowing tablets. We had to wait thirty minutes before we could even get one of the coveted study rooms. Thirty. Agonizing. Minutes. And to make matters worse, our group of four had unexpectedly become five.

Because, of course, Zephyr had invited Odessa.

We stood clustered outside the glass-paneled door, shifting from side to side as Sunna and Astrid failed miserably at whispering. They weren't even trying, really—every other sentence earned us a sharp glare and a pointed shush from the librarian, who, judging by the daggered look in her eyes, was two seconds from hexing us into silence.

I kept my gaze firmly on my feet, willing time to move faster. Finally, after what felt like an eternity, the previous occupants filed out, and we hurried inside. The second the door clicked shut, the soundproof walls cut off the chaotic noise of the library, leaving only the faint rustle of parchment and the scratch of quills against enchanted paper.

Three four-person tables filled the room. Sunna and Astrid claimed one, already pulling out their Battle Tactics and History assignments. Manifest had been a temporary stop for Zephyr, Sunna and me—once we'd manifested our abilities, we'd transferred to History, leaving only Odessa still enrolled in the class.

I took a seat at the second table, relishing the momentary solitude as I pulled out my overflowing stack of History homework. Weeks of missed lessons meant hours of catch-up, and I needed to focus.

Odessa made a move for the last table, but she hesitated when Zephyr kept walking—straight to my table.

He set his books down beside mine, then turned back toward her with a raised brow. "What are you doing?"

Odessa sighed, rolling her eyes. "Sitting."

Zephyr just gave her that blank, quizzical look of his that somehow conveyed more judgment than words ever could.

Odessa huffed dramatically and, with exaggerated reluctance, dragged herself over to our table.

"Let's start with History," Astrid announced. "Then we can split off for our separate assignments."

Odessa slumped into her chair, pouting. "Fine. I'll just do my work at the other table and come back when you guys are actually interesting."

She flounced off, leaving us blessedly alone—for now.

Hours passed, yet it felt like we hadn't made a dent in the mountain of work. Sunna, however, had other priorities. Every few minutes, she would lean in and whisper some grand scheme about sneaking away to Ereriath, brainstorming how we could vanish from classes without raising suspicion.

"Shh," I hissed, shooting her a warning glance. "We'll talk about it later."

My gaze flicked toward Odessa's table. She was slumped over her textbook, chin propped up on one hand, looking thoroughly unimpressed. She yawned dramatically, tapping her pen against the desk in an obnoxious rhythm. "You guys aren't done yet?

I'm getting bored."

I gritted my teeth. If I could get through this night without setting something on fire, it would be a miracle.

"Just come work over here," Zephyr said. "There was no reason for you to move."

"I am not in History yet, I haven't manifested." she pouted.

Something about the way she said it nagged at me. The way her eyes flicked toward Zephyr, the way her fingers drummed lightly on the table as if she were calculating something.

Zephyr shifted closer, leaning toward my textbook. "You're behind, right?" he asked.

I raised a brow. "Obviously."

He smirked, then reached for my notes. "Here, let me help. I already did half of this last week."

I blinked. "Wait—are you actually offering to be useful?"

His smirk widened. "I'm full of surprises."

His shoulder brushed against mine as he pulled out a spare sheet of paper his fingers moving smoothly as he began jotting down key points from the text. The warmth of his presence was distracting.

Focus, Selene.

I tried to, really, but then he glanced at me out of the corner of his eye and whispered, "You're staring."

My face heated instantly. "I am not."

"You kind of are," he teased, amusement dancing in his voice. "I get it. It's overwhelming, having me this close."

I rolled my eyes so hard they could have fallen out of my head. "Oh, please."

But the way he leaned in just slightly closer made my stomach flip. And I hated that it did.

Behind us, Odessa shifted, just slightly. I caught the movement out of the corner of my eye. Was she…watching? Listening? The sensation of being observed crept over my skin, making me sit up straighter.

Zephyr didn't seem to notice, too absorbed in the notes in front of us. But I did.

And I didn't like it one bit.

We needed a way to get rid of Odessa. After spending most of the night in the library, we had caught up—well, mostly. Everyone else was fine. I, on the other hand, had an outline of all the things I still needed to do.

"I'll walk you," Zephyr said suddenly. We were following the paths back to the dorms.

I jerked my head up, catching the tail end of his conversation with Odessa. My fingers immediately tightened around Astrid and Sunna's arms.

"What does that mean?" Astrid asked—too loudly.

I sucked my teeth, glaring at her. Subtlety was not her strong suit.

Zephyr glanced over his shoulder at us, brow raised. "I'll see y'all tomorrow. Well—" he checked his watch, "technically today."

"Yup," I said quickly, still gripping the other two. "See you then."

He gave me a lingering look before turning toward Odessa, and together, they disappeared through the doors.

The second they were gone, I hissed, "We need to talk."

Astrid nodded immediately, already catching on.

Sunna, however, frowned. "About what?"

"Can you come back to our room real quick?" I asked, lowering my voice. "We need to get to Caspian's phone so we can text him."

Astrid furrowed her brow. "We do?"

"Yes," I whisper-yelled. "How exactly are we getting to Ereriath? And what's our excuse for skipping class? Is there a time difference? What if it moves faster there—what if we lose whole days? We have no plan."

Astrid and Sunna exchanged glances before Sunna let out a slow breath. "Okay. Yeah. That's a fair point."

"Thank you," I huffed. "Now let's go before Zephyr comes back and decides to play twenty questions."

As soon as we got back to the room I went to my bed and grabbed the phone from the hiding spot. "Remind me again what we are looking for on Ereriath," Sunna asked.

"My dad left something there and I have to go get it," I said as I typed out a message.

"Left what?" she asked.

"See that we don't know. Something she needs."

Sunna smirked. "This is getting better and better. My transcript will look way better with quest on it."

"Okay," I said, far too loudly. "Caspian said he'll help us get there, so that's covered. But we need an excuse. If it takes three days, we'll be missing at least one day of classes." I looked up from my phone. "Any ideas?"

"The problem is, it's all of us," Astrid pointed between me, Sunna, and herself. "And Zephyr."

I sighed. She had a point. Disappearing alone was one thing, but all four of us? That was suspicious.

"What if we all caught a bug?" Sunna suggested, tapping a finger against her chin. "We're together all the time. No one would question it."

Astrid snorted. "Or—and hear me out—we just skip class."

I shot her a look. "Skipping class is not an excuse."

"It's an excuse," she countered. "Just not a very responsible one."

I pinched the bridge of my nose. "And what if it takes longer? What if something happens to us?" That was my real worry.

Astrid waved off my concern. "No one's going to miss us if we skip one class."

"All four of us?" I raised an eyebrow.

She and Sunna exchanged a look, then turned back to me with matching grins.

"I still feel like we need a cover," I said.

Astrid groaned, rolling her eyes. "Goody two-shoes Lee." She stretched her arms above her head like this entire conversation exhausted her. "Fine. Let me handle the excuse, okay?"

I hesitated. "Addy—"

"Lee," she smirked. "Trust me."

Something about that smirk made me nervous, but I let out a slow breath and nodded. "Fine."

She clapped her hands together. "Great! Now, let's go commit some light rule-breaking."

II

One Quest Down, I Hope No More To Go

Split Up, They Said. It'll Be Fine, They Said| Selene

We were back in the King and Queen's bedroom. I forgot how plain and normal it was.

Caspian stood close beside me, his warmth brushing against my skin every time he shifted. It was becoming harder to ignore.

Zephyr, leaning against one of the bookshelves, looked considerably less comfortable. His arms were crossed tight over his chest, his jaw clenched tight.

"So," Astrid drawled, tilting her head, "we step through a magic portal to an unknown realm, don't know where we'll land, and might die in the process. Sounds about right."

"Not *die*," Queen Grizél corrected smoothly. "You all will come back to me."

Sunna huffed. "Great. So it's a *wherever-the-wind-takes-you* type of journey."

Killian slung an arm over her shoulder. "Adventurous, isn't it?"

Sunna shot him a look. "That's one way to spin potentially falling out of the sky into certain doom."

Astrid was too busy inspecting one of the enchanted weapons a palace attendant had handed her. "Are we *sure* I'm not allowed to bring explosives?"

Grizél's eye twitched. "No."

"Just checking." she said with a shrug.

The Queen ignored them and turned toward me. "Selene, this is the part where I tell you to reconsider."

I straightened. "And this is the part where I tell you I won't."

King Victor sighed. "Then let's not waste time." He stepped toward the far wall, where an elaborate mural of constellations was carved into the stone. With a single word, the stars began to glow, shifting and rearranging themselves.

Caspian's fingers brushed against my wrist—so brief I almost thought I imagined it.

Zephyr pushed off the bookshelf, eyes flicking between us before settling on Caspian. He didn't say anything, but the sharpness in his gaze made something inside me twist.

Before I could think too much about it, the mural cracked open, revealing a swirling vortex of shimmering light. The portal.

Grizél exhaled. "Where you land will not be up to us."

Sunna huffed. "That's reassuring."

Killian grinned. "Come on, it's exciting."

Astrid rolled her eyes. "Says the guy who *likes* getting thrown through dimensions."

Caspian turned to me, voice low. "Are you ready?"

I wasn't.

Falling was the worst part.

It wasn't like flying. It wasn't graceful. It wasn't even *thrilling*. It was pure, untethered chaos.

I flipped. Someone screamed—maybe Astrid, maybe me. Zephyr was yelling something about stabilizing, but gravity had other plans.

I crashed through *something*, snapping through layers of vines and thick leaves, my limbs tangling in branches as I tumbled toward the earth below.

Pain exploded through my body as I hit the ground hard, my lungs wheezing in protest. A second later, Astrid landed directly on top of me.

"Oh," she groaned. "This is bad."

"You *think*?" I wheezed, shoving her off.

Zephyr landed next, rolling to his feet in an almost unfairly cool way. Killian dropped down after, grinning like he *enjoyed* that, because of course he did.

Sunna hit the ground with a yelp, landing in a thick patch of moss. Caspian was the last to appear. He landed near me, crouching just slightly before straightening and scanning the area.

The jungle was alive. Not in the normal, *oh, cool, lots of plants* way. No. This place *breathed*. The trees twisted unnaturally, their branches curling in strange, jagged angles, their leaves *shimmering* as if they were aware of our presence.

A distant roar echoed through the trees, deep and guttural, like something old and hungry.

Caspian's gaze was sharp. "Stay close. We don't know what's out here."

Zephyr sighed, muttering under his breath. "Of course we land in a cursed jungle."

Killian grinned. "Could be worse."

Astrid turned toward him, incredulous. "HOW? How could this be worse?"

Killian tilted his head, pretending to think. "I mean, we could have landed inside a monster's nest instead of just near one."

Astrid groaned. "You want to be thrown into something's mouth, don't you?"

Killian smirked. "You're catching on."

Astrid stared at him for a long moment. "I can't tell if you're flirting or just insane."

"Bit of both."

Sunna, pulling vines off her arm, shook her head. "This is either going to be hilarious or painfully awkward."

I sighed. "Both."

"Can we focus?" Zephyr rubbed his temples.

We started moving, pushing our way through the jungle, avoiding whatever was making that awful growling noise in the distance.

"So," Astrid piped up, stepping over a massive root. "On a scale from 'not at all' to 'definitely doomed,' how lost are we?"

Caspian sighed. "I'd say...a *seven*."

Killian smirked. "I'd say more of a *six*. We still have our *brains*."

"Debatable," Astrid snorted.

Caspian ignored them. "The first thing we need to do is figure out our bearings."

Sunna pulled out the enchanted map. She tapped the surface, watching as the ink shimmered. "Okay...according to this, we're somewhere near the River of Eshkan."

"That doesn't sound very *close* to the Seeker's stronghold," I frowned.

Zephyr crossed his arms. "Well, it's not like we chose to land here."

Astrid waved dramatically toward the wilderness. "We don't even know if this place is real. What if Ereriath is just a big magical hoax?"

I exhaled. "Alright, everyone shut up. We're in an unknown jungle, probably being hunted by something massive, and we definitely don't want to find out what."

"Told you we should've brought explosives," Astrid muttered,

And somewhere in the distance, the jungle growled again.

The jungle was a fever dream. Shadows stretched unnaturally long between towering trees, their thick trunks wrapped in spiraling vines that pulsed faintly with magic. Bio luminescent fungi clung to the bark, glowing in eerie blues and purples, casting a ghostly haze through the dense underbrush.

Every step felt like it disturbed something ancient. The deeper we pushed, the louder the jungle seemed to breathe. The leaves whispered, the branches creaked, and the ground shifted beneath our feet as if deciding whether to let us pass.

Then I touched the map.

The moment my fingers grazed the parchment, the ink pulsed like a heartbeat. Lines blurred, rearranging themselves into new pathways, new dangers. I felt the change before I saw it.

"The map just changed," I said, holding it up for the others.

Sunna's eyes darted across the shifting markings. "Wait, I just had it."

"Oh, because everything else about this situation makes sense?" Astrid muttered, peering over my shoulder.

Caspian stepped closer. "What does it say now?"

I squinted at the new path unfurling before us. "There's a divide up ahead. Two paths."

As if responding to my words, the jungle groaned. The trees twisted, roots ripping from the earth, reshaping the landscape. The path before us split violently in two, like a wound tearing open in the terrain.

A choice.

"Guess we're not turning back," Killian whistled low.

Zephyr rubbed his temples. "Of course not."

"We need to split up," Caspian decided, scanning the new routes. "We'll cover more ground and figure out where the hell we are."

"Splitting up in a cursed jungle. Great idea," I frowned.

"Not cursed," Sunna corrected. "Just...aggressively enchanted."

"Yeah, that's so much better," Astrid huffed.

The ground trembled beneath us, as if the jungle was impatient, urging us to move.

Caspian, Sunna, and I took the left path. Astrid, Killian, and Zephyr took the right.

We barely made it fifty paces before something moved in the foliage. A flicker of gold in the darkness, a slithering coil of something too fast to track. My heart lurched. "Did you see—"

A blur shot through the trees. A low snarl rumbled through the air.

The creature lunged. A mass of twisting limbs, jagged fangs gleaming in the dim light. Its eyes were hollow pits, reflecting nothing but hunger. It moved like liquid shadow, its body half-corporeal, slipping between solid and mist.

Caspian's blade was out in an instant, the enchanted steel gleaming as he slashed through the air. The creature shrieked, its form flickering. It split—one moment a singular entity, the next, three distinct figures, each more monstrous than the last.

"That's illegal," Sunna gasped.

I didn't have time to agree. One of them lunged at me. Fire surged to my fingertips, blazing to life just as the creature struck. Heat met darkness, and for a moment, the two forces clashed, twisting against each other in a violent storm of energy.

Then the creature screamed and shattered into nothing.

I stumbled back, breath ragged. "Okay. That worked."

Caspian drove his blade through the second creature's core, its form unraveling in a burst of dark mist. The final one hesitated, its hollow eyes flicking between us before it dissolved into the shadows, retreating into the jungle.

Silence.

The air crackled with residual magic. Sunna pressed a hand to her chest, exhaling shakily. "That was too close."

Caspian wiped his blade clean. "We need to keep moving."

We ran.

The jungle blurred around us, the oppressive heat pressing against my skin. My pulse pounded in my ears. Every branch, every rustling leaf, felt like another lurking threat. My fingers burned with leftover fire, my magic still thrumming with the fight.

Then I heard it.

A distant roar.

A scream.

Astrid.

We crashed through the underbrush, barely slowing as we barreled into the clearing where the others had been. My stomach dropped.

Astrid, Killian, and Zephyr stood in the center of a massive stone circle, frozen in place, their bodies rigid with unnatural stillness.

Surrounding them were statues. Dozens, their features twisted in expressions of horror, their hands outstretched as if reaching for help that never came.

Stone figures—trapped in mid-motion, locked in time.

And then I realized.

They weren't statues.

They had been people.

A sharp wind rushed through the clearing, stirring the dust around our feet. The air shimmered, reality bending at the edges.

A voice, deep as the earth, old as the sky spoke.

"You who trespass upon sacred ground—prove yourselves worthy, or become like those before you."

The wind howled, and suddenly, the air around us thickened. I tried to step forward—but my feet didn't move. A force, unseen but crushing, pinned me where I stood. My breath hitched.

And then I realized—I wasn't being held by magic.

I was holding myself.

The vines, the stones, the air itself—I could feel them, pressing, gripping, bending to my will. But it wasn't just fire this time. It was something else. Something deeper. My mother's gift.

My mom's power.

The statues around us began to shift, their stone hands trembling, dust falling from their frozen forms.

Jungle Spirits and Emotional Damage| Astrid

The jungle swallowed us whole the moment we stepped onto our path. Thick vines coiled like serpents, shifting underfoot, making every step a gamble. The air was humid, thick enough to choke on, and I swore the trees were watching us, their twisted limbs reaching, waiting.

Killian was the first to break the silence. "Alright, let's place our bets. What do you think tries to kill us first? Giant snakes? Flesh-eating plants? Or—" he paused dramatically, to face Zephyr, "—a cursed jungle spirit?"

Zephyr, unamused as ever, shoved past him. "How about we don't manifest our deaths?"

I rolled my eyes. "Great idea. Let's not invite whatever nightmare creatures live here to eat us."

But the jungle had other plans.

The path beneath us disappeared. Not in the normal way, just as if it had never existed. One second, we were walking. The next, we were sinking.

I screamed as the ground gave way, sucking us down like quicksand. My fingers clawed for something—anything—to hold onto, but all I found was empty air.

Then I hit the ground hard, my breath knocked out of me. The world spun and I barely had time to register the pain before I heard Killian groan beside me.

"Well," he wheezed, "that was unexpected."

I pushed myself up on shaky arms. "Where the hell are we?"

Zephyr landed last, rolling to his feet with unfair grace. He barely seemed fazed, brushing dust off his shoulders as he took in our surroundings.

The jungle above us was gone.

Instead, we were in a temple. The walls were smooth stone, slick with moss, carved with strange symbols that pulsed faintly with eerie blue light. The ceiling arched high above us, vines dangling like chandeliers of the damned.

"Okay. I take back my previous bet. It's a temple. Definitely cursed," Killian whistled low.

Zephyr exhaled sharply. "Fantastic."

I forced myself to stand, my muscles protesting. "Let's just find a way out before something decides to sacrifice us."

We started moving, each step echoing too loudly in the vast chamber. The air smelled ancient, like dust and forgotten things. The carvings along the walls stretched higher the deeper we went, the glow intensifying, as if sensing our presence.

A grinding sound echoed through the chamber, followed by the unmistakable click of something locking into place.

"Nope. I hate that sound," I froze.

Killian turned, his eyes wide. "Run."

The floor cracked open beneath us.

We bolted, just as stone pillars shot up from below, slamming into place where we had been standing a second before. The walls shifted, rotating like pieces of a puzzle, sealing off our path.

Zephyr cursed under his breath. "This place is alive."

"Gotta admit, it's kinda fun," Killian, ever the optimist, grinned.

I glared at him. "Your definition of fun is broken."

The shifting walls finally settled, leaving us in a new corridor, narrow and dimly lit. The only way forward was a single, ominous-looking door at the end.

"Alright. Who wants to bet on what's behind it?" I sighed.

Killian smirked. "My money's on a death maze."

"Just open it."

I reached for the handle and shoved it open.

Beyond the door was a chamber lined with statues—hundreds of them. Some were crumbling, half-broken, their faces frozen in expressions of terror. Others looked brand new, untouched by time.

And at the center, a pedestal. A single object sat atop it: an obsidian dagger, its blade etched with runes that pulsed the same eerie blue as the temple walls.

Killian tilted his head. "So, do we touch the obviously cursed artifact, or—"

The door behind us slammed shut.

"Of course," Zephyr groaned.

A deep voice boomed through the chamber, like the temple itself was speaking.

"Only those who prove their worth may claim the blade."

The statues moved.

I barely had time to react before the first one lunged.

I twisted away, ducking under a stone fist that would have shattered my skull. Zephyr's daggers flashed as he struck, but the statue barely flinched. Killian dodged another, grinning like this was the best day of his life.

"What the hell kind of trial is this?" I shouted, leaping onto the pedestal to avoid another strike.

Zephyr parried a blow, his expression grim. "One we're barely passing."

Killian blocked an incoming attack with his forearm, wincing. "Hey, if we die, at least we get to be statues in a cool evil temple, right?"

"Not. Helping."

The statues closed in. There were too many. My pulse pounded. We weren't going to make it.

Then my eyes locked onto the dagger.

A test.

I lunged.

My fingers wrapped around the hilt, and the moment I lifted it, everything stopped.

The statues froze mid-attack. The air shifted, the glow along the walls pulsing once before dimming.

Then, silence.

"Huh. That worked," Killian let out a breath.

Zephyr stared at me. "What did you do?"

I held up the dagger, its dark surface gleaming. "I think I won."

The walls groaned again, and the door behind us creaked open.

Zephyr rolled his shoulders. "Let's get out of here before it decides we failed after all."

I gripped the dagger tighter as we stepped through the doorway, my heart still hammering.

This wasn't over.

Not by a long shot.

Bound by Roots, Freed by Fire | Selene

The forms in front of us changed from frozen forms to people—gigantic people. I stared at Astrid, Killian, and Zephyr, wondering how they had been captured.

"You do have both," Caspian whispered.

I looked over at him, then down at the vines and roots in the forest.

"It's like they're moving on their own," I said.

"No, they're moving at your will," Caspian corrected.

The realization hit me like a crashing wave. The roots were obeying.

The roots lashed out, wrapping around the giants' feet like living chains, tightening, pulling, resisting their attempts to break free. The ground trembled beneath us as the massive figures roared in frustration, their struggle sending vibrations through my bones.

A deep voice boomed through the clearing. "Who are you?" His voice was thick with authority, as though the trees themselves bent to his command.

His gaze snapped up, locking onto Caspian, Sunna, and me.

And that was the opening Astrid needed.

She lunged forward, dagger flashing under the eerie light filtering through the trees. Her movements were quick, precise as she aimed for the nearest giant's exposed flank.

A roar of pain split the air.

The giant recoiled, its colossal hands swiping toward her. Astrid hit the ground with a sickening thud, rolling to a stop several feet away. My breath caught in my throat. She didn't move.

"Astrid!" I shouted, but before I could rush to her side, the earth beneath me rumbled violently.

The giant staggered back as golden blood seeped from the wound in its side. It clutched at its injury, its massive fingers trembling, enraged.

Another giant's cold, glowing eyes locked onto mine, and I felt the weight of its gaze like a crushing force against my chest. "You dare harm one of us?" it bellowed, voice like rolling thunder.

I swallowed hard. The roots around their legs were straining, barely holding against their strength. Sweat slicked my palms.

Caspian moved beside me, his power thrumming in the air. The wind picked up, howling between the trees, swirling around us in a powerful cyclone. "Selene," he called. "Focus."

I clenched my fists. Focus. Right. I could feel the pulse of the forest beneath me, the heartbeat of the land. The vines were waiting for my command.

"Hold them!" I shouted.

The ground obeyed.

Vines surged upward with new strength, twisting around the giants' arms, tightening like coiled serpents. Branches bent unnaturally, stretching down from the treetops to ensnare them, pulling their limbs away from their bodies. The giants roared in fury, thrashing against their bindings, but the forest held them fast.

Killian sprinted toward Astrid, dropping to his knees beside her. "She's breathing," he said, voice tight with relief. "But she's out."

Zephyr, still caught in the grasp of one of the remaining giants, grunted. "Not to interrupt this touching moment, but a little help here?"

Caspian flicked his wrist, sending a powerful gust of wind slamming into the giant holding Zephyr, forcing it to release its grip. Zephyr hit the ground in a crouch, shaking himself off before rolling his shoulders. "About time." His Armour of Ice slid into place.

The moment Zephyr's ice armor slid into place, the temperature around us dropped. Frost crept along the ground, his power surging in response to the growing chaos.

The giant that had grabbed him roared, shaking its massive arms free from lingering shards of ice. But Zephyr was faster. With a sharp inhale, he drew in the cold, then exhaled, sending a razor-sharp gust of icy wind directly at the giant's exposed face.

Ice spread instantly, creeping up its skin, freezing solid over its mouth before it could bellow another word.

Killian, who had been guarding Astrid's unconscious form, finally moved. His fingers brushed the hilt of his spear, and in the blink of an eye, golden light crackled around him, forming jagged streaks of electricity. He leaped forward, faster than I could follow, and drove his spear deep into the ground.

Lightning forked out in every direction, striking at the giants, running up their towering forms like electric veins. They howled in pain, staggering against their restraints.

Caspian flicked his wrist, the wind he had gathered in the air twisted violently, forming a howling vortex. He extended his arms, and the cyclone launched forward, slamming into the giants, knocking two of them backward, crashing into the trees with a deafening boom.

I couldn't let them recover.

The vines I had summoned earlier trembled, waiting.

I extended both hands and commanded, *Tighter.* The roots obeyed. They surged up, twisting higher, constricting the giants' arms, their legs, their throats. The trees themselves groaned as they bent toward my will, their branches tangling like woven chains.

The lead giant, the one who had spoken before, forced its glowing eyes onto me. "Enough!" he bellowed, his voice like a rolling storm. "You wield power, girl, but do you know what you wield?"

I hesitated for half a second too long.

With a deep growl, the giant flexed his muscles, shattering the vines around him. They ripped apart, torn from the earth like they were nothing but twine.

Caspian cursed under his breath, already redirecting the wind.

Zephyr narrowed his eyes, his hands lifting, gathering ice at his fingertips.

The lead giant lifted his hand, and the earth beneath us shook. I staggered, barely keeping my footing. Caspian cursed again.

"They have magic," he muttered.

"They have *what*?" Sunna lifted her hands, and suddenly, the air around us grew thick with moisture. Water surged up from the ground in twisting, spiraling whips, answering her call. "You mean to tell me we're not just fighting giants—we're fighting *magic-wielding* giants?"

Lightning flashed again as Killian struck, his spear slicing across another giant's exposed leg. "Oh, come on. That just makes it *more* fun."

Sunna groaned. "That's not the word I'd use."

The lead giant slammed his foot down, and the ground *split open.* Roots—my roots—ripped themselves free from my control, bending toward *him* instead.

"No—" I gasped.

The vines turned *on us.*

Thorned tendrils shot forward, coiling around Zephyr's ice armor, snapping at Caspian's whirlwind, slicing through Sunna's water like they weren't even there.

Killian barely dodged one that whipped past his head.

I clenched my fists. "No. *No.* That's *mine.*"

I *pulled.*

The vines *froze.*

For a split second, the world seemed to hold its breath.

Then, inch by inch, the roots reversed. They tore away from the giant's control and turned back against him. My power surged, *fighting for dominance.*

My hands burned with energy, not fire—something else. Something I didn't fully understand yet. But I felt it.

I pushed forward. "Yield!" I shouted.

The vines snapped upward, winding around the lead giant's throat, yanking him down.

The remaining giants roared, struggling against their own bindings.

We were winning.

But the giant leader just *laughed.*

"You are not ready," he rumbled. "Not yet."

And then he did something I never expected.

He stopped fighting.

He stilled. The others followed.

The vines still held them, the ice still froze them in place, the lightning still flickered in their wounds.

No one moved.

The lead giant locked eyes with me once more, and then, in a voice much quieter than before, he said:

"Release us. And I will tell you *everything*."

I hesitated, my breath shallow. The vines still wound tightly around the giants, pulsing with my magic, but my grip on them was as unsteady as my thoughts.

Caspian stepped closer, his voice low but firm. "Selene, think this through."

"They attacked first," Zephyr exhaled sharply, ice crackling as it retracted from his skin.

Killian spun his spear between his fingers. "Yeah, and we *won*. What's the harm in hearing them out?"

Sunna, her hands still raised, the remnants of her water magic hovering in the air, shot him an incredulous look. "The *harm* is that they could be lying."

I swallowed hard, fingers curling instinctively.

The lead giant shifted, his glowing eyes boring into mine. Something in his gaze had softened, just slightly, but it did nothing to still the rapid beat of my heart.

"You wield power beyond your understanding," he said, his voice deep as the roots of the trees. "If I wanted you dead, girl, you would already be gone."

That... was *not* reassuring. My magic thrummed, waiting. Testing. *It's your choice*, it seemed to whisper.

I let out a slow breath. Then, with reluctance, I lifted my hands. "Stand down."

The vines *shuddered*, hesitating for the briefest moment. They slithered back into the earth, retreating like snakes slinking into the shadows. Zephyr let his ice melt into mist, and Sunna dismissed the remaining droplets of water. Killian lowered his spear, though his grip never fully loosened.

The leader rolled his massive shoulders, stepping forward. His hand pressed against his bleeding wound, golden blood still seeping between his fingers.

"You fight well," he admitted. His glowing eyes locked onto mine. "Stronger than I expected."

My fingers twitched at my sides. "I'll take that as a compliment."

"It was not just a compliment." His voice darkened. "It was a warning."

A chill ran through me. "A warning about what?"

His gaze flickered toward the darkened treetops, as though he was searching for something unseen. "You are not the only one awakening."

I froze.

"The Seeker knows," he continued. "And he is already watching."

Caspian went rigid beside me. "What do you mean watching?"

The lead giant exhaled deeply, shoulders rising and falling like the slow shift of mountains. "Your presence here is not unnoticed. The Seeker has been waiting sixteen years for the child of fire and mind to awaken." His eyes flickered. "And now, you are within his reach."

My throat tightened. "That's not possible. He doesn't even know who I am."

The giant's gaze snapped back to mine. "You think so?"

The air turned thick, pressing against my skin like unseen hands.

Caspian moved closer, voice low. "Selene..."

But the giant wasn't done. "He has waited in the forgotten places, in the shadows where even the gods do not tread. He has spent a decade unraveling the chains placed upon your bloodline." His glowing eyes darkened. "And now, those chains have begun to break."

A wave of unease swept through me, leaving goosebumps in its wake.

Sunna swallowed hard. "Okay. Just to clarify—who *exactly* is The Seeker?"

"A hunter of magic. A collector of power. A thief of the gods' gifts."

Zephyr's arms tightened over his chest. "And what does he want with Selene?"

"To finish what he started with her parents."

My mind flashed to my father's journal, to the frantic warnings about something being *locked away.* The pieces cutting through me like shattered glass.

Caspian's voice was tight. "Why are you telling us this?"

The lead giant studied me for a long moment before finally speaking.

"Because I *must.*" His jaw tensed, as if the words pained him. Then, slowly, he lifted one massive arm.

Glowing golden sigils shimmered beneath his skin, curling up his wrists, shifting and pulsing like something alive. Not natural. Not *his.*

A binding spell.

Realization struck. "You're captive."

The giant exhaled. "I am bound to The Seeker's will, but not entirely." He was whispering now. "You wounded me, girl. And in doing so, you weakened his hold. The magic that chains me is fraying."

My stomach turned. "So that's why you're helping us."

"I will not remain free for long," he admitted. "Once he realizes what has happened, he will rebind me. And when that happens, I will once again be his pawn."

Killian let out a low whistle. "So, you're double-crossing him before he notices?"

The giant's mouth twitched into something that might have been a grim smile. "I am giving you what little time I can. There is a way forward. A path beneath the ruins of Erador's Keep. The tunnels will take you to what you seek."

Astrid, finally steadying herself, winced as she pushed herself up. "What's the catch?"

The giant's expression darkened. "The tunnels are old. The things inside...older. They do not *serve* The Seeker, but they do not serve *you* either."

Sunna groaned. "So, basically, we're walking into a death trap."

The giant simply nodded.

I clenched my fists. "We don't have a choice."

The giant took a step back. "You must move quickly. I do not know how much longer I will be myself." His glowing eyes met mine. "But remember this, Selene Trueshadow—if The Seeker reclaims me, I will be *forced* to hunt you."

The words settled over me like ice.

Caspian was already turning toward the trees. "Then we better start moving."

I exhaled and nodded.

The giant took one last look at me. "Go."

Then, without another word, he vanished into the darkness of the forest.

I turned to my friends, my pulse still pounding in my ears.

Astrid huffed. "So…who's ready to go underground and get eaten by whatever's in those tunnels?"

Killian grinned. "Oh, absolutely."

Zephyr just shook his head. "I hate this plan."

Sunna muttered, "Me too."

I exhaled and took the first step forward.

"Let's go."

Only One Lies

The world around us felt heavier the deeper we went into the forest. The path we followed wasn't really a path at all—just twisted roots and gnarled branches, weaving overhead like skeletal fingers. The ground, damp from the constant moisture that hung in the air, had turned to soft earth beneath our boots, swallowing the sound of our steps.

Somewhere in the distance, the eerie trill of an unseen creature echoed, fading just as quickly as it had come.

Astrid swayed slightly beside Killian, and I tensed, my fingers twitching. She was still off, still blinking too much, still moving like her body hadn't quite caught up with her mind.

"Head still bothering you?" he asked, his voice casual but his eyes sharp.

Astrid groaned, tilting her head slightly, like that would somehow shake off the dizziness. "It's *fine*."

Killian snorted. "Oh yeah? Because you just tripped over *nothing*."

She huffed, shifting her weight, but it was obvious now. "The ground is uneven."

Killian raised a brow. "Sure it is. *Totally* not a side effect of getting smacked across a forest by a giant."

Astrid shot him a glare, but the effect was ruined when she

winced, rubbing her temples.

Killian tsked, tapping her forehead lightly with two fingers. "Yep. That's a concussion."

Astrid swatted his hand away. "It is *not*—"

"Okay, sure," he cut in, his grip firm as he subtly shifted closer. "And I'm secretly a fairy prince. Listen, Astrid, you *whacked* your head. You need to take it easy."

She let out a slow breath, not quite arguing, but not quite agreeing either.

Killian sighed, then slung an arm over her shoulders. "Guess I'll just have to escort you myself. Lucky for you, I offer full-service concussion care."

Astrid stiffened. "Killian, I swear—"

"Nope. Too late," he said, as he guided her forward. "You're my patient now. If you start seeing double, just let me know—unless the double is *me*, in which case you should consider yourself blessed."

Astrid groaned, but I her shoulders sagged just a little in relief.

Killian adjusted his grip to make sure she wasn't leaning too far to one side.

At least *someone* was handling their feelings well.

Unlike me.

Or Zephyr.

The trees thickened as we moved forward, the moonlight barely making it through the dense canopy above. Strange flowers, bio luminescent and pulsing softly, lined the twisted trunks of ancient trees, their petals shifting from deep violet to a dull gold as we passed. The glow painted ghostly patterns along the damp forest floor, turning the winding roots into eerie silhouettes.

A thin mist clung low to the ground, swirling in lazy spirals around our feet. The air was damp, rich with the scent of wet moss, iron, and something else—something older. A scent that made my stomach twist uneasily.

Caspian had been walking beside me for most of the journey. Every so often, his shoulder brushed against mine—not enough to seem intentional, but enough that I noticed.

Zephyr was watching.

Not always directly, but I *felt* it. The weight of his gaze, the way his presence had shifted. He was keeping his distance, but I didn't know if it was intentional or if something had simply changed.

I hated that I was even thinking about it.

"Something on your mind?" Caspian's voice was low.

I blinked, snapping out of my thoughts. "What?"

"You've been staring at the ground like it personally offended you."

I sighed, shaking my head. "Just...thinking about what the giant said."

"Which part?"

"All of it."

I hesitated, then glanced up at him. "You're from Odreazah. Have you ever heard of The Seeker before?"

Caspian's jaw tightened. "Only in stories. Old ones. But if the stories are true...then The Seeker is more powerful than any of us can imagine."

"So, we're running straight into something we don't understand," I muttered.

Caspian smirked slightly, but it didn't reach his eyes. "Welcome to magic."

I huffed. "Not helping."

"Not trying to," he said. "But you *are* handling this better than most would."

I shot him a look. "You mean barely handling it?"

His gaze softened. "No, I mean holding your ground even when everything is shifting around you."

My stomach flipped. "You give a lot of speeches, you know that?"

"Only for you."

I opened my mouth—probably to say something awkward and unnecessary—but a sudden voice cut through the tension.

"So, uh...how much longer until we get there?" Sunna asked, a little too casual.

I turned just in time to see her give me *the* look.

The one that very clearly meant: *We're talking about this later.*

Astrid didn't push Killian away as he guided her toward the fallen log. That, more than anything, told me she was worse off than she was letting on. She dropped onto the moss-covered wood with a heavy exhale, closing her eyes for a long moment before muttering, "You get five minutes."

Killian grinned. "Oh, Astrid. I'm honored."

She cracked one eye open. "Don't push it."

"Me? Never." He sat down beside her, stretching out his legs. "Although, I could start making a list of all the ways I've saved your life recently."

Astrid scoffed. "One, I don't need saving. Two, you're exaggerating."

Killian tapped his chin, pretending to think. "Mm, let's see. There was the time I yanked you out of that collapsing bridge, the time I shielded you from that cursed arrow, and just now when I made sure your concussion-riddled brain didn't walk straight into a tree."

Astrid let out a reluctant chuckle. "That last one was barely a rescue."

"Still counts." He leaned back on his elbows.

She sighed, but when he shifted slightly, making sure her shoulder was propped against his, she didn't move away. She leaned into him just a fraction more, like she was finally letting herself rest.

His grin softened, just slightly, before he glanced up at the darkened sky. "Rest up, Addy. I'm keeping score, and you owe me."

Astrid huffed, but the fight had drained out of her. "Fine. But if I wake up and you've drawn something on my face, I will kill you."

Killian gasped dramatically. "I would never."

Zephyr scoffed from where he sat on a nearby rock. "That's a lie."

Killian smirked. "Okay, yeah, that's a lie."

Astrid let out a small laugh,.

While the others rested, Sunna paced, her eyes flicking to the trees. "Something feels *off*."

I frowned. "More than usual?"

She nodded. "It's like the air is...watching us."

I shivered. She wasn't wrong. The deeper we had gone into this forest, the heavier everything had felt. It wasn't just the mist curling around our ankles or the bio luminescent plants casting strange, ghostly shadows—it was something waiting.

Sunna sighed, raking a hand through her curls. "I hate this."

She tripped over something. Her hands flew out, but before she could hit the ground, water surged from the air itself—fluid and fast, wrapping around her like a guiding current. The water coiled at her back, softening her fall, then pushed her upright in one smooth motion, leaving only a faint shimmer of droplets in its wake.

Sunna exhaled sharply, regaining her balance. "Okay, that was close."

Astrid let out a low whistle. "You make that look way too easy."

Sunna flicked her fingers, and the remaining droplets dispersed into the air. "It's not my fault water likes me."

Astrid grinned. "Yeah, well, remind me to stick close to you next time I'm about to eat dirt."

Sunna smirked, tossing her hair over her shoulder. "Don't worry, Addy. I've got you."

Her gaze had snapped downward, eyes locked on the thing she had tripped over.

A flat slab of stone, nearly hidden beneath moss and tangled roots. The edges were unevenly carved and something faintly shimmered along its surface.

My pulse picked up. "That's not just a rock."

Sunna dropped to her knees, brushing the dirt away. The more she uncovered, the more the markings became clear—etched symbols, old and nearly worn away.

Killian, now fully alert, sat up. "What did you find?"

"Something important." Sunna traced the symbols carefully, her brows furrowing. "These are warding runes."

Caspian stepped closer. "For keeping things *in* or keeping things *out*?"

Sunna swallowed. "I don't know."

A chill passed through me. "So...what exactly are they warding?"

Sunna brushed away more dirt, more moss—until finally, we saw it.

The faint outline of a door, buried beneath centuries of earth.

Caspian exhaled slowly. "Well. That's ominous."

Zephyr stood, dusting himself off. "So let me get this straight—we've been following some cryptic giant's directions, and now we've found a sealed door buried in a cursed forest with runes that are barely holding?"

"Yup," Killian said. "Sounds like a great idea to open it."

Astrid groaned. "You're the worst."

Sunna glanced up at me, her expression serious. "Selene, this might be the entrance to the tunnel."

I bit my lip. The giant had told us to find the hidden path. That it would take us to what we needed.

But if these runes were meant to *keep something in*...

What exactly were we about to unleash?

Caspian met my gaze. "Your call."

I glanced back at Zephyr. Something in his stance—something in the way he was watching me—made my chest ache.

"Let's open it."

There was a moment—a breathless, flickering moment—where no one moved. The air felt like it had paused alongside us, holding its breath just to see what we'd do next.

Then Killian clapped his hands and rubbed them together. "Alright, let's crack open the haunted crypt-door of doom."

"Could we not call it that?" Astrid muttered.

He winked. "Too late. It's canon now."

Sunna pulled her fingers back from the runes, wiping her palms on her leggings like the energy had burned through her skin.

"Some of these symbols are decayed...but not dead. It's old magic. It won't open unless it's tested." Caspian said.

"Tested how?" Zephyr asked, arms crossed.

Caspian pointed to the center of the stone—where the etchings formed a circle, jagged lines curling inward like vines or claws.

"There's a riddle," he said, voice low. "A bad one."

I leaned in.

The script shimmered faintly, glowing pale gold beneath the grime as we read aloud together:

"Speak not of what you seek to find,
Lest silence strike and steal your mind.
Three must answer, one must lie—
Only then may truth pass by."

A very awkward silence followed.

"...So, like, is this an escape room thing?" Killian asked. "Because I excel at those."

Astrid gave him a flat look. "This is a magically-warded, ancient underground tunnel to somewhere that may or may not be full of secrets, curses, and probably skeletons. This is not an escape room."

Killian nodded thoughtfully. "But if it were, I'd win."

"I think we're missing the point," I said. "Three must answer. One must lie. It wants a test of truth."

Zephyr frowned. "So one of us has to lie on purpose?"

"Or maybe the magic chooses who lies," Caspian said. "Could be a compulsion. A misdirect."

Sunna glanced at me. "Or worse—it might not let us *know* who's lying."

My stomach twisted.

"So," Astrid muttered, crouching beside the runes, "how exactly do we even begin that?"

A faint rumble echoed beneath us—like something was listening. Waiting.

Then, the center of the stone slab shifted. A small square

section rose up, clicking into place. Four stone discs appeared, each with a sigil carved into the surface: a flame, a crescent moon, a raven, and an open eye.

And below them...a single line etched deep into the stone:

"Choose your symbol. Speak your truth. The liar will be claimed."

Killian whistled. "Oh. *Oh*. This just got fun."

"No," Zephyr said, stepping back. "This just got dangerous."

"What happens if we get it wrong?" Sunna whispered.

I stepped forward, heartbeat like thunder in my ears. "We're not going to get it wrong."

Astrid gave me a look. "Lee..."

But I wasn't backing down. Not after everything. Not now. I placed my hand on the flame.

The stone warmed under my touch, and a quiet hum thrummed through the ground.

One by one, the others moved.

Astrid chose the crescent moon.

Sunna pressed her palm against the open eye, her breath catching.

Killian grinned and slapped his hand onto the raven, like it was a game show buzzer.

And just like that, the forest around us vanished. Like mist blown back to reveal something hidden beneath it.

We were standing in the same spot...and also not.

The trees were frozen. The air buzzed with static, like the moment before a lightning strike. And from the earth beneath us, a voice rose—not loud, but *inside* us.

"Speak your truth."

The magic wanted an answer. And I knew, somehow, what it was asking.

"Why are you here?" the voice asked.

My mouth opened. "To protect the people I care about."

My symbol glowed.

The others followed.

Astrid: "To make sure Lee doesn't do something reckless alone."

Sunna: "To find out who I am—what I'm really capable of."

Killian: "Because I love a good mystery. And also, I may or may not owe a talking mushroom a favor. Long story."

All four symbols pulsed—then dimmed.

Then the voice spoke again.

"One of you lies."

The stone rumbled. And the door began to crack open. The forest wasn't done with us yet.

From the shadows just beyond the trees... something moved.

The rumbling deepened—low and guttural, like the forest had a heartbeat and we'd just messed with its rhythm.

I turned slowly, every nerve screaming at me *don't look, don't look*, but I did anyway.

Beyond the shifting mist, something uncoiled.

It wasn't huge, it was worse. It was *humanoid* in the way a shadow is shaped like a person—roughly the right form, but wrong. Like someone had taken the idea of a person and sculpted it out of smoke, bone, and grief.

It had no face, just a smooth, hollow surface where its features should've been, but I felt its eyes on me. Like fingers dragging across my thoughts.

The shadow-creature stepped forward.

"What the hell," I say as my muscles tense. I feel the tingle in my hands and they warm.

"We're not supposed to fight it," Sunna said suddenly in a

different voice.

I glanced at her, and the mark beneath her hand—the open eye—was *glowing*.

"It's a guardian," she continued, staring straight at the thing. "Part of the magic. It's not here to hurt us… unless we lie again."

Astrid shot her a glance. "Define 'hurt.' Like, minor inconvenience hurt or we-lose-a-limb hurt?"

Killian raised his hand lazily. "If it takes a limb, I'd prefer it go for my left arm. Not that I'm volunteering, but just—y'know, logistics."

The shadow-creature stopped just short of the edge of the runes.

It tilted its head.

Then the voice returned—cold, smooth, and echoing like it came from *inside the bones of the trees.*

"One among you lies.
Step forward, or be revealed."

Everyone turned to look at me.

"Why me?" I demanded. "It could be any of you!"

"Because," Astrid said carefully, "you're the one who volunteered us for this cursed forest side quest in the first place."

The symbols under our hands began to pulse again—slower this time, like a countdown. The runes on the stone slab were glowing brighter.

The creature stepped closer.

My throat dried out. "Okay! Okay. Let's talk this out."

"We did talk," Killian said, watching the creature like it might lunge at any moment. "Pretty sure we're out of words."

"Maybe the lie wasn't intentional," Sunna offered. "Maybe someone doesn't even know they lied."

The symbols pulsed faster.

The creature moved again.

One step.

Two.

It reached the edge of the circle.

And pointed.

At Killian

The forest went silent. Even the mist stopped moving.

Killian didn't flinch.

"What?" I breathed.

His expression didn't change. "That's a mistake."

"You lied," Astrid said sharply.

Killian turned his head. "You think I don't know how this magic works?"

"You're not denying it," Astrid said slowly.

The runes beneath *his* hand—the flame—glowed blood-red.

"The lie has been spoken," the voice said. **"He may not enter."**

The creature stepped between Killian and the stone door.

It didn't touch him.

He stepped back once, twice, until he was outside the circle.

The door opened.

Just a sliver—but enough for us to feel the pull.

Cold air swept out from within. Not the kind that made your skin shiver—but the kind that tugged at your soul, like something inside had been waiting for you all along.

"Go," Killian said quietly. "I'll wait here."

I stared at him.

"You lied," I whispered.

I suddenly knew *exactly* what his lie was.

He didn't come here to help me find answers.

He came because he already *knew* them. I looked over at Astrid who was staring back at Killian. His gaze went dark until his eyes shifted, searching. He must can see the forest now too.

"You know what this means?" Sunna began. "Only us three can move on. Caspian, Zephyr and Killian have to stay."

I took a deep breath, looked forward and stepped through.

Not the only Bloodline | Selene

The door yawned open just enough for the mist to coil through it like it was alive, beckoning us in. Cold air swept out—sharp and heavy with memory.

Sunna stepped forward first.

I followed.

Astrid hesitated at the threshold, her fingers brushing the stone frame like she expected it to bite.

"Addy?" I asked.

She exhaled. "If I get snatched by some creepy magical entity, I expect an actual rescue effort."

"You'll get a dramatic speech and everything," I promised.

She grinned faintly and stepped through.

The moment we crossed the threshold, the door sealed shut behind us with a *hisss* of air and stone. The light outside vanished.

We were in.

The passage ahead was narrow—barely wide enough to walk side by side—and the walls were slick with something that shimmered faintly. The air buzzed, the magic here... *off*. Not hostile, just different.

"Why does it feel like we're walking through someone's bloodstream?" Astrid muttered.

"Whose blood shimmers?" Sunna whispered back, her voice edged with awe.

The path sloped downward, winding like a serpent. Runes flickered along the walls, but they didn't stay still—each time we passed one, it rearranged itself, as if...reacting to us. Judging us. Or maybe *recognizing* us.

Then we entered a chamber.

It was circular, the ceiling high and domed with pale crystal, casting a soft glow across the space. Four tall pillars stood in a perfect square, each carved with a different set of runes—none of which matched any script I'd seen before.

In the center of the room stood a pedestal.

And on it—

A book. Bound in dark, smoky leather. Its surface moved like it was breathing.

"Well that's not unsettling," Astrid said, crossing her arms.

Sunna circled the pedestal slowly. "This is it. The clue the giant mentioned."

I swallowed, stepping closer. "How do you know?"

"Because this room wasn't made to hold treasure," she said. "It was made to hide something."

My eyes scanned the runes again. They were ancient. Powerful. And beneath the pedestal, etched in neat, spiraling script, a single phrase burned in golden light:

"The Seeker devours what is remembered. Only what is *written* may survive."

I blinked. "Wait—what?"

Sunna read it again aloud, slower.

"The Seeker...devours what is remembered. Only what is written may survive."

"So he can erase memory," Astrid said. "But not ink?"

"Which means this book...it's a memory someone didn't want forgotten," Sunna whispered as she reached out and touched the book, running her hands over the cover. Suddenly she jerked her hand back. "Ouch!"

I reached out and rested my fingers against the cover.

It was warm. Alive.

And then—without warning—the book opened.

Pages fluttered rapidly before stopping near the center. And there, written in a hand I recognized from my father's old notes, was a short entry:

"Ereriath is not lost. It sleeps beneath the Hollow.
The map must be fed. The bloodline must wake."

Silence.

Astrid leaned in. "Please tell me that wasn't metaphorical."

Sunna looked at me. "You're the bloodline."

I stepped back from the book, heart pounding.

If the *map must be fed...*

"What does that mean?" I whispered. "What map?"

The moment the words left my mouth, a drawer slid out of the pedestal.

Inside it, lying perfectly still was a thin stone slate, etched with the same serpentine script from the wall. When I picked it up, it felt warm—then suddenly, *hot.*

I gasped and nearly dropped it, but the light flared and a glowing map began to form in the air above it.

It was a living map that revealed aerial view of the forest. Then deeper. Down past the earth, the stone, the roots—revealing a sunken city, broken and half-consumed by vines.

Ereriath.

My voice cracked. "It's real."

Sunna stepped beside me. "The Hollow is under us. We're not

in a forest. We're walking across the roof of a buried realm."

Astrid was still staring at the book. "So, if this is what the giant wanted us to find...what happens if The Seeker gets here first?"

Suddenly, the map shifted—zooming in on a flicker of motion far beneath the surface.

A shadow, moving.

* * *

The deeper we followed the glowing trail, the more the forest started to *change.*

The trees were taller here—pale and smooth like bone, with leaves that shimmered faintly in the dim light. The air had taken on a strange metallic taste, like lightning had kissed the ground and never left.

Zephyr kept checking the edges of the path like he expected something to leap out of the trees. Sunna was staring at the map like it might shift again if she blinked. Astrid kept pace beside me, silent and coiled, like she was waiting for a fight she couldn't name.

Killian was too quiet.

Not in the usual way, where he was scheming or making a bad joke. This was different. Heavy. His eyes weren't scanning the trees—they were locked on the path ahead, jaw tight, brows drawn.

"You're thinking very loudly," I said quietly, falling into step beside him.

He didn't look at me. "Am I?"

"You only walk like that when you're either overthinking...or hiding something."

He gave a half-hearted shrug. "That's slander. I'm an open book."

"Killian."

He sighed and finally glanced my way. "You ever have a secret you wanted to tell... but knew the second you did, things would never go back to the way they were?"

"Is this about the time you tried to tame a wyvern with a sock puppet?" I asked. "Caspian told me," I shrugged.

A faint smile tugged at the corner of his mouth. "Okay, that was a noble attempt. And Socko deserved better."

"Killian."

The humor faded. He looked forward again, the gold in his eyes catching on the fading light.

"My mother was from Ereriath."

I stopped walking.

He kept going, slowly, like if he said it too fast, the truth might catch fire.

"She left before the collapse. But not because she foresaw doom or wanted a new life—she left because of me."

He exhaled hard. "She didn't belong to the court. She wasn't the queen. She wasn't even noble."

"Wait—are you saying...?"

He nodded, jaw clenched. "King Victor had a son with someone who wasn't his wife. Someone from a city that no longer exists."

The pieces slammed together in my head.

"Your mother was from *Ereriath.*"

"That's the part no one knows." His voice dropped. "Victor covered it up. Buried it under layers of diplomacy and silence. The queen raised me as hers. Publicly, I'm the perfect heir.

Privately...I'm a secret no one wants dug up."

I stared at him, heart thudding. "You've known this the whole time?"

"I suspected. Then I found proof. Letters. Old sigils sealed in magic only Ereriath used. And when the dreams started—when the pull toward this place got too strong to ignore—I knew I had to find it for myself."

"Why didn't you tell me?"

Killian finally looked at me. And I saw it—under the jokes and bravado and lazy charm—the weight of someone who's been living with a truth that could unravel everything.

"Because I didn't come here for the mission. Or even for you. I came for her. For what she left behind. For what I am because of her."

Behind us, the others had slowed—listening.

Killian's voice turned quiet. "The bloodline must wake. That's what the giant said. But I don't think it meant just yours."

His hand rested lightly over his chest.

"There's another bloodline in this forest. One it wasn't supposed to remember."

I swallowed, throat tight. "And now it does."

Sunna stepped closer, her voice like a warning. "Then we need to get to the city first. Before it calls back anything that should've stayed buried."

I looked down at the map. The glowing trail had curved ahead into a jagged dip—a fault line, marked by a pool of still, dark water.

A sinkhole. Or an entrance. We were walking into Killian's inheritance. His mother's legacy. A truth even the king never wanted found.

I turned to look at Caspian. I waited for him to catch up and grabbed his hand.

He looked down at me.

"You okay?" I asked. "You knew that, right?"

"No," he scowled. "I just found out like you."

I glanced back at Killian who was now walking with Astrid, her hand mirror mine in his.

"Uh, so you wanna hold hands Zephyr?" Sunna asked.

Astrid and Killian laughed, my cheeks heat up and I moved my hand from Caspian's.

I will not, cannot, must not look back at Zephyr.

* * *

The sinkhole shimmered behind us, the surface now calm and still, like it hadn't just swallowed six reckless idiots with boundary issues and unresolved trauma.

The staircase wound down into shadow, each step lit by eerie lanterns that didn't burn, but glowed. The deeper we went, the cooler the air became.

"I swear," Astrid muttered, "if we walk into a crypt and there's another creepy riddle waiting for us, I'm sitting down and letting someone else die first."

"Noted," Killian said. "You can be the dramatic sacrifice. I'll be the one who sings at your funeral. Poorly."

"You're assuming I'd invite you," she snapped.

"I'd crash it anyway. In black velvet. With a sword."

Caspian snorted behind them. "You do own an embarrassing amount of velvet."

"You're just bitter because I pull it off better than you."

"You don't," Caspian said. "No one does."

Killian turned mid-step and raised a brow. "Jealousy doesn't suit you, big brother."

"I'd say the same about humility," Caspian muttered.

"I wouldn't," Killian said cheerfully. "I wear arrogance like a crown."

Sunna rolled her eyes. "I keep forgetting you two are literally royalty. And then you open your mouths."

Astrid snorted. "More like a royal pain."

Killian gave a dramatic bow. "I accept this honor on behalf of our entire dysfunctional bloodline."

"Just don't try to take the throne with that attitude," Caspian said dryly. "Or the fashion sense."

"The throne can wait," Killian replied. "We've got glowing staircases and possibly cursed instruments to investigate."

The staircase ended in front of a wide stone archway. The floor leveled out, revealing a vast, echoing chamber beyond—pillars like ribs, walls lined with murals of starlight and shadow.

At the far end of the room, resting on a pedestal of obsidian, was something that did not belong.

It looked like a harp. But the strings were made of light. And it was playing itself.

"Okay," Zephyr said slowly. "I did not see that coming."

Astrid squinted. "Is it enchanted?"

Killian tilted his head. "Or possessed."

Sunna stepped forward. "Or both."

The harp shifted. Its strings began to vibrate—faster.

"Cas, you getting flashbacks to music class with Miss Virell?" Killian asked.

Caspian blinked. "The one who turned into a raven mid-lesson and flew out the window?"

"The very same."

"Didn't you hit her with a recorder?"

"She lunged first."

"Fair."

The music crescendoed—then stopped.

Dead silence.

The floor beneath the harp shimmered, then crumbled in a perfect circle.

A staircase spiraled downward.

Again.

Because of course it did.

"Well," I said, staring at it. "I guess the harp liked us."

Caspain sighed. "You mean *you*. It liked *you*. I just stood here and made snarky comments."

That's basically your entire skillset."

"Not inaccurate," he admitted.

The stairwell pulsed faintly with light. Below, something stirred—too far to see, too deep to guess.

But whatever waited at the bottom…

It *knew* we were coming.

We Are Not Ready | Selene

The others moved toward the staircase, their voices fading into the low hum of the chamber—Caspian calling for a formation (which everyone ignored), Astrid muttering about cursed acoustics, Sunna silently studying the harp like it might bite.

Killian stood just off to the side, half in shadow, gaze fixed on the spiral staircase like it had personally insulted him.

"You good?" I asked softly.

He didn't look at me at first. "Define 'good.'"

"Functioning. Not actively spiraling. Only mildly emotionally compromised."

He huffed a laugh. "Then yeah. I'm fantastic."

I stepped closer. "You didn't have to tell me. About your mother."

His jaw flexed. "I know."

"But you did anyway."

He finally glanced at me. "You deserved to know. Especially before we walk into the city that remembers everything."

I tilted my head. "Is that what this is about? Getting ahead of the secrets?"

He looked away again, and for once, the gold in his eyes wasn't dancing with mischief. they was guarded.

"She told me never to come here," he said quietly. "Said this place would eat me alive if it ever remembered who I was."

"Then why come?"

"Because I have to know," he said. "I have to know what she left behind. What he left buried. I spent my whole life being part of something and never belonging to it. If there's any part of me that actually fits somewhere... maybe it's down there."

I didn't speak for a moment. "You belong here," I said finally, the words slipping out before I could second-guess them.

He looked at me then.

Not with his usual smirk. Not with deflection or armor.

Just... *Killian.*

"And what about you?" he asked, voice lower now. "When this is over...what do you want?"

I blinked. "Survival?"

He arched a brow.

"Answers," I amended. "The truth. Whatever's waiting down there that ties all of this together."

"And if it doesn't?"

"Then I lie really convincingly about what we found and write a book that sells moderately okay."

He laughed, quick and genuine, and for a second, the tension between us softened.

Then his smile faded, and he took a step closer. "Selene. If something happens—"

"Don't," I cut in, voice sharper than I meant it to be. "We're all making it out."

He didn't argue.

Just reached out and brushed his knuckles against mine. Not a grab. Not a grip. Just a touch. Real and quiet and steady. I didn't pull away.

"Ready?" he asked.

"No," I said honestly. "Let's go anyway."

And together, we stepped toward the spiral.

We barely made it ten steps down before the air shifted.

It was just a ripple. A pressure change. The kind of thing you'd miss if you weren't paying attention.

But Killian felt it too.

He stopped mid-step, one hand brushing my arm. "Selene."

I stilled.

The space around us... *twitched.* That's the only way I could describe it. Like reality hiccuped and tried to blink us out.

The light from the lanterns dimmed.

And then we heard it.

The staircase leveled into a smaller chamber, round and echoing, walled in dark stone. Twelve statues stood in perfect formation—tall, cloaked figures with blank faces and arms folded across their chests.

Guardians.

The second Killian and I stepped onto the floor, the door behind us vanished.

Zephyr cursed under his breath. Astrid drew her blade, though what good that would do against stone, I had no idea.

Two of the statues moved.

Their heads turned, stone groaning with the sound of centuries waking. Their empty eye sockets burned with violet light—and something colder beneath it.

One pointed at me.

The other pointed at Killian.

"Why am I always the one being pointed at?" Killian muttered, but I could hear the tightness in his voice.

Then the voices came. Not aloud. Inside us.

"Blood returned. The city remembers."

It felt like the words had been carved into my bones. Killian flinched beside me.

"I don't like this," Sunna said, edging closer to the wall.

"Join the club," Astrid muttered.

The statue on Killian's side shifted again. The violet glow in its eyes flared—

—then turned gold.

The one facing me turned silver-blue. The chamber pulsed.

"One belongs. One is the reckoning."

Killian inhaled sharply. "What does that mean?"

"I don't know," I said. But my heart was racing. "It knows us. It knows who we are."

Or worse, it knew something we didn't.

Caspian moved. "We need to leave. Now."

Before I could argue, the staircase behind us rebuilt itself. The stone twisting in reverse as if it had never collapsed at all.

An invitation.

Or an exit.

Sunna's hand glowed faintly with waterlight. "This room is holding back. It doesn't want to kill us. Yet."

Killian looked at the statues again. "They said I belong. That has to mean—"

"They also called you the reckoning," Zephyr snapped. "I don't care how noble that sounds, it's never good."

I turned to Killian. His expression had gone still.

"Killian," I said softly, stepping into his line of sight. "We don't run. But we *retreat* when the ancient stone guardians start whispering death riddles."

We backed up, step by step. The statues didn't move. But I could still feel them.

We passed the threshold and the voice followed us.

"Return when you know who you are."

We weren't ready.

We didn't speak until the forest swallowed us again.

Not even Killian.

The staircase behind us had vanished entirely, buried under roots and moss and stone as if it had never existed. The harp chamber, the spiraling descent, the statues who spoke without voices—it was all *gone*.

But the weight of it clung to us like mist.

Astrid kicked a nearby root. "Okay. I officially hate that city."

"I second that," Zephyr muttered. "That was not an entrance. That was a warning."

Sunna crouched beside a patch of stone, tracing a lingering shimmer of magic with her fingers. "It's closed but not locked."

Caspian stood a few paces away, back to a twisted tree, arms crossed tight across his chest. Watching Killian.

He hadn't said a word since we left the chamber. Not even a sarcastic quip. And that was almost more unnerving than the guardians pointing at us like we'd woken something best left buried.

"Killian," I said quietly, stepping closer.

He didn't look up.

"They knew who you were."

"I know."

"They called you—"

"I know," he snapped. Then closed his eyes, exhaling hard. "Sorry."

When he finally looked at me, something behind his eyes had cracked wide open. Not panic. Not fear.

Recognition.

"Did they mean reckoning like a threat," he said. "Or did they mean consequence."

"For what?"

"For existing," he whispered. "My mother was from a city that wasn't supposed to survive. My father is the king who buried that truth so deep no one would ever dig it up."

"Until now," I wanted to reach for his hand. I didn't. I wasn't sure who that would be for—him, or me.

Sunna stood suddenly. "We need a new path."

"The map's still active," I said, pulling the slate from my pocket. Its glow was dimmer now.

Astrid leaned over my shoulder. "It's showing a second trail."

A new path, branching off from the one we'd followed. One that hadn't been there before.

Zephyr narrowed his eyes. "How does a map *change*?"

"It's reacting to us," Sunna said. "To what the city learned."

I frowned. "So...we failed the first test."

Caspian's voice was low. "Or we triggered the next one."

Killian finally stood straighter. "Either way, we follow it."

"You sure?" Zephyr asked. "Because last time we followed a path, we almost got judged into a spiritual coma."

Killian looked at me. Then at the glowing trail ahead.

"No more running," he said. "This time, we're going to learn who we are before we go back."

I Feel Stupid | Astrid

I sat with my back against a tree, a blade spinning slowly between my fingers, catching the firelight in quick flashes. I looked relaxed, which meant I was trying very hard not to punch her own thoughts.

Zephyr sat a few feet away, sharpening his spear. The scraping of metal against stone filled the silence.

"You're going to grind that thing down to a toothpick," I said without looking at him.

Zephyr didn't stop. "Maybe I want a toothpick."

I snorted. "A very stabby toothpick."

He said nothing.

I sighed, finally glancing his way. "Alright. Out with it."

Zephyr paused, tension winding through his shoulders like pulled thread. "Out with *what*?"

"Whatever's got your jaw clenched and your emotions leaking out like a bad stew."

"...I don't leak."

I just arched a brow.

He set the spear down.

For a long time, he didn't say anything. Not until the fire cracked loud enough to startle a moth from the brush.

Then, quietly, so quiet I almost didn't hear it:

"I likes him."

I tilted her head. "Selene?"

A nod.

"Caspian."

Another nod.

"Ohhhhh."

Zephyr's jaw ticked. "You didn't see the way I looked at him. When they talked earlier. It's different."

"Yeah. It is."

"She listened when I talked," he winced, voice rough. "Not just heard me, *listened.* And I thought maybe…maybe she saw me."

"She does see you," I said. "Just not in the way you wanted."

Zephyr looked down at his hands. "I feel stupid."

"You're not."

"Then why does this feel like I am?"

I blew out a breath, then nudged his leg with her boot. "Because you gave a piece of yourself to someone and didn't get one back. That doesn't make you stupid. That makes you real."

I leaned forward, arms draped over my knees. "For what it's worth… I don't think she knows what she wants. She's caught in something bigger than all of us. Bigger than feelings."

Zephyr looked up. "And Caspian?"

I shrugged. "He's like a mirror. He reflects what people want to see. But Selene…" I paused. "She might be the only one who actually sees him. That's dangerous. And kind of beautiful."

Zephyr gave a weak laugh. "That's very poetic of you."

"Don't get used to it."

He ran a hand through his hair, sighing. "You ever get tired of feeling things?"

"Constantly," I said as I stole a glance over to Killian. "But we're cursed with hearts and a penchant for dramatic friend-ships, so here we are."

I Regret Nothing | Selene

The portal spilled us into the center of Odreazah's southern courtyard, casting a wash of violet light over the polished stone and waking the guards stationed along the outer walls. They reached for weapons before recognition set in.

Six soot-smudged, blood-dried, slightly limping messes stepping out of an unstable realm?

Killian went first, his jaw set tight. I followed close behind, my fingers curled around the slate tucked into my satchel. Still cold. Still silent.

Behind us, Zephyr scanned the rooftops like he half-expected an ambush, and Sunna didn't let go of the water still pooled around her fingers until we reached the great hall doors. Astrid limped just enough to worry me, but she waved off help with a sharp glare .

We were led straight to the war chamber.

King Victor stood coldly at the far end of the obsidian table, his hands clasped behind his back. queen stood just beside him—elegant as ever, wrapped in silken shadow, one hand resting lightly on the edge of the table.

Her eyes betrayed her cool demeanor when she looked at Killian.

"Report," Victor said. His voice cracked the silence like a blade against ice.

Astrid didn't hesitate. "We reached the Hollow. The ruins are real."

Victor's gaze sharpened.

Sunna squared her shoulders. "There are statues. Guardians. Stone constructs with ancient sentience. They knew we didn't belong."

"They *tested* us," Zephyr whispered. "Spoke to us without speaking."

Victor's fingers twitched—barely noticeable, but I caught it.

"And what did they say?" he asked.

"They remembered us," I said, my mouth dry. "Or something in us. They said the blood had returned. That the city remembers."

Astrid shifted beside me. "They reacted to Selene and—"

"They reacted to all of us," Killian cut her off calmly, as he moved closer to the table.

The queen studied him closely. Not blinking. Not breathing.

Victor narrowed his eyes. "And?"

Killian held his ground. "They told us not to return until we understood what we were."

The queen finally spoke after a long silence.

"And did you understand?"

Killian hesitated. Just for a breath. Then—

"No."

Victor turned away, motioning to a nearby scribe. "We'll speak again tomorrow. Separately. All of you. Now, please leave."

The moment the doors closed behind us, Killian exhaled. "They know something's off," he said.

"They know you're holding something back," Zephyr countered.

"They always knew that," Astrid muttered.

We walked in silence for a few moments.

Then Killian slowed, just enough to match my stride.

"You're not going to tell them," he said.

"No," I said. "Not yet."

He looked at me, and for the first time since we returned, the weight of it all cracked through the edge of his voice.

"They saw me. The guardians. The city."

I nodded. "They saw me too."

He reached out, like he meant to take my hand—then stopped.

"We're not done with it," I said.

"No," he agreed. "But we're not walking in blind next time."

The marble halls echoed with our footsteps, as we crossed the bridge to the portal tower.

"You'll be okay?"

I nodded. "You?"

He smirked, but it didn't reach his eyes. "I'll make sure my father doesn't try to 'strategically' vanish the truth while you're gone."

Caspian was already speaking with a steward at the end of the hall, his muffled tone angry.

"Don't let him pull that 'I'm fine' thing for too long," Killian added, nodding toward his brother. "He's not."

I looked at him. "And you are?"

He tilted his head. "I'm complicated."

I didn't argue. Instead, I turned and stepped toward the swirling portal, with Sunna, Zephyr, and Astrid behind me.

"Try not to get crowned without us," Astrid called over her shoulder.

Killian gave a lazy two-finger salute. "I make no promises."

And then we stepped through.

* * *

"Two days," Professor Harth snapped not ten minutes sooner, his voice slicing down the hallway like a guillotine. "Two. No excuse. No contact. No documentation."

I glanced at Sunna.

"Sunna," I whispered out the side of my mouth. "You said you sent it."

"I meant to!" she hissed back. "Then we were getting judged by magical statues and possibly about to be erased from reality. It slipped my mind!"

Harth's eyebrow twitched. "You will be expected in the Headmaster's study this evening. All four of you."

"Wouldn't dream of missing it," Astrid muttered as he stalked off, his robes billowing behind him.

It did not feel like we were gone that long, but if Odreazah is a little slow maybe Ereriath's time is more different.

I sighed, the weight of exhaustion settling back. " So... we survived a cursed city, returned with unspoken magical trauma, and now we're in trouble for truancy."

"Academy life in a nutshell," Zephyr said, dragging a hand through his hair. "Near-death experiences: fine. Miss two days of class? Unforgivable."

Sunna groaned. "Do you think he'll expel us?"

Astrid rolled her eyes. "No, he'll just make us polish every gargoyle on campus with a toothbrush enchanted to scream if you miss a spot."

"That actually sounds like something he'd do," Zephyr

smirked.

"I'm still stuck on the fact that the excuse was your only job, Sunna," I said, eyeing her.

"Addy asked me last minute to come up with something," she moaned, clutching her bag like it could protect her. "I failed the group. I accept my fate. Just promise me if he turns me into a plant, you'll water me."

Astrid patted her head. "Once a week. Max."

We retreated to our dorm room like soldiers who'd survived battle only to be court-martialed for coming back late. The door slammed shut behind us with a bit too much finality, and Astrid collapsed on her bed.

"Well," she declared, "I guess this is how we die."

"You're being dramatic," I said, though I wasn't exactly disagreeing. I made a beeline for the snack drawer. Crisis coping step one: sugar.

"I am not," she replied, pointing toward the ceiling like the gods themselves were to blame. "We're about to face a Headmaster with the emotional range of granite and a track record for assigning detention that makes students cry in three languages."

There was a knock before the door creaked open—Sunna tiptoed in. "Do you think we're getting actual punishment? Or just, you know, a stern talking-to with bonus guilt?"

Astrid groaned. "You clearly don't know the man. The last time someone missed a single class without notice, he assigned them a week of cataloging cursed scrolls in the Restricted Archive. With gloves that scream if you handle anything out of order."

Sunna winced. "So...not a warning, then."

"I'm still stuck on the fact that it was your only job," I said, pointing a cheese chip in her direction.

"I know, I know," she groaned, dropping onto the armchair we mostly used for clean laundry and dramatic sighing. "I panicked, alright? We were almost erased from reality! I was spiritually multitasking!"

Astrid rolled to her side. "Did you at least *start* the form?"

"I opened the tab," Sunna muttered. "That counts."

Zephyr texted me. I glanced at my tablet, then held it up for them to see.

Zephyr: *Are we screwed?*

Astrid snorted. "Tell him yes. Tell him we're writing our last wills in scented ink."

Sunna perked up. "Ooh! Should we leave magical objects to each other? I got dibs on Addy's wind ring. It's cute."

"You're not even a wind mage," Astrid grumbled.

"Doesn't mean I can't accessorize," Sunna replied sweetly.

I bit back a laugh and flopped onto my bed, pulling a blanket over my face. "Someone wake me when the apocalypse is over."

"Only if we survive first hour tomorrow," Astrid replied, tossing a pillow at my legs.

Sunna stood up with a dramatic stretch. "I should go. Text me after?"

"You'll hear the screaming," Astrid said.

Sunna grinned as she backed toward the door. "Good luck, delinquents!"

The door clicked shut.

I peeked out from under the blanket. "We are so doomed."

Astrid nodded solemnly. "Honestly, I regret nothing."

The Things She Didn't Say | Leia

I walked into the room from the attached bathroom, wet feet padding across the cool tile until they sink into the plush carpet of the bedroom. The shower cap still clings to my head, and the robe I pulled on is soft and heavy.

The scent of vanilla and old magic lingers in the steam. I let it settle over my shoulders like armor, like memory.

Kofi is on the edge of the bed, elbows on his knees, holding a smooth obsidian stone. A focus charm. It hasn't held power in a long time. None of them have. Not since ours were taken from us. But he holds it anyway.

He doesn't look up when I enter.

"She's back," I say softly, like saying it too loud might shatter something fragile between us.

His jaw tightened, just slightly. "I know."

I crossed the room, tugging the cap from my head. Damp strands cling to my neck as I stop by the window, looking out over the quiet courtyard below. The floating lanterns cast a soft, blue glow across the stone, painting the castle's bones in dream light. I wonder if she passed through there. If she looked up. If some instinct told her that we were near.

But of course not. She still thinks we're on Earth.

She thinks we're safe. Far away.

Three sharp, insistent raps interrupt the silence.

Kofi moves without a word and opens the door.

Queen Grizél enters first, cool and composed, followed by Victor.

"She's returned," Grizél said without preamble.

"She's unharmed," Victor added.

Kofi closes the door behind them.

"She found it, didn't she?" I asked,

Grizél nods. "They reached the relic. Stood before the seal."

"But?"

Victor's voice is clipped. "It didn't let them in."

I blink. "It rejected them?"

"It tested them," Grizél said. "Then shut them out. They didn't make it far enough. The relic didn't accept them. But it didn't ignore them either."

"So, it's still asleep."

"For now," Victor says. "Selene knew it. She said it herself—they'll have to go back."

I lowered myself into the velvet chair by the window, the weight of that truth settling in my chest.

"She said she wasn't ready," Grizél added, her voice softer now. "But she intends to return."

"She always goes back," Kofi murmured. "She's your daughter, Lei."

"She's *our* daughter," I corrected quietly.

Grizél lifted her hand, conjuring a memory bubble above the table. Selene's image flickers into view tall, flame-light in her eyes, her hand pressed flat against the seal's inscription. Her shoulders are squared. Her jaw, set.

"She's asking questions," Victor said. "Spoke of whispers from the relic. A name that shouldn't exist."

Kofi straightened. "The Seeker?"

Grizél nodded. "She didn't say it aloud. She asked why there's no record of the relic at the Academy," Grizél continues. "Why it bears the Trueshadow seal. Why it's hidden in Ereriath."

Victor folded his arms. "She's not guessing anymore. She *knows* something's wrong."

"She doesn't know we're here," I said. "Not yet."

"She suspects," Kofi murmured. "If not where we are—then what we've done."

Grizél hesitated. "She said she doesn't know who to trust."

"She thinks we're still on Earth," I whispered. "Still blind. Still innocent."

"She thinks *you're* innocent," Victor said. "And that makes her angry."

I nodded slowly. "Of course it does."

"She's changing," Grizél said gently. "The relic responded. The seal didn't open, but it reacted. Her pyromancy flared without thought."

"She's pulling from my line now," I mumbled.

"Yes," Grizél said. "The boys said she moved earth and all it bares while they were in combat.

Victor nods. "Something old moved through her. Something even we haven't seen."

Kofi shifted. "If The Seeker senses it..."

"He hasn't yet," Grizél said. "But he will."

When they leave, it's without a word. Just the soft click of the door, and then it's only me and Kofi again. I slumped beside him on the bed, leaning into his warmth like a lifeline.

He wrapped his arms around me just as his phone buzzes.

We both freeze.

A deep breath. He swiped answer and put on a voice I haven't heard in a while.

"Hey, baby," he says.

My heart stuttered, trying to catch her voice on the line. Her cadence. Her words.

She asked about us.

Kofi answers with careful warmth. "We're good. Your mom's right here."

She mumbles something. I can't make it out.

"You manifested," he said, brightening. "That's great. Wow. Both me and your mother...a Trueshadow indeed."

His pride is clear, glowing right through his voice.

"Alright. Call us if you need anything, okay? I'll tell her. Bye."

He sets the phone gently on the nightstand.

I stared at him.

"She didn't ask to talk to me?"

He looked at me for a long second, then says, "She started to ask about my journal. But it wasn't the spellbook I gave her. She changed the subject." He smiled again, softer this time. "She's manifested both our powers. She's brilliant, Leia."

Pride bloomed in my chest, but it's quickly smothered by something else.

"She didn't ask to talk to me," I say again, quieter this time.

"Don't read into it," Kofi murmured, wrapping me back into his arms. "She's a teenager."

I grumbled into his chest. "Yeah, yeah. Whatever."

But the ache doesn't go away.

Her Voice, Not Mine | Selene

I stared at the ceiling, eyes wide open in the dark.

Astrid's already out cold across the room; one arm flung dramatically over her pillow. She passed out mid-rant about relic security, magical ethics, and how she absolutely could've pried the seal open with five more minutes and a crowbar.

I haven't spoken to Zephyr since we got back. Not really. Not the way I should have.

I pressed the charm Dad gave me to my chest. It's warm again. Like it knows I've been clutching it all night.

The room feels too small.

I slip on a hoodie over my sleep shirt and step into the hall.

Zephyr's out on the east balcony, hood up, legs swinging, perched on the railing. A half-empty soda bottle sits beside him. When he sees me, his expression shifts, but only slightly.

"Well hello, stranger," he said, voice light.

I dipped my head, guilt pressing at my collarbones. "Sorry," I mumbled.

He bumped his shoulder into mine. "You okay?"

I wanted to say yes. I wanted to toss out something flirty and breezy like I always do. Something easy. Instead, I murmur, "Do you think we failed?"

He tilted his head, silver eyes reflecting starlight. "We didn't die."

"Not dying doesn't mean we didn't fail."

He's quiet for a long beat. Then, "You're not the kind of person who gives up after being shut out."

"Maybe I should be."

He nudged his hand against mine, close enough to make it feel like lightning could arc between us if we dared. "You had a vision, didn't you?" he asks. "When you touched the seal."

I swallowed hard. "I heard something."

"You're changing," he whispered. "That's not failure, Selene."

I glanced at him, and for a heartbeat, we didn't look away.

Instead, I took a breath and forced my voice steady. "Thanks for waiting out here."

His lips twitched into a crooked smile. "Didn't want you brooding alone. You're a menace when you brood."

"Wow. Romantic."

"I try."

He hopped down from the railing and stretches, neck rolling until it pops. Then he glanced toward the hall.

"I'm waiting for someone," he said.

The words hit hard. My mouth opens. "Oh," I say. "Sorry. I didn't mean to—"

"Selene—" he starts, but I'm already turning.

Already walking away.

Back in the room, Astrid's snore could level a bookshelf. I slipped under the blanket and pulled it over my head like it'll shield me from the way my stomach twists.

I waited

And waited.

My mind won't quiet.

I'm waiting for someone.

Maybe it's a roommate. A friend. Maybe it's a girl.

I have no claim over Zephyr. I don't even know if I *want* one. At least, that's what I tell myself.

But that doesn't stop the ache from blooming sharp and stupid in my chest.

I reached under my pillow and pulled out the phone wedged into the corner, the hidden one.

Caspian: So. You're not dead.
   Caspian: Slightly disappointed, if I'm honest. I was preparing a dramatic eulogy.

A reluctant grin slipped across my lips. I text back:

Me: Not dead. Not impressed by your concern, either.
   Me: No eulogy needed. The relic just...didn't want me.
   Caspian: Wow. Rejected by a rock. That's rough.
   Me: Ancient stone artifact, actually. Very powerful.
   Me: Unlike you.
   Caspian: I'll have you know I've been called powerful before.
   Me: By who? Your reflection?
   Caspian: I missed you.

My smile faltered and becomes something soft.

Me: You're being sentimental. It's suspicious.
   Caspian: You nearly got erased from existence. I'm allowed one moment of weakness.
   Me: That was my *first* almost-erasure this semester.

Caspian: That's not comforting.

I hesitate. Then type:

Me: I thought about you when the seal flared.
   Caspian: Did it show me in a glowing vision, or was I just a comforting thought in the void?
   Me: You're never comforting.
   Caspian: I know.

A beat. The typing bubble flickers.

Caspian: Did you find what you were looking for?
   Me: Not yet.
   Caspian: You will. Or you'll burn the world down trying.
   Caspian: And for the record… I'd still follow you through the ashes.

My breath caught.

Me: You shouldn't say things like that.
   Caspian: Why not?
   Me: Because I might start believing you.
   Caspian: Maybe I want you to.

My heart flipped.

Me: I should sleep.
   Caspian: Probably. But if you dream about me, I expect a full report.

Me: Goodnight, Caspian.

I rolled my eyes as I type it. But the smile is still tugging at the corner of my mouth.

Caspian: Goodnight, Selene.

I tucked the phone back into its hiding place, deep under my pillow.
   It's reckless, whatever this is between us.

* * *

The morning hits me like a ton of bricks.
   Not even poetic bricks. Just regular, concrete, soul-crushing ones.
   The only good thing about today is that detention is finally over.
   It was brutal. Over-the-top, backbreaking, totally unnecessary. Whoever designed that punishment definitely woke up and chose violence.
   From the bathroom, music is blasting through a speaker. Astrid's bouncing around in there like she's prepping for a music video, not getting ready for class.
   I groaned and yanked the pillow over my head.
   "Addy," I mumbled, voice half-lost in the fabric. "Turn it down."
   No response—except the music gets *louder*.
   A few seconds later, her head pops around the doorway, eyebrows arched. "Did you say something?"

I lifted the edge of the pillow and squinted. "Why are you so chipper?"

She shrugged, stepping fully into the room. "Why are you so not?"

Before I can answer, she walked over and snatched the pillow clean off my face.

"Hey," I protested, squinting against the daylight like a vampire.

"Seriously," she said, hands on hips. "Did you sleep at all? You look like you've been hit by a freight train."

"I feel like I got hit by two."

She turned back to her dresser, digging through one of the drawers. "You need concealer. Maybe caffeine. Or both. Do your face, girl. You look tired."

"I *am* tired," I mumbled, sitting up just enough to lean against the wall.

She tossed a tube of lip balm onto my bed. "Here. Fix your vibe."

"Thanks," I said dryly. "Just what I needed, chapstick and judgment."

Astrid shoots me a grin in the mirror. "Judgment is free. Chapstick is a gift."

I groaned and flopped back down. "You're impossible."

"No," she sings, swiping mascara onto her lashes. "I'm fabulous. You're just grumpy."

She's not wrong. Her chaos was the only thing keeping me from sinking too deep into everything else.

By the time we make it to the café, I at least *looked* like a functional human. I slicked my hair back, pinned it in place, slapped on some skin tint and concealer, and added a little of that lip balm. Astrid called it a "makeup resurrection."

We headed toward the tables by the windows—our usual spot—and my stomach immediately dropped.

Sunna and Odessa are already there, laughing like they've been best friends for years.

Astrid wrapped her fingers around my arm. "Be cool," she whispered, dragging me forward before I can change course.

"Hey everyone!" she chirped, voice bright like she didn't just give me a look that could kill.

I slid into the seat next to her and immediately start eating, stabbing my fork into my food.

The conversation dies. No one says anything.

"Please, don't stop the fun on my behalf," I said dryly, not bothering to hide the edge in my voice.

"Hey, Selene," Odessa said, her tone so sweet it could rot teeth.

"Hey, Odessa," I mumbled, eyes glued to my plate.

"And hello to you too," Astrid said, throwing her a look.

Odessa blinked, then smiles. "Sorry. Hey, Astrid."

Sunna picked up the conversation again, pulling Astrid and Odessa into a heated discussion about *Calder Academy: The Series*. Apparently, the dorm has weekly watch nights in the common room, which is...news to me.

I pushed food around my plate.

I'm not sure if I'm hungry or just trying to stay occupied.

The only person at the table not saying anything is Zephyr. He's sipping his drink, eyes fixed somewhere out the window like he's not even here.

"We should go Lee," Astrid said, pulling me into the conversation.

"Yeah," Odessa giggled. "Me and Zephyr went last night, it was fun. I mean when he got finished asking me a million questions.

I knew it.

"Uh, I haven't seen the other episodes. I would be confused." I said, trying to back out of it.

"Zephyr was too, hense the million questions," she said with an attitude. "Yall in for next week?" she asked.

"Yes," Astrid said. "And that gives us time to catch up so we are not an embarrassment like Zephyr."

Zephyr's eyes sparkled and his lip twitched with a smirk, but he stayed quiet.

"Why so quiet?" Astrid asked. "Suspicious," she joked.

I tried not to roll my eyes too obviously. Because if he *was* being suspicious, we were just going to pretend we didn't notice?

"Maybe he's trying to avoid saying something embarrassing," I said, raising an eyebrow in his direction.

Zephyr just shrugged, his smirk deepening. Which somehow only made him more suspicious.

And irritating.

And…annoyingly cute.

"I vote the three of us watch the first episodes together," Astrid declared.

"Oh, are we doing group screenings now?" I asked, half-joking, half-bracing myself for more of Odessa's smugness.

"Absolutely," Astrid said, already pulling up a calendar app on her tablet. "No one's getting left behind."

"Then it's a date," Zephyr finally said, just loud enough for only me to hear.

And I absolutely did *not* blush.

I just had warm cheeks. From the room. From the lights.

Not from him.

Fire Donuts

Battle Tactics was held in one of the oldest wings of the Academy.

A massive chalkboard stretched across the front of the room. It was currently scribbled with diagrams of battlefield layouts and glowing runes that moved slightly.

The Professor stood at the front, arms behind his back, his storm-gray cloak dragging softly across the stone floor. He didn't need to raise his voice, the silence he carried was enough to quiet a thunderstorm.

"Battle," he said, pacing slowly, "is not about power."

His eyes swept the room; each student held in place by the weight of his stare.

"It's about intent."

Astrid, sitting next to me near the middle row, leaned in and whispered, "He practices in the mirror, doesn't he?"

I choked back a laugh, which earned me a glare from Odessa, three rows ahead, sitting with posture so rigid it looked like she'd swallowed a staff.

"As mages and warriors of the Academy," he continued, "you will not just learn to fight. You will learn *why* you fight, and *how* to win before a single spell is cast."

With a flick of his hand, the chalkboard shimmered and

changed. Now it showed the battlefield of Varnok's Stand: jagged cliffs, a narrow valley, and a lone stronghold at the center.

"Odessa," he said suddenly, "explain how the battle of Varnok was won."

She straightened like a pulled string. "Through vertical control," she recited. "The defenders used the cliffs to force bottleneck engagement, eliminating the enemy's numerical advantage. They also rigged the southern ridge with explosive sigils, causing a collapse mid-charge."

The professor gave a small nod. "Correct. And Selene?"

I froze mid-note-taking. "Sir?"

"If you were leading that charge, what would you have done differently?"

The room tilted slightly. I felt Odessa's satisfaction three rows away.

"Uhh..." I cleared my throat. "I would've sent a decoy unit up the western incline while using illusion magic to conceal an underground push through the dry ravine at the base. Once inside, my mages could trigger reverse pressure and collapse the cliffs *on* the defenders."

Silence.

Then he—*actually* impressed—nodded once. "That would've changed the outcome."

Astrid pumped her fist beside me. Odessa slowly turned to glare.

Sunna raised her hand two rows back. "Question. Wouldn't collapsing the cliffs risk your own units?"

The professor turned, his cloak swishing dramatically. "Hence the importance of timing. That, Miss Flatbash, is what separates a tactician from a hopeful."

He waved his hand again and the board changed once more—

this time showing stick figures falling into fiery pits.

"Today," he announced, "we will begin dissecting the core combat roles used during the Siege of Ironfield. Initiators, Support, Anchor, and Specialist."

Zephyr raised his hand. "No Defender?"

The professor smirked. "In Ironfield, they didn't last long enough to earn a name."

A few people laughed. Odessa didn't.

"Your desks will now adjust."

We yelped as the seats shifted beneath us. Rows suddenly rearranging into four-person tables. Ours was me, Astrid, Sunna, and—of course—Zephyr. Odessa landed at the table to our right and looked offended by the seating algorithm.

"Each table will analyze how one side lost, and the other won," he instructed. "You have fifteen minutes. Then: presentations."

Astrid clapped her hands. "Group project!"

I flipped open my textbook. "Okay, so Ironfield. What do we know?"

Sunna tapped her screen. "They tried to fortify from the inside but forgot the back gate was enchanted. A thirteen-year-old necromancer walked in through the pantry."

Zephyr snorted. "That's what happens when you put your weakest shield on the kitchen."

Astrid started drawing furiously on a scrap of parchment. "This is their defense layout."

I peeked over her shoulder. "That's...a doughnut on fire."

"It's a metaphor," she said proudly.

Zephyr leaned back and flicked two fingers toward her sketch. A tiny breeze picked up, curling the corner of the parchment until it spun like a lazy tornado and drifted dramatically onto my lap.

"Very tactical," I said, handing it back.

He grinned. "Just visualizing their collapse."

Sunna pointed at one stick figure. "That's the Anchor. He lasted about eight seconds."

"What role did they mess up?" I asked, scribbling notes.

"Anchor," Zephyr and I said at the same time.

We paused, blinking at each other.

He grinned. "You're learning."

"I already knew," I muttered.

From across the room, Odessa raised her hand.

"Yes?" The professor said without looking.

"I'd like to volunteer to present first."

"Fine," he said, gesturing.

Odessa stood like she was preparing to accept a trophy. "The losing team failed because of poor communication and lack of trust. The support units spread too thin, and the Anchor couldn't cover multiple entry points. Their tactics lacked precision."

She sat.

The professor turned to our table. "Selene. You're next."

I rose, heart hammering, and walked to the front. I could feel Odessa's eyes stabbing me between the shoulder blades.

"The winning side," I said, keeping my voice even, "used misdirection. They created the illusion that they were retreating, baited the attackers into a tighter position, then used their Specialists to collapse the enemy's spell lines from the back. It was psychological warfare."

He nodded, slower this time. "Excellent. Sit."

As I returned to my table, Odessa tilted her head and said sweetly, "Well done. Did you read the summary in the back of the book?"

I smiled. "Nope. Just have a mind for strategy. You'll catch up."

Zephyr coughed into his sleeve. Astrid cackled.

The professor looked up sharply. "Next class, you will simulate this. No safety enchantments."

The room froze.

Sunna raised her hand. "Like…simulate as in fake, or simulate as in…survive?"

He smiled faintly. "Survive. Class dismissed."

We all sat there for a beat.

Zephyr stood first. "I suddenly regret not signing up for Gardening."

Odessa bounded over and hooked her arm into Zephyr's. "Studying with me, right?" she asked.

Zephyr narrowed his eyes at her. "We all study classes we have together, together."

She pouted but recovered quickly. "Fine," she looked over to us. "Where to today?" she asked sweetly, but her eyes flicked to our books like she was already scanning for intel. "Someplace strategic, I hope. I'd hate to waste the rest of the afternoon on small talk."

Astrid fake-coughed, "Trap," into her sleeve.

I smiled, already gathering my things. "We were thinking the library. You know…where the real strategies are."

Nothing Suspicious, Just Totally Normal Students | Selene

There are exactly thirteen steps from the dining hall to the West Stairwell and I hit every single one of them at a full sprint.

"We're late," I hissed, clutching my bag to my side as Astrid matched my pace, boots slapping against the stone floor.

"We're not late," she said, not even winded. "We're strategically misaligned with the schedule."

"That's not a thing."

"It is if you say it confidently enough."

We veered left, ducking beneath the archway that led to the East Wing corridor. Somewhere behind us, a professor's voice echoed with a suspicious, "Miss Selene?"

I didn't turn around. "Go, go, go!"

Astrid and I bolted around the corner, nearly sliding into a suit of armor. It wobbled dangerously and let out a groan.

"Did that thing just sigh?" Astrid asked.

"Focus!"

Halfway down the corridor, the worst possible thing happened.

Odessa turned the corner. Her eyebrows lifted as she caught sight of us. Her mouth opened.

Astrid didn't hesitate. She threw her arm around my shoulders and said loudly, "There you are! Come on, we're going to be late for our private session with Professor Vinocia."

"Private session?" Odessa echoed.

"Yep," Astrid chirped. "Lineage-based magical diagnostics. Very hush-hush. Totally above board. We even have a form."

Odessa squinted. "Let me see it."

I pulled it out slowly, making sure the signature glimmered. She leaned in to inspect it, eyes narrowing. Then, reluctantly, she stepped back.

"Fine. But if I find out you skipped Battle Tactics again—"

"We only did that once," I muttered.

She looked unconvinced, but before she could say anything else, Zephyr appeared at the end of the hall.

"There you are," he said, walking toward us. He nodded at Odessa. "You okay?"

Her posture softened slightly. "They're acting sketchy. Again."

Zephyr glanced at me, then back at her. "They always act sketchy. It's their thing. Don't take it personally."

She rolled her eyes but didn't argue. "You're still on for training later, right?"

Zephyr smiled. "Wouldn't miss it."

She turned and walked off.

Astrid exhaled like she'd been holding her breath for a week. "You two dating now?"

Zephyr shrugged. "We're talking. Training. Talking while training. Possibly flirting. Hard to tell with her."

He peeked over at me, and I looked everywhere but at him. It's fine that he's dating.

We hurried back to our dorm. Astrid flung the door open, and the familiar warmth of our room wrapped around me like a spell. The armoire in the corner shimmered faintly, its frame glowing with residual magic like it had been waiting for us.

Sunna was perched at my desk, flipping through a rune-bound notebook. Zephyr dropped onto my bed.

"Did it work?" Sunna asked.

"Barely," I said. "Odessa was two seconds away from demanding a wand duel."

"She always does," Astrid muttered. "It's how she says hello."

Zephyr lifted his head. "She's not that bad."

Sunna blinked. "You serious?"

"She's intense," he said evenly, "but not wrong. Most of the time."

I held up the forged Independent Study form. The signature shimmered faintly with borrowed enchantment. A flawless copy of the Headmistress's hidden predecessor. Sunna had pulled it from some restricted archive and polished it up with a charm that would make even a truth stone blink.

"Unless someone knows he's not technically alive anymore, we're good."

"Technically," Zephyr smirked. "My favorite…"

Astrid moved to the armoire and brushed her fingers along its edge. "Still stable?"

Sunna nodded. "Stable-ish. Might be a little snippy, but it should hold."

I pulled out the enchanted phone Caspian had given me. The screen flickered to life with soft golden light.

On the way.

It pulsed once. No reply yet.

"Think he'll be waiting again?" Zephyr asked. "Or are we landing in mud this time?"

"Hopefully not his bathroom," I muttered. Astrid burst out laughing.

Sunna had already stepped inside, boots crunching against the surface.

Zephyr followed with a sigh. "I was promised snacks."

"You promised yourself that," Astrid said, climbing in after him.

I lingered a moment longer, hand on the frame. Ahead, Odreazah waited—with Caspian, and questions that hadn't stopped whispering since the last time I left.

I stepped through.

The door shut behind us with a soft click.

The sensation of stepping through the armoire never got easier. It was like being squeezed through a keyhole made of starlight—sharp, cold, and impossibly bright.

When my boots hit solid ground again, I stumbled forward, caught myself on a marble column, and blinked against the sudden shift in light.

We were in the entrance hall of the eastern wing of the royal residence. A wide space filled with warm golden chandeliers, polished stone, and the subtle hum of enchantments woven into the floor. The scent of wild lavender and firewood clung to the air.

Astrid appeared behind me. "Ten out of ten landing. Very regal."

Sunna stumbled next, muttering something about portal nausea, and Zephyr rolled in after, hands tucked in his coat pockets like he'd just taken a casual stroll through a magical tunnel.

Killian and Caspian walked into the room a beat later. Caspian brushed off his sleeves and glanced around the room.

He looked at me and smiled. "Hey, Selene." Seeing him smile at me turned my gut upside down. Yeah, I was a little more cool with Zephyr and Odessa dating.

"Hey," I said.

Killian walked up to Astrid. "Is it our time to look into each other's eyes all in love?" he asked.

I glared at him. Astrid laughed and punched him in the arm. "You aren't glad to see me?" she asked.

"Or me?" Sunna said. "Zephyr and I are here too."

Caspian led us out of the chamber and down a side corridor lined with arched windows and climbing ivy frozen in magical stasis. Every few steps, a soft light pulsed, like the castle itself was breathing. The deeper we went, the quieter the air became.

"We can debrief in the solar Room," he said over his shoulder.

Astrid groaned. "Please tell me that doesn't involve sunbeams and emotional vulnerability."

"No promises," Caspian replied with a smirk.

I walked beside him, careful not to let our arms brush. My fingers were still tingling from the portal—or maybe it was the memory of what the creature in Ereriath had said last time:

"The Hollow requires more than blood. It responds to memory. To bonds. To things not easily faked."

We entered the solar room moments later—a wide circular room bathed in the late-afternoon glow that filtered through enchanted stained glass. The shifting colors danced across the walls in slow, mesmerizing waves. Plush velvet seating, a round central table, and a spell-sealed door made it clear that this was a room designed for quiet conversations and guarded truths.

As soon as we were settled, Killian summoned the map. It unfurled on the table, a golden glow tracing its edges.

"It reacted again," I said, pulling a folded scrap of parchment from my bag. "Right before we left, when I touched it in the dorm. It burned through my satchel."

Astrid leaned over, eyebrows raised. "Yeah, it was crazy!"

I nodded and tossed the scrap down. The center of it had darkened slightly, like something had scorched through from the inside.

He slid a page forward—not from the map itself, but clearly torn from something related. The ink shimmered faintly: a riddle, written in two overlapping languages.

Sunna leaned over to examine it. "That's Old Erereiath and originator script. But it's not just a riddle. It's layered magic."

"What kind of layered?" Zephyr reached for a biscuit from the tray a steward had quietly delivered.

"Memory-based," she said. "It looks like the riddle only works if you're remembering the right thing...at the same time."

"Shared memory," I murmured, looking at Killian, who was already looking at me.

Astrid frowned. "But you two don't have any shared memories, do you?"

There was a long silence. Killian didn't answer. He looked at the map instead.

Caspian cleared his throat, his voice softer than usual. "We don't have to figure it all out now. My mom said she'd open the portal tonight. We can approach the Hollow fresh."

Sunna tapped her fingers against the table. "There might be another way. If it's about memory, then maybe you don't need an exact moment. Maybe you need an echo. Something shared that neither of you knows you share."

"Like what?" I asked.

She gave a slow shrug. "That's the riddle, isn't it?"

Zephyr tossed a biscuit in the air and caught it in his mouth.

"Well, I for one hope this Hollow has decent lighting. I don't do well with dramatic darkness."

Astrid kicked him under the table. "We're going into a sacred, possibly haunted, magic-infested relic space, and you're worried about ambiance?"

"Everyone needs a hobby," he said through a mouthful of crumbs.

Caspian turned to me again. "If it starts acting up again, let me know. My mom may be able to stabilize it if we're out of time."

I nodded, though a knot curled in my stomach. I hated not knowing what the Hollow wanted. I hated even more that I might already know the answer and just didn't want to say it aloud.

I could feel the map pulsing faintly beneath the surface of the table, like a second heartbeat.

Whatever was waiting in the Hollow wasn't just calling.

It was remembering us too.

* * *

Night in Odreazah settled like velvet. The palace halls dimmed to a golden hush, lanterns floating near the ceilings casting soft pools of light that drifted like starlight down the walls.

We gathered in the Moon Atrium—a vast open space framed by crescent-shaped columns and glass that shimmered with starlit reflections. The Queen stood in the center, her gown a sweep of midnight blue that shimmered like oil on water. She wasn't wearing her crown, but somehow that made her look even more powerful.

"You're certain?" she asked, her voice echoing across the

marble floor. "You know what you're walking into."

No one answered immediately. Then Killian stepped forward.

"We don't know everything," I said. "But we have to go back to get the answers."

Her expression softened. "Very well."

She raised her hands, and the air shifted. Magic rolled across the room like a wave—old, resonant, and woven with more than power. Runes ignited beneath our feet, spiraling outward in a language older than speech. The center of the atrium cracked open, revealing a swirling pool of gold and shadow.

The portal.

I felt it before I saw it. A pull low in my chest, like something calling home.

The Queen exhaled slowly. "This path will not be straight. You may not return the way you came. The Hollow tests more than magic."

Zephyr whistled low. "We remember."

Astrid elbowed him. "Not the time."

Caspian stood at my side now, close enough that our arms brushed. "We go together. No splitting up this time."

Sunna stepped closer to the edge of the portal. Her eyes were fixed on it with something I couldn't read, curiosity, maybe. Or hunger.

Killian held out the map. It shimmered, responding to the portal's energy.

"The Hollow knows we're coming," he said quietly.

We stood in silence for a breath longer. Then the Queen said, "Go."

One by one, we stepped through.

The sensation was colder this time. Harsher. Like the Hollow knew we were closer to uncovering something it had buried deep.

When we landed, it was on cold soil, laced with veins of glittering rock that pulsed faintly beneath our boots.

The air smelled like frost and old books—not the pleasant kind, but the ones that whispered even when closed.

We stood in a forest clearing, surrounded by spindly black trees, their trunks etched with glowing runes that flickered in time with our breathing.

"Well," Astrid said, brushing moss off her shoulder, "this is cozy."

"It's definitely the Hollow," Killian said. "Look."

The map floated between us, glowing softly. Its surface showed not roads, but paths etched by memory—shifting trails that only appeared when someone focused hard enough.

Caspian frowned. "It's not showing us a way forward. Just fragments. Symbols."

There were images: a broken compass, a burning book, a half-open door.

Sunna stepped beside me. "It's showing us choices. Not directions."

Zephyr glanced around. "And do any of these choices include going back? Because I don't love the vibe here."

"No turning back," Killian said quietly. "We need to figure this out."

I took a step forward. The moment I did, the trees shifted, parting like curtains to reveal a stone archway tangled in thorned vines.

We moved as one.

The Hollow had opened.

And it was waiting.

Mama Said Knock You Out | Selene

The map pulsed softly in the dim clearing, floating just above Caspian. It didn't show paths anymore, just images. A broken compass. A burning book. A half-cracked open door. And something new now: a circle with overlapping lines through the center, like a seal or crest I couldn't quite place.

"What are we even supposed to do with this?" Zephyr asked, hands deep in his coat pockets. "This looks like the kind of thing you wake up from in a panic after eating cursed stew."

Astrid crossed her arms. "It's not directions. It's symbols. A message."

"No," Sunna corrected. "It's a riddle. The Hollow isn't giving us a trail. It's giving us a memory test."

I frowned. "But it's not our memories."

Sunna gave me a strange look. "Are you sure?"

The symbols shimmered, shifting slightly. The broken compass rotated once, then pointed east. The door began to glow with a faint golden light, and the lines on the seal rippled like water. In the center of the map, ancient script formed.

"What's that?" Caspian asked.

Sunna read aloud: "Only those who remember what was never spoken can unlock what was never sealed."

"Awesome," Zephyr muttered. "It's a brain teaser wrapped in an existential crisis."

Killian stepped up beside me, his gaze fixed on the rotating compass. "It's a layered riddle."

Astrid nodded slowly. "There's something here. Something beneath the symbols."

I stepped closer to the map and focused. The compass stopped moving. Its face cracked slightly, and a word appeared faintly along the rim: *Origin.*

"The compass leads to where something began," I said aloud. "Something we were supposed to remember."

"But we didn't live it," Killian said. "So how are we supposed to remember something we weren't part of?"

"Maybe you were," Sunna said quietly. "Not you exactly. But your bloodline."

A long silence followed.

Killian and I exchanged a look, both instinctively stepping toward the map at the same time. The seal glowed brighter when we did, its overlapping lines rearranging themselves into a tree. Not a literal tree—a family tree. Branches intertwining, some of them pulsing with faint light.

Zephyr squinted. "Okay, that's…creepy."

"It's a diagram. A record," I said.

Astrid stepped between us and pointed to a name at one of the glowing branches. "That's in Originator script. Can you read it?"

Caspain squinted at it. "It says *Taranith.* That's…that's a royal name. From Ereriath."

Killian's face went pale. "That's my mom's name."

The map pulsed again, and the door icon swung open slightly. More script spilled across its frame.

What one forgot, the other must remember.

"This is about you two," Sunna said, matter-of-factly. "You're the key to the Hollow's next phase."

I shifted, uncomfortable. "But why us?"

Caspian stepped to my side, his hand brushing mine briefly. "We'll figure it out."

"I think," Zephyr said slowly, "the map is telling us to trigger something. A memory between them. Or...from them."

"I don't share memories with Killian," I said. "We've barely know each other."

"But maybe your families did," Astrid said, voice soft. "Maybe it's not about *you* remembering. Maybe it's about something inside you recognizing what's already there."

The compass image flashed suddenly, and a pathway illuminated beneath our feet—runes lighting up one by one, leading eastward.

Killian glanced at me, then at Astrid. "I'll go."

"I'm going with you," I said before I could stop myself.

Astrid didn't protest. She just looked at Killian a moment longer, then nodded.

The others stayed behind to study the seal and the tree-symbols. Killian and I followed the runes.

The path wound between spindly black trees etched with pulsing runes, the ground soft under our boots. The air buzzed faintly, like we were inside something that had been asleep for centuries and had just started to stir.

"This reminds me of something," I murmured.

"What?"

"A dream I used to have. My mom would sing about a valley with burning stars and a river that whispered names. I always thought it was just a story."

Killian was quiet. "My mother told me something similar. She used to hum this tune when I couldn't sleep. Said it came from her homeland."

"Ereriath?"

"Yeah."

The runes led us into a stone circle—like an altar—at the center of which stood a monolith covered in the same script we'd seen on the map. It pulsed when Killian stepped closer.

The compass symbol reappeared briefly in the air above it. Then the vision hit.

I saw two figures standing on opposite cliffs. One in royal blue, the other in white. They held hands across a rift of light, and below them, a tree burned gold without catching fire. The figures smiled at each other, their faces blurring and resolving and blurring again.

Then the vision shifted.

The two were seated in a chamber—laughing, teasing, weaving braids into each other's hair. One of them looked like my mother. The other...

Killian inhaled sharply. "That's her."

"You see it too?"

"I do, but I don't know who the other one is," he said.

"My mother," I mumbled turning my attention back to the image.

He nodded. "I think...I think our mothers knew each other. Maybe more than that."

The runes glowed brighter, drawing him in.

"Killian, wait—don't—"

He reached out and touched the monolith.

His body jerked once, violently, then stilled. His eyes went wide—unseeing—and his knees buckled.

"Killian!"

I caught him as he collapsed, his weight heavy and limp in my arms bringing me to my knees. His breathing was shallow. His skin was ice-cold.

His eyes were open but blank

I shook him gently. "Killian. Hey. Come on, don't do this."

Nothing.

The monolith was still glowing, but the compass had gone dark.

I pressed my hand to his chest. "Please."

Behind me, I heard footsteps—Astrid's voice calling my name, Zephyr's quick stride crashing through brush.

Astrid dropped beside him, voice sharp with panic. "What happened?!"

"He touched the monolith," I said numbly. "The map led us here. He saw something. I saw it too."

"What did you see?" Caspian asked.

"A valley. Two girls. Our mothers, I think. They were close. They knew each other."

Zephyr gave a low whistle. "So that's why the map needed you two."

Sunna crouched near the stone and ran her fingers across the runes. "It wasn't just a memory. It was a trigger. He unlocked something too deep."

Astrid held Killian's hand tightly. "Can we undo it?"

Sunna hesitated. "Maybe. If we solve the next part of the riddle."

Caspian touched the map. The door symbol was now glowing.

And underneath it, new script appeared: *The door will open when the bond is remembered.*

I stared at Killian's still form.

Somewhere in his mind, the Hollow was searching.
And we had to find the answer before it took him completely.

They didn't ask for the truth | Leia

The candlelight flickered across the stone walls, catching on the gold trim of the Queen's crest above the hearth. I sit at the small writing desk near the window, my tea long gone cold. It doesn't matter. My thoughts are far too loud for warmth tonight.

I heard them talking. I wasn't meant to. But old habits die hard.

Victor's voice carried through the corridor just outside the library—low, clipped, serious.

"They've gone," he said. "Selene touched the map again. And this time...Killian reacted too."

My heart hasn't stopped pounding since.

"You're thinking about her again."

"She's in the Hollow," I said, standing slowly.

She nodded. "Tonight."

"And you're letting them go through with it?"

"They volunteered," she explained. "They believe they're ready."

But I know what the Hollow does to people who think they're ready.

I walked to the hearth and placed my hand on the stone. The cold seeps into my skin, grounding me. "You always said the map would find its way back to blood."

"I did," she replied.

I stare into the fire, and suddenly I'm seventeen again, crouched behind a crumbling stone wall in the ruins of Ereriath, my wand drawn, heart hammering in my throat. Kofi was beside me, sharp-eyed and steady. We were on a mission from the Headmaster—one of the last before we made the choice to give it all up.

The Academy never told us what we were really doing. They just said we were good at uncovering hidden things. And we were. Especially together.

But that mission in Ereriath wasn't about politics or relics.

It was about her.

I went because I knew she was there.

My sister.

We were separated at birth—divided by war, by prophecy, by choices made before we were old enough to have names. I was raised in the Earth Realm. I trained at the Academy, worked for the Headmaster, and spent my life moving between lies.

She was raised there as royalty.

By the time I found her, she was already a princess. Already the heir to Ereriath's fractured crown. Already beloved by people I'd never met, tied to a world I didn't understand. She didn't know who I was. I never told her.

I told the Headmaster that the lead had been false. That the mission had failed. And I buried the truth.

Years later, she stood in front of me again. Older, wiser, crowned. And still, she didn't know.

She was Queen. And I was nothing more than a ghost at her door.

"She never forgave me," I whispered. "Not really."

"She didn't know what you gave up," Grizél said gently.

"No. Because I never told her."

Outside, wind rustles the ivy along the tower windows, brushing against the edges of old magic laced in the stone. The same kind that hung in the Hollow. The same kind that remembers bloodlines even when names are forgotten.

"And now our children are walking straight into it," I said.

"They're stronger than we were."

"Maybe," I murmured. "But the Hollow doesn't just want strength. It wants truth."

Grizél remained quiet.

"I still remember him as a baby," I said. "Killian. Crying all through the naming ceremony. And she just laughed. She said he was cursed with curiosity. Just like Selene. She used to say they'd change the world—our children. That they'd undo what we broke."

I closed my eyes. And now, they're the key to a puzzle none of us finished.

"I knew," I whispered. "Even before the map reacted. I knew the Hollow would call to Selene. And I should've known it would pull Killian too."

Grizél steps beside me. "You couldn't have stopped it."

"Maybe not. But I could've prepared her. I could've told her who she really is. Who her aunt is, why the Hollow remembers her name."

"What would it have changed?"

"Everything."

The fire crackled. Somewhere beyond the castle walls, night stretches deep into Ereriath's wilderness.

"She's going to survive this," I said finally. "She has to."

Grizél's voice is quieter. "She's not the only one you're

worried about." I glanced toward the door. "If the Hollow takes him—"

"Then we make sure it doesn't."

I nod, but my heart's already somewhere else.

With Selene.

With the son of the sister who never knew me.

And with the truth neither of them asked for—but are about to uncover.

The Bond Beneath | Selene

Killian hadn't moved in hours.

He lay on the moss-covered stone like the Hollow had claimed him as its own. His skin was too pale, his lips faintly blue, his eyes wide open—but blank. Astrid hadn't left his side once. She held his hand with both of hers, whispering his name like it was a warding spell.

Caspian crouched nearby, the air around him humming faintly from the last of the spells he'd tried. "The binding charm didn't take. Same with the memory tether."

He ran a hand through his hair, jaw tight. "It's not just a mental lock. This is blood-magic level—ancestral. The Hollow's got its roots in him."

"So what," Zephyr muttered, pacing at the edge of the circle. "It hijacks your brain if you're too related to someone?"

"It's not that simple," Sunna said, frowning at the shimmering projection of the map. "This place doesn't care about logic. It cares about memory."

I knelt beside the map, staring at the rotating images: the compass, the burning book, the half-cracked door. And now a fourth one—dim and flickering. A key. I hadn't seen that before.

I remembered the first clue. The one that started all of this. The riddle from my father's journal.

"Four doors, four keys, four paths untaken," I murmured. "A hidden truth in shadows shaken. One who seeks but does not see will find the lock, but not the key."

Sunna looked up sharply. "That's what was in the journal?"

I nodded. "It was written in the margins,"

Zephyr tilted his head. "Four doors. Four keys. We've seen three symbols so far, right?"

"Four," I said. "The last one just started flickering. The key."

Sunna flicked her fingers across the floating map, cycling through the symbols. "They're not just metaphors. They're tests. Memory-based riddles, linked to lineage. And Selene and Killian triggered the first major one."

"The tree," I said quietly.

The projection shimmered again, blooming into the twisting branches of a glowing lineage diagram. I stepped toward it, and two names pulsed instantly—*Leia* and *Velastra*.

Caspian pointed to them. "That's your mom, and that—Velastra—that's Killian's. She's the former Queen of Ereriath."

"And she's my mother's sister," I whispered. "My aunt."

Sunna gave a grim nod. "That's what the map's been showing us all along. It didn't need your magic—it needed your memories. Your family's forgotten bond."

Killian knew. Somewhere inside him, I realized now, he must have felt it. That moment in the forest when we both saw that vision—the valley, the girls on opposite cliffs—it wasn't random. It was a memory the Hollow preserved.

"Okay," Astrid said, standing abruptly. "So, we've got magical cousin connections, shared ancestral trauma, and a psychic plant that eats secrets. What do we do now?"

"We speak the vow," Sunna said. "We finish what their parents started."

"I don't know the words," I said. "Just pieces."

"You don't need the exact words," she replied. "You already remember the feeling."

Caspian stepped to my side. "If you do this, do it fast. That pulse—it's spreading."

He was right. The runes beneath Killian's body were glowing brighter now. The map buzzed like it was tuning to a frequency only blood could hear.

I took a breath, stepped forward, and placed my hand over *Leia's* name.

The shift was instant.

I stood on the cliffs again. Wind roaring. Stars scattered across the sky like broken glass. Across the chasm stood Velastra—Killian's mother, younger, her hair unbound, her hand stretched toward me.

"We made a vow," she said.

"To return," I answered.

"To remember."

The wind carried the words like an echo.

I blinked—and the Hollow roared.

Killian gasped. His chest arched as if pulled by invisible threads. Astrid was leaning into him, cradling his shoulders, crying openly. "You're okay. You're okay, you idiot. Don't ever do that again."

He looked dazed but alive. His eyes—still unfocused—found mine. "We were there. The cliffs."

"I saw it too."

Sunna turned to the tree. The compass and the door symbols pulsed once—then slid together, forming a new image: a circular seal with a starburst core and four runes orbiting the edge.

Four keys... I thought.

The map flared, and new text burned across its center:

The memory has been reclaimed. The Hollow has marked you.

I stepped back, pulse ringing in my ears.

"Does that mean we passed?" Zephyr asked. "Or, like... we triggered some kind of cosmic alert?"

"I don't know," Caspian said slowly.

The air around us seemed to tighten, like it was folding in on itself. Killian jumped to his feet just as a wind howled to life, spiraling in from all directions. Zephyr and Astrid raised their arms, their powers crackling outward, trying to counter the growing force. But the harder they pushed, the more furious it became, as if it was feeding on their resistance.

It shoved us back toward the door, the ground groaning beneath our feet.

"What the hell?" Caspian yelled, throwing his hands up. A ball of pulsing energy formed between them, then shot forward—straight into the churning air.

It vanished on contact. The storm didn't even flinch.

I clenched my eyes shut. *Stop*, I commanded silently, pushing the thought out like a pulse from my chest.

When I peeked, the wind hesitated. It hiccuped—just for a moment—but then surged again.

Taking a deep breath, I stepped forward, grounding my feet. "I command you to stop!" I shouted.

This time, the wind screamed like a creature in pain, spinning violently in place before slowing. It coiled and twisted inward, folding in on itself until something began to form in its center—tendrils of smoke wrapping together into a shape.

A figure.

"Holy shit," Astrid whispered.

The form solidified—wispy robes, a face cloaked in shadow, and eyes that glowed like twin embers in a storm.

"Finally," the figure hissed, voice low and serpentine. "A Trueshadow and a Taranith, both within my reach."

"Uhh, I think now would be the *perfect* time to get out of here," Astrid muttered.

"Who are you?" Killian demanded, stepping up beside me.

The figure tilted its head. "The answers you Seek shall be revealed soon enough."

"Caspian," I called, never taking my eyes off the figure. "The portal."

He dug into his pouch and pulled out a carved stone, pressing it to the floor. The runes lit up—but sputtered.

The figure raised its hands—and everything exploded.

A cyclone ripped through the chamber, throwing Zephyr back into the far wall. Astrid caught herself mid-stumble, knees scraping the stone as she slammed her palms down, sending a sharp *shockwave* of air toward the figure. The gust made it stagger, but only for a second.

Zephyr recovered with a grunt, eyes glowing icy blue. He thrust both hands forward—one swirling with wind, the other frosting over with ice. Twin torrents blasted across the room, colliding into the figure in a storm of razor-sharp hail and air pressure.

The figure inhaled the magic—devouring it.

"It's feeding on it," I gasped. "Our powers—it's absorbing them!"

Killian raised both arms, summoning a flare of energy. His magic shimmered strange—almost unstable—but he held it, palms radiating with raw force. "Then we don't give it one source—we hit it *together*. Overload it!"

Astrid gritted her teeth. "On your count, Killian!"

"Three—two—one—now!"

We all launched at once.

Zephyr sent a barrage of frozen needles slicing through the air, while Astrid compressed a wave of air so tightly it shimmered like a blade. I focused inward, pulling at the strange thread inside me—the one that had stopped the wind before—and pushed it outward in a blast of pure command, forcing the figure to recoil. I raised my hands and set my fire flying towards him too.

Killian's power crashed down in powerful waves. It hit the figure like a thunderclap, staggering it backward.

The creature screamed—an otherworldly, broken sound—and wavered. For a moment, it flickered like a flame in the wind.

"*Now*, Caspian!" I shouted.

The portal surged to life, glowing bright. Zephyr grabbed Astrid, pulling her toward the light. I went next, Caspian close behind.

"Killian, go!"

He turned—but the shadow moved faster.

A tendril of darkness whipped out, slamming into Killian's chest.

"Killian!" I screamed.

His body convulsed before stumbling through the portal. The figure let out a hiss as the gateway closed with a thunderous *crack*.

We landed in a heap in the family room of the castle.

But Killian didn't move.

His hands trembled, and when I reached for him, I saw it—the faint shimmer of dark tendrils beneath his skin, pulsing like veins of shadow.

And then his eyes fluttered open...glowing faintly with that same sickly light.

We'd escaped the chamber.

But whatever that thing was—whatever it had done—part of it came with us.

Not My King | Selene

King Victor and Queen Grizél paced opposite sides of the war room like two storms circling the same eye. The tension between them crackled, hovering like lightning, ready to strike.

"We have to send you home—for now," King Victor finally said, stopping mid-step to point directly at Zephyr, Sunna, and Astrid. His voice was low and absolute. It was a royal decree.

"What?" Sunna's voice cracked across the room like a whip. "We were out there too—risking our lives, nearly torn apart by that...*thing*. Why do we have to leave?"

Victor's gaze whipped to her like a blade drawn in silence. With a flick of his fingers, a portal split open behind them, the light pulsing and twisting like a warning rather than an invitation.

"Wait," I cut in quickly, stepping forward before anyone could move. "That portal leads back to our room—our dorm. We should go with them."

Victor didn't spare me a glance. "You do not trust these friends of yours to travel to the Academy realm alone?"

I narrowed my eyes. "That's not exactly what I said," I muttered under my breath. "But... point taken."

I turned to Astrid, who looked caught between confusion and frustration, her fingers twitching like she was barely holding her air magic back. "Addy stays," I said firmly, returning my gaze to Victor and standing straighter. "Not up for debate."

Caspian's brows lifted in surprise, and Killian's lip twitched, his eyes gleaming like he'd just witnessed something amusing and dangerous all at once.

King Victor looked like he might challenge me, but then Queen Grizél raised a single, elegant hand. "It's fine," she said softly, her voice calm but commanding.

"Then we all stay," Sunna said firmly, stepping protectively beside Astrid.

With a second flick of his wrist, the portal surged forward, sweeping Sunna and Zephyr into it in a rush of wind and magic. Their surprised gasps echoed faintly as the light sealed shut behind them.

My mouth fell open. "That was *rude!*" I shouted, whirling on him.

King Victor's eyes narrowed, his gaze sharp and cold as steel. "Do not press your luck, girl."

"My name is *Selene*," I said, voice trembling with fire. "And you are *not* my king, Victor. I do not bow to you."

The silence felt like the room had inhaled and forgotten how to exhale.

Caspian let out a slow breath through his nose. Killian's posture shifted beside me—rigid, like he was caught between loyalty and us. Astrid leaned closer to me without saying a word, grounding me even when the air had turned icy.

Victor stared at me like I was a puzzle he hadn't decided whether to solve or destroy.

And I didn't blink.

Then, like water pouring over fire, Queen Grizél stepped in. "Alright, now," she said, her voice smooth but firm. "Everyone, let's sit. We need to talk this through properly."

She gestured toward the long obsidian table that dominated the room, littered with maps etched in glowing ink, magical sigils suspended above it like floating constellations, and a few half-drunk glasses of tea left untouched.

Reluctantly, we moved. I took my seat beside Killian, our shoulders nearly touching. His leg bounced; mine trembled with tension I didn't want anyone to see.

"For the sake of clarity," the Queen continued, folding her hands gracefully, "Selene, begin at the top. Don't leave anything out."

Killian and I exchanged a glance.

So we told the story. Again.

The war room filled with the low hum of our voices as we recounted it all—every gust of corrupted wind, every pulse of devouring magic, every twisted word from the shadowed figure, and finally, the way Killian had collapsed just after we made it through the portal. I felt it all over again as I spoke—the fear, the power, the helplessness.

I leaned forward, pressing my hands flat against the table. My voice came out quieter than I expected, but sharp. "So... what exactly is going on?"

No one answered.

The silence stretched too long. I wasn't going to let it win.

"Who was that?" I asked again, more insistent now.

My eyes scanned their faces—Queen Grizél, poised and unreadable. King Victor, stone-faced and unmoved. Caspian, staring at them, like he'd heard just enough to begin forming the questions he wasn't sure he wanted answered.

"Because I know you know something," I said. "Don't act like that was just some random spirit. You've been feeding me breadcrumbs this whole time."

Queen Grizél's eyes flickered—just for a second. Guilt? Regret? Fear?

"Selene..." she began gently, but that calmness only made my anger flare hotter.

"Don't *Selene* me," I snapped. "I need answers. I deserve answers."

Victor spoke.

"Then it's time," he said grimly, his voice lower than before. "She deserves to know who she really is. And what that creature wants with her."

"You're right," a voice said from behind us.

I turned fast, magic buzzing at my fingertips—not because I was afraid, but because in *this* place, surprises rarely meant anything good.

"Mom? Dad?"

They stood just inside the chamber, framed by the arched doorway. My mother's posture was composed, but I caught the tension in her shoulders. My father's expression was guarded, the way it always got when things were complicated—which, clearly, they were.

"You're in *Odreazah*?" I asked, blinking. "Since when?"

"For a while now," my mom said, stepping forward. "We have a lot to tell you."

I looked between them, disbelief settling like a weight in my chest. "So you've been here... this whole time. While we were out there getting nearly torn apart?"

My father sighed. "There is not much we can do. There is much you don't know."

I took a step back, the realization still sinking in. "And no one thought to *mention* this part?"

III

Oh, when it all (yeah), it all falls down
(this the real one, baby)

Spiderweb of Lies | Selene

"You're in *Odreazah*?" The words slipped out before I could even begin to process the sight in front of me.

My mother and father stood just inside the war room, cloaked in silence like they were part of the stonework. My mother's green velvet cloak trailed behind her. My father's arms were folded tightly across his chest, jaw tense, shoulders stiff. They didn't look shocked to see me.

And yet I felt like the floor had just dropped out from under me.

"For a while now," my mother said gently, as if that explained *everything*.

I stared at them, arms locked across my chest, trying to anchor my thoughts before they scattered. "You've been here. In this realm. In this castle. While we were nearly dying trying to unravel truths you kept from me?"

Neither of them answered.

I took a step forward. "I've been here so many times. Stayed in the halls, walked through the same corridors. I *called* you. You were here the whole time?

My father stepped forward, his voice as steady as ever. "Selene, it's not that simple."

A bitter laugh slipped out. "Of course it's not."

They exchanged a look before Mom spoke. "You're right to be angry," she said quietly. "But watch your tone. We should've told you sooner. But the truth was dangerous. And the longer we waited, the harder it became."

"Then tell me *now*," I said, my voice softer. "No more cryptic warnings. No more breadcrumbs. I want the *whole* story. Please."

They hesitated before Mom started. "Her name was Velastra. She was your aunt. My half-sister. Killian's mother."

The world tipped. I sank onto the nearest bench before my legs gave out.

"We shared a father," she went on. "A mage named Elion. He wasn't loyal to anyone but his own ambition. He fathered Velastra with the Queen of Ereriath. A few years, he crossed into the Earth Realm during a covert mission, met my mother, and…I happened."

"You were born in the Earth Realm?" I asked, blinking.

Mom nodded. "Raised there. Hidden. I didn't even know Velastra existed until I was sent to Ereriath while at the Academy—part of a diplomatic exchange between realms. That's when I met her."

"What—instant sister bonding over war stories and spellbooks?" I asked.

She gave a sad, crooked smile. "Not exactly. She was guarded. But there was something between us. We shared the same spark. The same…core. We weren't close. But we trusted each other. Eventually."

Her smile faded, replaced by tension.

"And then came the Seeker."

Dad's voice dropped. "He was never meant to rise. He was created out of desperation after the Realm Wars has begun.

Built by magic, born from blood. Part weapon, part watchdog. Designed to track power across dimensions."

Mom's expression hardened. "At first, he did as commanded. Until he realized the truth: magic wasn't something to track. It was something to *own*. Bloodlines were his currency."

"He found out about them," Dad continued. "Two daughters of Elion. If he could merge that bloodline... he believed he'd unlock something ancient. Something the Hollow still whispers to."

"He wanted to *consume* us," Mom said bitterly. "Not just physically—our essence. Our magic. He thought we were keys to dominion. Over the Hollow. Over this world."

I felt my stomach turn. "So what did you do?"

Mom's voice cracked. "I ran."

She took a slow breath before continuing, "I begged Velastra to come with me. I was already pregnant with you. But she was Queen. She had little Killian. Her duty kept her rooted. She couldn't leave."

"So, you did," I whispered.

She nodded. "I left her behind. I crossed back into the Academy realm with your father. I refused the Headmaster's orders, abandoned every mission, every oath. We severed all contact with Ereriath. Wiped all records of you. Buried you in protection spells. And made a pact with Queen Grizél to shield your existence."

"You knew about Killian this whole time?" I asked bitterly

"Yes. I didn't tell you because the more you knew, the easier it would be for the Seeker to find you. I hoped—naively—that Victor would protect Velastra and her son. That the bloodline would be safe...even if we were fractured."

"But Velastra died," I said quietly, turning toward Killian.

His jaw clenched, but he didn't speak.

"We believe the Seeker found her," Dad said gravely. "Or someone he controls. Her death was called natural, but nothing about it ever sat right. And now..."

That made me think about the Hollow. The binding spell that I fractured.

"He's after me," I said aloud, voicing the fear I'd tried to ignore.

"And Killian," Mom confirmed. "It's not just one of you he needs. It's *both*."

"Because of Velastra?" I asked, still not fully able to grasp it.

"Because of what you *both* are," she said. "You two are bonded. Two pieces of the same legacy. One line split by fate, reunited by the Hollow."

Killian stepped closer. "That's why the Hollow responded to us."

Dad nodded. "The Hollow isn't just a destination. It's a mirror. A keeper of what was lost. And it knows you two belong to something that was never meant to be broken.

"So what now?" I asked quietly, my thoughts a chaotic mess of names and realms and powers I wasn't ready to wield. "What am I supposed to do with this?"

Mom knelt in front of me and reached for my hand. "I wish we could hide you. But our powers are gone. Stripped when we chose to disobey the Seeker's design. And he's already found you."

She looked at the spiderweb of dark veins now creeping up to Killian's neck.

"See?" she said, voice trembling. "He's marked you."

I yanked my hand away, heart slamming against my ribs.

"No," I said, voice barely more than a rasp. "No. We can fight this. We have to."

Killian's eyes met mine, dark and glassy, like he already knew something I didn't. He didn't flinch. That scared me more than anything.

Mom rose slowly, "We hoped you would have more time. That he wouldn't find you so soon. But the Hollow was never meant to heal. It was always a trap. A mirror. A weapon."

Kofi's jaw tightened. "It doesn't offer protection. It magnifies what's already inside and if he controls even a piece of you, he'll control it too."

Silence strangled the room. Even the flames on the sconces seemed to flicker lower, retreating from the truth.

Killian looked at me, the black veins along his neck dark and pulsing. His voice was low.

"Then we don't run. We don't hide. We end it."

"Don't be reckless," Dad said sharply, stepping forward. "You're already marked. The Hollow will strip away what's left of you."

"So what?" I demanded, my voice slicing through the heavy air. "We do nothing? We let him hollow us out piece by piece while we wait for some miracle that isn't coming?"

Mom pressed a trembling hand to her chest. "We wanted to keep you safe," she whispered. "But hiding only delayed the inevitable. The Seeker always knew what to look for. He was always coming."

I swallowed hard, anger and terror and something fiercer rising inside me.

"And now he's not coming," I said. "He's already here."

Mom reached for me, desperate, but I stepped back. "No more half-truths. No more waiting."

Another sharp knock rattled the door.

"We'll come back," I said, my voice iron-clad. "But right now…we fight."

I turned, not waiting for their reply, and pushed through the door—into the chaos already spiraling into motion.

Into the storm we were born from.

The Path Beneath | Selene

I didn't expect the room to feel this... hollow.

The portal in the back of my armoire snapped shut behind me with a low hiss. I stood in the center of the room, half-drenched in war room shadows, half-hearing my mother's words still echoing through my head.

Your aunt. My half-sister. Killian's mother.

"Anything you wanna unpack, vent, exorcise?" she asked. "Or should I just assume we're going to repress until it explodes on someone's head later?"

"I don't know," I said quietly. "It's just...a lot."

Astrid's voice softened, losing its usual edge. "Yeah. I get that."

I sank down at my desk, the weight of it all pressing into me. My fingers found my father's journal almost without thinking. Magic hummed against my skin.

The runes across the cover shimmered. A violet light spilled across the pages as I flipped to the last section, the one that should have been blank.

Fresh ink bled across the parchment in Hollow script— symbols I hadn't seen since I was a child. Letters no one alive should be able to call back.

"Addy..." I said slowly.

She turned, immediately on alert. "What did you do?"

"I didn't do anything." Which was true. The journal had done something to me.

The lights overhead flickered once. Then again. A pulse, low and rhythmic, thrummed under the floorboards.

Astrid was up and armed in an instant. "That's not normal Academy magic."

I nodded, heart thudding against my ribs. "I think it's reacting to what happened in the castle. To what I am."

As if summoned by my words, the secret phone tucked into my desk drawer buzzed sharply, then sparked. I snatched it up, but the screen was dead, blackened at the edges like it had been burned from the inside out.

"Caspian?" I muttered. "Or Killian—?"

"Did something curse the signal?" Astrid asked, pulling out her own phone. Hers was fine.

Before I could answer, a sharp knock rattled the door.

Astrid grabbed the dagger she kept under her pillow. My palms already tingling with spellfire.

"Open up!" came a familiar voice. "Lee, it's me!"

Astrid yanked the door open.

Zephyr stumbled inside, out of breath, hair sticking up at odd angles like he'd been sprinting through portals sideways.

"Listen," Zephyr panted. "The Queen sent a message."

My blood ran cold. "Through the secret phone?"

His brows knitted. "Secret phone? No. Through the mirror."

Astrid dropped the dagger with a sharp clatter. "I'm sorry, *what?*"

"She used the Dormant Glass. The one my parents gave me. I have no idea how she knew I had it."

I rose, the journal still glowing faintly in my hand. "What did she say?"

Zephyr's voice dropped. 'The Path is open. And it remembers.'"

Astrid and I exchanged a look.

"And Caspian?" I asked. "Why didn't he text?"

"Don't know. But..." Zephyr hesitated. "I saw Killian in the mirror for a second. He looked... wrong. Distracted. The black veins were active."

My mouth went dry.

"The Path," I said aloud. "She means Erador's Path, doesn't she?"

Astrid crossed her arms. "Is this the part where we pretend it's not our responsibility and go get snacks? Or the part where we lace up our boots and risk death again?"

"Option B," I muttered.

Zephyr glanced at the journal still faintly pulsing in my grip but said nothing.

"Let me change," I said. "We portal in five."

As I moved toward the armoire, I could feel their gazes trailing after me and beneath it all, the journal's thrum growing louder.

We stepped through the portal together.

The Academy vanished in a wash of violet light. When we landed, it wasn't in our dorm, or the courtyard, or the safe halls of Odreazah.

We were standing at the threshold of the war room corridor.

And we weren't alone.

Queen Grizél stood waiting, the hem of her indigo gown brushing the stone floor.

Flanking her were my parents cloaked in deep navy, armed, ready. They didn't smile. They didn't reach for me. They simply nodded — two warriors acknowledging another.

I swallowed hard, tightening my grip on the journal.

Before I could move toward them, footsteps echoed from the side hall.

Caspian.

His cheeks flushed with cold air, and his eyes locked onto me in an instant.

"You're okay," he asked, voice low enough that no one else could hear.

I nodded once.

Caspian fell into step beside me naturally, as if he belonged there. His presence steadied the floor beneath my feet even as the rest of the world shifted.

Queen Grizél's gaze hardened. "You felt it?"

"We saw it," I said.

She gestured toward the wall behind her, where glowing runes carved themselves into ancient stone.

"This," she said, "is Erador's Path."

Behind us, Killian rounded the corner, his movements slower. The veins at his neck pulsed faintly under his skin.

I stepped instinctively toward him, but he gave a small shake of his head.

Not yet.

Queen Grizél's voice dropped lower. "The Path was sealed after Velastra's death. It was meant to stay buried."

"Why open now?" Zephyr asked.

She looked to me. To Killian. To the journal burning softly in my hands.

"Because you carry what she did," she said. "Because you are what the Seeker still hunts."

The air around us thickened, vibrating slightly.

Killian stepped forward first, pressing his hand against the door. Nothing happened.

I followed, placing my palm beside his.

This time, the wall responded.

The stone hissed and split open, revealing a spiral staircase descending into darkness. Faint, pulsing vines snaked around the edges of the steps, glowing violet blue.

"I hate stairs," Astrid muttered, pulling her dagger free.

"I hate cursed basements more," Zephyr added.

Killian looked at me. "You sure you want to do this?"

"No," I said. "But we're doing it."

Caspian caught my eye just before we stepped forward. A silent promise there: *You won't face this alone.*

We descended into the dark together, leaving the last scraps of safety — and everything we thought we knew — behind us.

Where Shadows Remember | Selene

The spiral staircase swallowed the light behind us.

Every step downward, the world narrowed—the air tightening, the stone closing in, the magic thrumming deeper under our skin. The walls were etched with strange grooves, spirals at first glance, but they shifted with the light, forming runes—sentences in a language that shimmered and retreated.

Behind me, Astrid's boots scraped softly against the stone. Zephyr moved with a little too much bounce for someone descending into possibly cursed ruins. Caspian was just behind me. Killian walked ahead, the glow from the vines in the walls casting green shadows over the sharp lines of his jaw.

The deeper we went, the thicker the air became. It was like breathing in magic. Ancient magic. The kind that had a shape and a will of its own.

"You feel that?" Zephyr muttered. His voice bounced oddly off the walls.

Astrid grunted. "Like the tunnel's listening."

"No," Caspian said quietly. "Like it's remembering."

The staircase leveled off into a wide, arched corridor. The air shifted, colder, tinged with ozone. My hand brushed the edge of the stone wall—power buzzed along my fingers like static.

Ahead, a black stone door blocked the path. Except when Killian stepped forward, the runes across it lit up.

"Wait," Caspian said, catching his breath. "This wasn't supposed to be sealed."

Killian frowned. "They never mentioned a door."

"No." Caspian tilted his head. "That's because this wasn't made to keep things out."

I stepped beside Killian and laid my hand on the stone next to his. It was cold. Then hot. Then neither. A thrum passed through my wrist, like it was testing me.

A deep click echoed through the chamber, and the door split down the center. The corridor beyond was revealed, lined with massive stone columns. Between them floated dozens of objects. A dagger. A ring. A cracked mirror. A vial of blood. A weathered crown.

"Don't touch anything," Caspian said softly at my side.

Zephyr had already wandered closer to a golden coin etched with Hollow markings. "What is this stuff?"

"Temptations," Caspian answered. "Anchors. Warnings."

Killian brushed past an urn and flinched. "They're not just magical. They're personal."

I turned. "Personal how?"

Before anyone could answer, Astrid stumbled back from a pedestal. Her face was pale.

"I saw my brother," she whispered. "He was holding that blade. I watched him die with it."

There was no blade now—only a cracked stone with a faint echo of smoke curling around it.

I moved toward a pedestal holding a fractured mirror.

At first glance, it was nothing. But when I leaned closer— Velastra stared back at me. Her crown was broken. Her mouth moved soundlessly.

I stepped forward—

"Selene," Caspian said sharply, grabbing my wrist.

The image shattered. Only my reflection remained, distorted and cracked.

"They're not just testing us," I said. "They're trying to show us. What we want. What we fear."

Farther down the corridor, Zephyr stood frozen before another pedestal—a leather bracelet floating above it.

His shoulders stiffened. His mouth moved, but no sound came out.

I rushed forward, yanking him back just before his fingers could close around it. The relic dissolved into ash.

"My mother" he muttered hoarsely. "It showed me her."

"They're using our memories against us," Astrid said, voice tight. "They're learning our weak points."

The corridor narrowed, forcing us closer together as we moved forward.

Then, the world shifted.

Just the sudden, jarring sensation of the ground giving way to grass, the scent of flowers filling our lungs, a sky stretched too wide overhead.

We were in a field.

Violet grass rippled underfoot. The stars above pulsed like living things. A false peace lay over everything, and underneath it, the cold, knowing thrum of Hollow magic.

At the center of the field stood a figure cloaked in black.

The Seeker. His presence was enough to freeze the breath in my lungs.

Astrid darted forward, her twin daggers flashing, aiming for the Seeker's throat in one smooth, deadly strike.

Behind her, Zephyr flung a burst of slicing wind — the air rippling with sharp, cutting force — trying to pin the Seeker down. His Ice Armour falling into place seamlessly.

Caspian surged in next, sword gleaming with a faint shimmer of battle magic, ready to drive the blade through the Seeker's chest.

I stretched out my hands, summoning a coil of spellfire— and reached into the space between us with my mind, grabbing for the heavy stones scattered across the field, hurling them straight toward him.

Killian lifted his hand too, shadows gathering in his palm, dark veins glowing faintly.

The Seeker moved only slightly. The air around him seemed to bend.

Astrid's daggers disintegrated before they touched him— turning to ash mid-strike.

Zephyr's wind slammed into an invisible barrier and shattered backward, nearly knocking him off his feet.

Caspian's blade froze a hairsbreadth from the Seeker's body, stuck fast in the air like it was encased in invisible stone.

My spellfire splintered and faded the second it neared him. The stones I threw crumbled to dust before they even reached his cloak.

Killian's shadows, instead of striking him, coiled back— twisting around Killian's arm like a serpent.

The Seeker simply watched us, his expression almost amused.

"Children," he intoned. "Still clinging to the illusion of power. Still thinking you can wound the inevitable."

He lifted his hand, palm open.

The magic we had thrown at him—wind, stone, darkness, firelight—was drawn toward him, sucked into the blackness gathering in his center like water into a whirlpool.

Caspian was the first to pull away, dragging Astrid with him. "Fall back!" he barked.

I yanked at my magic, reeling it back before the Seeker could siphon more of it.

One by one, we retreated, weapons lowered, magic stifled.

And still, the Seeker stood motionless.

Smiling.

Killian stepped forward before anyone could stop him.

"You're late," the Seeker said. His voice was soft. "You've already unlocked the first gate," he continued. "Now you'll open the second."

He turned toward us. His face blurred—shifting between a stranger's, Killian's, Velastra's, even my own. Each flicker worse than the last.

"You think your blood protects you," the Seeker said. "But blood remembers. And it always collects its debt."

The field shuddered. The stars dimmed. The violet sky cracked, threads of blackness spreading outward.

Beside me, Caspian reached for his blade. Astrid's daggers were out. Zephyr's hands sparked with ice.

But Killian—he just stared.

"You feel it too," the Seeker said, smiling now. "The pull. The truth they've hidden from you."

He turned his gaze to me next.

"And you," he said. "The Hollow's favorite daughter. So full of fire. So desperate to be more than your blood."

My fists curled at my sides. "You won't win," I said.

The Seeker's grin widened into something monstrous.

"I already have. You're here."

He lifted a hand.

The field twisted. The sky screamed. The ground beneath us splintered.

And for one terrible moment, I saw it—

A vision of what could be.

The castle in ruins. The Hollow bleeding into every realm. Killian on his knees, black veins swallowing him whole. Caspian lying motionless, his sword broken at his side. Astrid and Zephyr torn apart by magic.

And me—at the center. Hollowed out. Powerless. A puppet.

I stumbled back, gasping.

Caspian caught me before I fell, his arms steady around me, his voice a low murmur in my ear.

"Selene. Breathe. It's not real."

The Seeker's voice echoed through the collapsing illusion:

"You can't stop what was promised."

The field dissolved into dust. The stars blinked out. The sky crumbled.

We were back in the Hollow's true heart—cracked stone, endless dark, walls pulsing with a magic older than memory.

But something had changed.

The runes along the walls now blazed bright gold, forming words I could read:

"The Second Gate Awaits."

Killian staggered beside me, clutching his head. The veins along his neck darkened, spreading like ink under his skin.

Caspian shifted, half-blocking me from view, hand tight around the hilt of his blade.

Astrid pulled Zephyr closer, her face grim.

We weren't just being hunted anymore.

We were being *called*.

And something deep in the Hollow was answering.

The Seeker's Game | Selene

The Path didn't just wait for us.

It swallowed us.

The second we stumbled deeper into the corridor, the air tightened, like invisible hands pressing against my chest, my spine, my skull.

Every torch lining the walls flickered once—and died.

Darkness slammed into us like a wall.

I reached for magic, but the Hollow pushed back, twisting the spellfire gathering in my palms into something cold and brittle.

"Don't separate!" Caspian barked, but his voice sounded wrong—like it was stretched too thin.

One step forward—and they vanished.

Astrid. Zephyr. Caspian. Killian.

Gone.

I spun, heart hammering, but the mist had swallowed them whole.

I was alone.

"No, no, no—" I whispered, forcing down the panic rising in my throat.

Then I heard it.

A voice.

Soft. Familiar.

"Selene."

I turned.

Velastra.

Whole. Smiling. Reaching for me.

"Come, little star," she said. Her voice was honey-thick with love and something sharper hidden beneath.

Tears blurred my vision.

The woman I'd only known through whispers and dreams. She looked so real. So right.

"You don't have to fight anymore," Velastra said, beckoning with one outstretched hand.

I wanted to believe.

Gods, I wanted to believe.

I took one step forward.

Selene, it's not real!

Caspian's voice ripped through the fog, sharp as a blade.

I froze.

The world around Velastra flickered—her smile twisting, warping.

Not real.

I clenched my fists and reached inside myself—not for spellfire, but for the colder, heavier thing coiled deep inside.

I *yanked* the edges of the illusion,.

It fought me, screaming in Velastra's voice, pulling back with all the weight of my own longing.

But I pulled harder, harder, until the world cracked around me and the illusion shattered like glass under a hammer.

Velastra's form disintegrated into black mist.

I staggered back, gasping, hands trembling.

Caspian caught me before I could fall, one hand steadying my shoulder.

"You're back," he said quietly.

I nodded, even as my chest ached from the force it took to tear myself free.

Astrid stumbled towards us, dragging Zephyr by the wrist. Astrid's daggers were still out, but her arms were bleeding—thin lines slicing up her skin where illusions had cut too deep.

Zephyr's skin shimmered with patches of ice; his hands shook.

"They showed us," Astrid muttered. "Our families. Alive. Whole."

Zephyr's voice was hoarse. "My sister, she…she told me she was waiting. That I could save her." His face twisted, raw and broken. "I almost stayed."

Caspian stepped forward, scanning the mist warily. "It's not over. The Path will push harder now."

The mist thickened again—dense, suffocating.

And then—

Killian screamed.

A raw, animal sound that ripped through the corridor.

We ran.

We found him crumpled against a jagged wall, hands tangled in his own hair, the black veins along his neck crawling up his jaw, his temple, his cheekbone.

I dropped to my knees beside him, grabbing his face between my hands.

"Killian," I forced him to look at me. His skin was freezing cold. His pulse, when I found it, fluttered like a trapped bird under my fingers.

His eyes were wide, wild, black flooding the whites like ink spilled across a map.

Astrid crashed down beside us hard enough to rattle the stone. Her hands framed his face too, more demanding than gentle.

"Killian," she growled. "Listen to me. Look at me." Her thumb brushed the hollow of his jaw. "You're not lost," she whispered. "You hear me? You're still you. You're still here."

His panicked gaze jerked toward her. The black swirling through his eyes quivered, cracked—just enough for him to see her. His chest heaved like it hurt to breathe.

"There you are," he rasped, his voice tearing raw from his throat.

"Duh," Astrid's face twisted.

Killian sagged forward, exhausted, his forehead pressing into her shoulder. His whole body shook like he was barely holding himself together.

Astrid caught him, arms locking around him like a shield. Her hands trembled — but she didn't let go.

And still, the Hollow around us didn't retreat.

It coiled tighter, pressing against the walls, slithering through the cracks in the stone, tasting the fear bleeding off us like smoke.

I forced myself to stay standing, even when my legs threatened to give out. Astrid held Killian together with her hands; I held the rest of us together with the sheer force of will.

But the mist ahead of us shifted—and for a split second, I saw her.

Sunna's back was turned, her figure vanishing into the mist like she belonged to it.

She wasn't fighting the Hollow.

She was leading it.

I swallowed the fury clawing up my throat. She had offered herself to it.

And if we didn't move fast—

she wouldn't be the only thing the Hollow devoured.

The Second Gates Open | Selene

The runes carved into the stone pulsed like a heartbeat, bleeding dark light across the cracked floor. Mist thickened at our feet, coiling upward like skeletal hands reaching for whatever warmth we had left. We stood frozen, waiting for the gate to demand something more.

It didn't make us wait long.

The runes brightened, then flared outward in a sudden burst of hollow wind. The air tasted like iron. Magic crackled through the corridor, thick enough to choke on.

Caspian shifted closer to me as the mist thickened, his arm brushing mine. The contact was accidental but it still sent a jolt through me that had nothing to do with magic.

"You good?" he asked, voice low enough that only I could hear it.

"Define good," I muttered, trying to sound normal, but my heart was hammering.

He gave a half-smile, the kind that was more reflex. "Breathing counts."

"I'm definitely still breathing," I said, managing a crooked smile back.

His eyes softened, just for a second, and something in his posture shifted.

Like if I leaned even half an inch closer, he'd catch me without question.

I caught myself staring and tore my gaze away, heat rising in my cheeks.

This was *so* not the time.

"Stay close," he said, softer now, like it was more than a tactical suggestion.

The ground under our feet shuddered, a low pulse of magic vibrating through the stone.

"This is wrong," Caspian muttered beside me, his hand tightening on the hilt, though even he knew a blade wouldn't save us here. "This isn't an entrance."

Astrid was half-holding Killian upright. His head lolled against her shoulder, the black veins now spiderwebbing all the way up his throat, creeping toward the fragile skin under his eyes. She shook him once, but he barely stirred.

Zephyr paced a few feet away, muttering under his breath, his fingers sparking tiny wisps of frost into the air that vanished as fast as they formed. He shot a glance at the broken pendant lying at the base of the gate—Sunna's—and scowled.

"She already gave herself up," Zephyr said tightly. "She's gone. That should've been enough."

"It's never enough," Astrid grunted, shifting Killian's weight against her.

Zephyr whirled on her, frost sparking at his fingertips. "You think she volunteered for this? You think she *wanted* to leave us?"

Astrid stood, shoulders squared. "She wasn't dragged screaming into the mist, Zephyr. She walked through it."

"You don't know that!" Zephyr shot back, his voice cracking. "Maybe she didn't have a choice!"

"She did," I said, stepping between them before the argument could spiral further. My voice cut through the rising panic like a blade. "I saw her."

They turned to me.

"In the mist," I continued, forcing the words out. "She wasn't running. She wasn't calling for help. She was walking away. Like she knew exactly where she was going."

Zephyr opened his mouth—then closed it, shoulders sagging.

Caspian moved closer too,. "Taken or not, it doesn't change what's happening now. The gate's still hungry. And it's not going to wait much longer."

The gate moved.

The mist thickened around our ankles and from its center a tendril of black magic uncoiled, lashing toward us with a sound like a hundred whispers crammed into a single breath.

Zephyr shouted as the tendril wrapped around his chest and yanked him off his feet. Snarling, he thrust both hands outward, a violent blast of ice and wind exploding from his palms. Frost raced up the tendril, crackling and splintering. For a heartbeat, the magic hissed, retreating under the sudden cold.

But the Hollow adapted.

The tendril absorbed the ice like it was nothing, tightening with a sickening creak around Zephyr's ribs.

I hurled a blast of spellfire toward it, violet flames catching along the tendril's edges. The mist screamed—high and thin, almost human—but it didn't let go.

Astrid lunged in next, daggers flashing as she slashed across the tendril's thickest part.

Caspian followed her a second later, his sword arcing downward in a clean, brutal strike that carved through the magic with a blinding crack.

The tendril recoiled, hissing, snapping back toward the gate.

Zephyr hit the ground hard, coughing, his arms coated in frost, the remnants of his magic sparking weakly around him.

I stumbled back toward Killian, reaching him just as his knees buckled.

The black veins were crawling higher, twisting under his skin like roots. I caught him under the shoulders before he could collapse fully, my magic coiling instinctively around both of us, shielding him from the mist still curling across the stones.

Ahead of us, Zephyr dragged himself to his feet.

The gate shuddered, furious, the runes now pulsing like a heartbeat out of rhythm.

"It's not going to stop," Caspian said, breathing hard. His eyes met mine.

I looked at the runes again, forcing myself to focus. They weren't warnings; they were instructions. Blood answers blood. One opens. One is taken. My stomach turned cold as realization set in.

It didn't just want a life.

It wanted a specific life.

Mine.

Killian's.

Tied by bloodlines, by Hollow magic, by something older we still didn't fully understand.

"I have to do it," I said, stepping forward.

Caspian caught my arm, his grip iron-tight. "No. Absolutely not."

"You don't understand," I said, trying to keep my voice calm even as my magic coiled restlessly under my skin. "It's keyed to me. To Killian. If I don't—"

"I'm not letting you sacrifice yourself," he said fiercely.

Astrid looked up from where she was still crouched over Killian. "There has to be another way."

"There isn't," I said, feeling the truth of it settle like a stone in my gut. "Not anymore."

Another tendril lashed out from the gate, faster than the first. It grabbed Astrid around the waist, yanking her backward.

She cried out, slashing at it wildly, but the magic tightened, dragging her toward the stone.

Killian, barely conscious, threw himself forward, wrenching Astrid free with a raw, animal strength that should have been impossible given how broken he already was. They both collapsed hard against the floor, gasping.

I shoved Caspian back with a blast, not hard enough to hurt him, but enough to get free. He shouted something—my name, maybe—but I didn't stop.

I stepped toward the gate, magic building in my hands, in my chest, in my bones. I gathered every shred of spellfire, every scrap of will I had left, and threw it outward.

The mist recoiled. The runes flared.

The gate screamed.

But I didn't let go.

I reached out with my mind, wrapped invisible fingers around the foundation of the spellwork embedded in the stone, and *ripped.*

Pain exploded behind my eyes. Magic surged through my veins. The gate resisted, howling, but I yanked harder, dragging at the very fibers of the Hollow's construction.

The stone cracked with a deafening roar. A fissure split the gate in two, golden light pouring through the seam. The gate buckled.

The Hollow screamed in fury, the Seeker's rage pressed

against the edges of my mind like knives.

Caspian was at my side again, arms braced around me as I stumbled, my vision already swimming at the edges.

"You're not doing this alone," he said, low and savage.

The world exploded.

Magic tore through the corridor like a hurricane. The ground dropped out from under us. I felt myself falling, yanked by a force too big to fight, Caspian's arms the only thing keeping me from being torn apart by the pull.

I tried to speak—to warn him,—but the words caught in my throat.

The last thing I felt was the fierce, steady grip of his hand against mine.

And then everything went dark.

The Hollowed Bargain | Caspian

Selene collapsed against me just as the gate ripped itself apart.

I barely caught her before the blast of magic nearly knocked me off my feet. Her weight was nothing—the problem was the deadness of it. Her head lolled against my shoulder, her body slack, like someone had cut the strings that held her upright.

I gritted my teeth and locked my arms around her.

The others shouted but the wind howling through the broken gate swallowed the sound.

"Move!" Astrid screamed somewhere behind me.

We were out of time. I shifted Selene higher against my chest and ran straight into the storm.

The Hollow met us head-on.

Mist slammed into my face, sharp and stinging, tasting of metal and cold earth. Every step felt wrong, like walking through a place that hated you just for existing. I could feel the magic clawing at Selene, trying to pull her away. I tucked her tighter against me, forcing every ounce of battle magic I had left into a thin shield around us.

Astrid appeared at my side, half-dragging Killian, whose boots barely touched the ground. Zephyr staggered a few steps behind, his face paled, frost trailing from his hands as he struggled to keep his balance.

"Keep going!" Astrid shouted hoarsely.

The gate—if you could still call it that—shrieked as the last of it buckled behind us, collapsing into nothing but mist and ruin.

We stumbled through the threshold together, half-carried by momentum, half-dragged by sheer will.

And then—

Silence.

We stood in a cavern of stone and shadow, the air so heavy it felt like it was pushing down on our lungs.

I staggered to a halt, adjusting my grip on Selene. She didn't stir. Her forehead was burning against my collarbone, magic still flickering weakly under her skin like dying embers.

I didn't realize I was holding her too tightly until Astrid touched my arm.

"She's breathing," she said, quieter now. "Just unconscious."

I nodded, jaw clenched so tight it hurt.

We weren't safe. Not even close.

Across the cavern, a figure stood waiting.

Sunna.

But it wasn't the Sunna we knew.

Her posture was wrong—too still, too perfect. Her smile was hollow, stretched too wide. And the magic around her shimmered wrong, tinted with a familiar, terrible darkness.

Behind her, deeper in the mist, another figure began to emerge.

The Seeker.

He moved like he owned the ground under our feet, the air in our lungs, the magic thrumming against our skin.

"I should've seen it," Astrid growled as she helped Killian

shift his weight against her shoulder. "We should've seen it."

Zephyr cursed under his breath, pacing a jagged line in front of the broken gate.

"What are you talking about?" I asked sharply, tightening my grip on Selene.

Astrid stared across the cavern—at Sunna's distant silhouette standing proudly by the Seeker. "Breakfast. The first day," Astrid's voice was tight. "She knew about Selene's parents. She knew before Selene ever said anything. Played it off like it was gossip."

Zephyr stopped pacing, realization dawning. "And Manifest classes. She *made sure* she ended up in the same ones."

"Study groups, too," Astrid added. "She always volunteered to 'help' when the riddles came up. Like she already knew what the Hollow wanted."

"She wasn't just lucky," I said grimly.

"She was setting us up." Astrid's hand tightened around her dagger hilt until her knuckles whitened. "From the start."

Zephyr's jaw clenched. "And we fed her everything. Our powers. Our plans. Our weaknesses."

I shifted Selene higher against my chest, the rage rising in my throat so fast it almost choked me.

They had targeted her from the beginning. While we joked and studied and planned, the Seeker had been using Sunna to dismantle Selene's defenses one piece at a time.

Selene trusted so few people.

And she had let Sunna in.

I curled my free hand into a fist, forcing the fury down. There would be time for rage later.

Right now, I had only one job:

Keep her breathing.

Keep her standing.

And kill anything that tried to take her from me again.

Astrid shifted closer to me, ready to strike.

Zephyr cursed under his breath, ice cracking along his arms again.

I adjusted my stance, shifting Selene's weight so I could move faster if I had to—shield her if I needed to.

The Seeker took another slow step forward, his cloak whispering across the ground. Sunna stayed rooted at his side, her hands loose at her sides, her chin tilted in silent, smug defiance.

"Welcome," the Seeker said again, voice rich and poisonous. "You've fought long and hard to reach this place. Truly admirable."

Astrid shifted, her daggers flashing briefly under the Hollow's strange, pulsing light. Zephyr muttered something savage under his breath, ice misting off his fingertips again.

I tightened my grip on Selene, feeling the uneven flutter of her heartbeat against my chest. She was still unconscious. Every second we stood here, the Hollow breathed closer, wrapping itself around us like a noose.

The Seeker's gaze slid lazily across our broken group, pausing briefly on Killian's sagging frame against Astrid's shoulder.

Then it landed on Selene.

And stayed there.

"You bring me what I asked for," he said, amusement curling at the edges of his words. "Though not in the condition I would have preferred."

Astrid stepped forward before I could, daggers raised. "You're not getting her. Not now. Not ever."

The Seeker's smile widened.

"Oh, but you misunderstand." He spread his arms, as if

offering a gift. "I am merciful. Generous, even. I offer a bargain."

"No deal," Zephyr snapped immediately.

"There are two bloodlines I seek," he said calmly, watching Selene. "Two keys fractured by time and fate. Velastra's line. And Leia's line. Both parts of Elion's linage."

He tilted his head slightly, like a wolf studying cornered prey. "You," he whispered, "have the chance to choose which one I take."

A chill slammed down my spine.

What the hell are you talking about?" Astrid spat, stepping forward, her daggers trembling.

The Seeker smiled wider.

"Selene or Killian."

The words dropped like stones into the silent cavern.

"You give me one," he said, as if discussing weather, "and the other walks free. Untouched. Unharmed."

"No," I said instantly, tightening my arms around Selene. "Not happening."

Astrid's face betrayed a flicker of fear she. Killian, half-conscious, managed a soft, choked sound.

Zephyr stepped forward, fists clenched so tightly his knuckles turned white. "You think we're going to hand over one of our own to you?"

The Seeker chuckled—a sound like rotting silk tearing apart.

"You misunderstand," he said, the mist swirling tighter at his feet. "I *do* need both. But I do not need them alive. Only... willing."

The words hit like a gut punch.

"If you offer one to me freely," he continued, maliciously, "the bond between them severs. The survivor's spirit fractures.

Easier to control. Easier to consume."

Behind him, Sunna smiled faintly—an empty, hollow thing full of triumph.

I could feel the group fraying around the edges, panic rising like water in a sinking ship.

Selene shifted weakly against me, a soft whisper escaping her lips.

She was waking up. Not fast enough to stop what was coming.

The Seeker's voice dropped lower, roughened by something ancient and hungry.

"Refuse me," he said, "and I will take both."

Astrid's breathing hitched, panic flaring behind her stubborn mask.

Zephyr muttered another curse, his hands trembling with barely restrained magic.

I bent lower, pressing my forehead briefly against Selene's.

"I'm not letting them have you," I whispered, so low only she could hear.

Even if it killed me. Even if it meant dragging her broken through the fire and the blood and the Hollow itself.

The Seeker took another step forward, mist rolling like a tidal wave behind him.

The ground beneath us trembled.

The choice had been offered.

The trap had been set.

And time was running out.

The Shattered Choice | Selene

The world tilted dangerously, but I stayed on my feet, breathing through the ache that threatened to fold me in half.

"You don't get to choose," I repeated, my voice rough.

The others stood frozen around me—Caspian half-reaching, ready to catch me if I stumbled again. Astrid holding Killian up with one arm, ready for anything with the other. Zephyr tense and paled, magic sparking faintly at his fingertips.

Guilt hung in the air like smoke.

They had meant to protect me.

But protection was just another kind of cage.

Across the cavern, the Seeker's smile twisted.

"So much spirit," he said, voice dripping with amusement. "It will make consuming you all the sweeter."

I ignored him.

I turned to Astrid and Zephyr, forcing them to meet my eyes.

"We don't survive by making bargains with monsters," I said. "We survive by standing together."

Astrid nodded once, sharply. Zephyr squared his shoulders, frost curling from his hands.

Caspian stayed silent, but the fierce look in his eyes said everything.

He would follow me, wherever this led.

The Seeker's gaze darkened, the mist curling tighter at his feet.

"You think you are defying fate," he said softly. "But you are only delaying it."

I lifted my chin, even as my knees threatened to buckle again.

"Maybe," I said. "But we choose how we fight. Not you."

The ground trembled, cracks spiderwebbing across the floor, dark light bleeding up through them.

"So be it," The Seeker's patience snapped, his voice no longer human..

The mist exploded outward.

Astrid shoved Killian toward the wall and stepped in front of him, hands flying out. Zephyr flung out a wall of ice, but the mist tore through it like paper.

I braced myself, magic flaring hot and unsteady around me, the taste of spellfire thick on my tongue.

Caspian stepped in front of me, dagger raised.

The mist slammed into him first, knocking him back against me, but he didn't fall. He gritted his teeth and pushed off the ground, forcing himself upright.

For a sickening moment, I felt it too—

—not just cold, but a thousand broken echoes flooding through us.

Visions of failure.

Of hands slipping from mine.

Of Killian lying cold and still on a battlefield I didn't recognize.

Of Astrid screaming my name as the Hollow devoured her.

Of Caspian's voice, raw and begging, as I turned away from him, choosing someone else.

It wasn't real.

Caspian gritted his teeth, shaking visibly, and forced himself upright, shoulders squared, eyes burning with a stubbornness the Hollow couldn't corrupt yet.

I stumbled after him, magic clawing against the rising tide of despair, refusing to let it win.

"We need a plan!" Zephyr shouted, casting another freezing blast across the cavern.

"Plans are for people who aren't about to die," Astrid snapped, slicing through a tendril of mist trying to snare her ankle.

I threw out a pulse of telekinesis, buying us half a breath of space.

"We're not dying," I said, voice shaking with the effort. "We're not done yet."

The Seeker stepped forward, the mist thickening around him, taking on shapes—half-formed shadows, faces twisted in agony.

The Hollow wanted us broken before it devoured us.

Sunna moved behind the Seeker like a loyal shadow, her eyes gleaming with something colder than victory.

I could feel the magic inside me—thin, frayed, barely holding—but it was still there.

Still mine.

"You can't have us," I whispered, more to myself than to him.

The Seeker smiled, and the cavern floor shattered beneath our feet.

We fell—not into air, but into swirling, choking mist.

I grabbed for Caspian blindly and felt his hand close around mine.

Astrid's scream ripped through the darkness, Zephyr's magic flaring blue-white somewhere to my left.

Killian's voice—raw, broken—called my name.

And the Hollow closed over us like a mouth snapping shut.

Tendrils of black shot through the air, fast and sharp, snaring Killian first, yanking him out of Astrid's grip with a vicious crack.

He shouted—pain, fury, fear all tangled up—and reached for me, hand outstretched across the swirling dark.

I threw out my own hand, magic crackling weakly at my fingertips.

Our fingers brushed—only brushed—

and the world twisted violently, wrenching us apart.

I saw Killian's face, pale and panicked, disappearing into the mist.

Felt the blood bond between us snap tight like a cord.

"Killian!" I screamed, lunging forward, but the ground beneath me gave way to a yawning, endless pit, pulling me down with a force stronger than gravity, stronger than magic.

Caspian dove after me, his hand clamping around my wrist before I could vanish.

Above us, the mist coiled and churned, furious, robbed of its prize.

It had tried to claim us together.

Failed.

But it wasn't finished.

It would never be finished.

Not until it hollowed us out from the inside.

I tightened my grip on Caspian's wrist with everything I had left.

And together, we fell into the dark.

The Fractured Hollow | Selene

I dropped to my knees beside Killian, hands trembling, panting. He was barely conscious—his body twisted, the black veins burning brighter now, like they knew they were winning.

"Killian," I whispered, brushing his hair back from his face. "Stay with me. Please—just—stay."

His eyes opened, just barely, clouded and unfocused. "Selene…"

"I'm here," I said, trying to sound stronger than I felt. "You're okay. We're going to find the others. We're going to finish this. Just hold on."

But The Hollow had done what the Seeker couldn't.

It had shattered him on the inside. His power—his life—was unraveling. Slipping into the mist around us.

If I didn't act now, the Seeker would claim it. Absorb Killian's magic into the Hollow and turn it against us.

"No," I whispered, shaking my head. "You don't get to have him. Not like this."

My hands hovered over Killian's chest. I felt the pulse of his magic deep inside him—barely there, flickering like a dying ember.

"Killian," I said, voice breaking. "I can take it. I can keep it safe. But only if you let me."

He didn't speak.

But his hand found mine—weak, trembling.

And he nodded.

It was all the permission I needed.

I closed my eyes and reached for the fragile bond between us—and pulled.

His magic hit me like lightning—cold and fire all at once, flooding my body, my bones, my blood. I screamed as it carved through me, stitching itself into every hollowed-out space the Seeker had ever tried to claim.

When it was over, I couldn't breathe.

Killian lay still beneath my hands.

The black veins were gone.

And I was something else now.

I thought it was leftover magic—just a burn beneath the skin. But then I looked down and saw them.

The veins.

Dark and pulsing, curling up my wrists like ink beneath glass. They moved with the same eerie glow that had once spread across Killian's skin. Like they were alive.

My breath caught, but I didn't look away. Because I understood now. I hadn't just taken Killian's power. I had taken his curse, too.

The Hollow shifted.

It felt the change—felt the magic burning through my bones like wildfire and storm. A legacy doubled. A bloodline corrupted and crowned.

It coiled around me, slower this time. Almost cautious.

I stood, the weight of my grief anchoring me—but something deeper buoying me upward.

I was no longer just Selene.

Not anymore.

I was the last daughter of two realms.

The bearer of his blood.

And the one thing the Seeker hadn't planned for.

Killian's hand went slack.

The weight of his magic still burned through me—white-hot, violent, too big to hold. It wasn't like channeling a spell or building a shield. It was like drinking lightning.

It was too much.

But I didn't let go.

The Hollow trembled around me, sensing the shift. A new bond forged through fire and grief. A bloodline severed…then doubled.

"I'm sorry," I whispered, my voice a raw echo in the dark.

His body was still, peaceful in a way that made me ache. Killian—who cracked jokes when he shouldn't, who rolled his eyes at danger, who always stepped forward first—was gone.

And I was still here.

Alone.

I felt the shift before I heard it. The air around me tightened, grew colder—sharper.

A figure stepped through the mist like she owned it.

Sunna.

She looked the same, and yet completely wrong. Her hair still braided down her back, her boots still caked in dirt from fake battles. But her empty eyes gleamed with Hollow light.

I stood, slowly, letting Killian's weight slip from my lap to the ground. My limbs screamed. My heart felt like shattered glass.

Sunna smiled.

Triumphant.

"You finally broke," she said, almost warmly. "I was starting to think you never would."

I didn't answer. She circled me slowly, boots scraping against stone. "Do you want to know what he saw?" she asked, nodding toward Killian. "Right before the end? The Hollow let me watch. Said it was a gift."

"Shut up," I said, my voice low, steady.

"Oh, he called for you," she continued. "Begged for you, actually. But you were too slow. Again."

I didn't move. But the power inside me surged—Killian's magic pushing forward, for protection.

Sunna's smile widened. "You feel it now, don't you? What he left behind. The potential. The danger."

"You don't know anything about him," I scowled.

"I know enough," she said coolly. "Enough to know the Seeker only needed him alive if he stayed loyal. But dead? Dead works fine too—as long as you break with him."

"I didn't break," I whispered.

"No?" she tilted her head. "You look broken."

I let the spellfire rise—Killian's lightning braided with my own. It buzzed in my fingertips, kissed the air in sparks.

"I'm still standing," I said.

"For now," she replied.

Then she moved.

Not with the training we had—this was faster, sharper. Hollow-taught. Her blade gleamed as it sliced toward me, but I met it with a wall of pure force. She staggered back, barely keeping her footing.

"You're not stronger than me," she hissed.

"No," I agreed. "But I'm not fighting alone."

And I let the Hollow feel the fused power inside me. The line of magic threaded through two realms, two legacies. One forged in light. The other born in blood.

Sunna stepped back, she wasn't expecting resistance.

Not now.

Not from me.

"Fine," she spat. "Then die fighting. It'll make what comes next more fun to watch."

She lunged again—faster, this time. But I was ready.

I had nothing left to lose.

Flood and Flame | Selene

Sunna didn't hesitate.

The second I raised my hands, she sent a whip of blackened water slicing through the mist like a blade.

I threw myself aside, the arc missing my shoulder by inches. The force of it carved a deep scar into the stone, steam hissing and curling from the impact.

That wasn't water.

It slithered across the floor, alive, hungry, soaking into the cracks of the Hollow like it belonged there.

"You always needed saving," Sunna mocked, circling me like a vulture. "Now look at you. Drenched in his power. Still too soft to use it."

The black veins on my arms throbbed so hard it hurt, visible through my skin, pulsing in rhythm with the fury building in my chest.

"I'm not the one who sold my soul for secondhand magic," I spat back.

Sunna's vicious smirk widened.

"It wasn't a sale. It was an upgrade."

She raised both hands—and the mist rushed inward, folding over itself like a living wave, forming a serrated wall that hung in the air, unnaturally still—impossibly dense.

Then it dropped.

I planted my feet, lifting both palms, and let Killian's storm rise.

Lightning ripped from my hands, lancing through the mist.

The impact detonated the wave midair—an explosion of scalding mist and acidic droplets. They peppered my skin, burning deep, and I screamed.

The pain lit up the Hollow-forged magic inside me, stoking it hotter, wilder.

I lunged, rage and desperation coiling inside me like a living thing.

I shoved my hands forward. The magic ripped out of me, not neat and sharp like a trained spell, but raw and wild. It roared into the space between us like a storm unleashed, cracking the ground beneath my feet.

Stone split under the force.

The air screamed.

The blast wasn't just my mother's powers anymore.

It was something born of two bloodlines colliding.

It slammed into Sunna's chest with a sound like thunder, lifting her off her feet and hurling her back against the stone wall hard enough to make the entire Hollow shudder.

I stumbled after the force of it, my arms burning, my magic flaring out in uncontrolled surges.

Sunna hit the ground, rolled, and came up laughing—wild and breathless.

"Finally," she said, her voice rough. "You're done pretending you're better than us."

"I am better than you," I said through gritted teeth. "Because I didn't become a puppet."

Her smile vanished.

This time, when she moved, it wasn't water she summoned.

It was a noose.

Black tendrils of corrupted mist shot from either side of the room, twisting into a loop that snapped around my throat mid-step.

Sunna yanked her fist back.

I dropped, gasping, the loop tightening cruelly, squeezing the breath from my lungs.

"Feel that?" she whispered, stalking closer. "That's not just magic. That's inevitability."

The veins across my neck and wrists flared, burning white-hot.

The Hollow tried to crush me.

Killian's magic fought back. My magic fought back.

Electricity sparked from my skin, crackling against the choking mist.

The noose shattered with a sound like breaking glass, and I dropped forward, coughing, blood in my mouth.

Sunna's face twisted with fury.

She charged as mist solidified into two jagged blades in her hands, edges humming with venom.

I caught one mid-swing with a psychic shove—barely.

The second slashed across my arm, burning cold.

We collided in the center of the Hollow like two storms forced into the same sky.

I slammed a palm into her shoulder, releasing a surge of raw lightning that lit up the cavern like a second sun.

Sunna flew back, hit the ground with a brutal thud, and for a heartbeat, I thought she might stay down.

She didn't.

Instead, her body arched sharply, the mist sinking into her

skin, her mouth opening in a silent scream. When she rose, her eyes weren't hers anymore.

They glowed Hollow-white.

"You think I fight for him," she said—or whatever hollow thing was speaking through her said. "But I fight for what comes after. When the weak are erased."

"You're not chosen," I snarled, my voice cutting through the rising noise. "You're just the last to fall."

I lifted both hands.

Killian's power.

My power.

A storm braided through blood and vengeance.

Sunna roared—a sound not fully human—and threw herself at me.

We met mid-strike, spells slamming into each other with a force that cracked the stone under our feet. Mist exploded around us. The air twisted, thick with electricity and corrupted magic.

The Hollow screamed—high and shrill, a sound that rattled my bones.

The floor splintered, spiderweb fractures racing out in all directions.

The cavern shook.

Above us, a second pulse hit the air—deeper, colder.

The Seeker was coming.

* * *

The Seeker's smile was wrong.

It didn't stretch his face—it hollowed it. Like he was wearing his own skin too loosely.

He moved forward, the mist folding back like obedient servants before him.

Sunna tried to rise—her hands trembling, her face twisted in a snarl—but she collapsed before she could take two steps.

The Hollow had burned through her already.

She was a broken and discarded tool now.

And I was all that remained.

"You're stubborn," the Seeker cooed, as if it was meant to soothe even as it scraped along my bones. "It's almost admirable."

He stepped closer, mist curling from his fingertips.

"Your mother was the same. So was her sister."

The words slid under my skin like needles.

"Leia ran," he said, seeing the crack in my armor savoring it. "Velastra stayed. And it didn't matter. They both lost."

The mist thickened, curling around his boots like vines.

"Velastra thought duty would save her. That loyalty would protect her bloodline. She died begging for a future that never wanted her."

I clenched my fists so hard my nails dug into my palms.

"You lie," I said, but my voice shook.

He tilted his head, feigning sympathy. "I don't have to lie, little Hollowborn. I was there."

The mist surged forward.

"And now, so are you."

I kept my hands clenched at my sides, forcing the wild magic thrumming in my blood to stay down.

If I unleashed it now, without control, I'd tear myself apart before he even touched me.

He circled lazily, studying me the way one might study a flawed gemstone—debating whether it was worth keeping.

"You think taking his power saved you?" he asked. "You think doubling the bloodline will stop what's already begun?"

I shifted my stance slightly, bracing myself against the tremble in my legs.

He smiled wider.

"You're bleeding from the inside, little Hollowborn," the Seeker said, his voice curling like smoke through the broken cavern. "Every second you hold that power, you unravel faster."

I staggered slightly, I could feel it. The burn under my skin. The crackle at the edges of my magic that wasn't mine alone anymore. The black veins pulsing stronger every time I lashed out.

I hadn't just taken Killian's strength. I had taken his curse too. And the longer I held it, the more it hollowed me out from the inside.

I gritted my teeth, forcing the thought away. Maybe I was bleeding. Maybe I was already breaking. But I would break on my own terms. The mist curled tighter at my feet, hungry.

"I'd rather burn myself down," I said, as I dug my heels into the broken stone , "than let you touch a single piece of it."

The Seeker tilted his head, amused.

"You may yet get your wish."

He lifted one hand—and the Hollow answered.

The mist thickened into spears—sharp, crystalline, aimed at my chest, my heart, my head.

I raised my hands instinctively, trying to summon a shield, but my magic faltered—Killian's power roiling too hot, too fast under my skin.

Pain lanced through me—white-hot.

The first spear struck.

I barely deflected it, the force of it shoving me two steps back.

The second grazed my arm—searing cold carving a line across my skin. I hissed, stumbling, blood slipping from my fingertips that stained the cracked stone black.

The Seeker advanced slowly, savoring it. "This is mercy," he said. "You were never built to carry this legacy. It will devour you."

I forced myself upright. Every part of me screamed to run, to hide, to surrender. But I remembered Killian's face—broken and brave.

I remembered Astrid's steady hands. Zephyr's wild laugh.

Caspian's voice, whispering I'm not letting them have you. And I found something deeper than magic.

I found fury and I slammed my palms into the ground.

The magic exploded outward. The Hollow recoiled, shrieking. The ground cracked wider, glowing with golden veins that pulsed in time with my heart.

The Seeker's smile faltered.

Just slightly.

"Stupid girl," he hissed, his voice rippling with fury. "You can't break the Hollow.

I rose slowly, the black veins blazing up my arms like living fire.

"Then maybe," I said, my voice a rasp of storm and iron, "it's time the Hollow learned fear."

I lifted my hands again—Killian's lightning surging.

My spellfire flaring wild.

I called every earth element up, out and towards The Seeker.

And I charged.

Straight at him.

The Cost of Power | Selene

The moment I charged, I knew it wouldn't be enough.

My lightning tore through the air, fused with spellfire, surging wild and bright. But the Seeker barely moved. He lifted a single hand and summoned the Hollow. Mist slammed into me like a tidal wave—thick, suffocating, and cold enough to numb bone. I pushed against it, my body already screaming from the inside out. My magic was bleeding into the open air in wild, untethered waves.

My footing slipped. Cracks splintered beneath me, the stone groaning under the weight of what I carried. My vision blurred. The veins on my skin glowed black and violet, curling like fire beneath the surface, searing every nerve.

He wasn't even trying. He was waiting. Watching me break.

"You think taking his power saved you?" He mocked. "You think doubling the bloodline will stop what's already begun?"

The mist trembled with his fury. His plan was unraveling, slipping from his grip, and he hated it. Hated me.

My knees nearly gave. His words weren't wrong.

I was literally burning from the inside. The magic I'd stolen from Killian was fracturing me. It had never been mine. Not fully. My body wasn't made to hold it, and every second I kept it locked inside was another second closer to losing myself entirely.

"You're bleeding from the inside, little Hollowborn," he said, as if he could read the pain I tried not to show. "Every second you hold that power, you unravel faster."

I forced myself to move, lifting my hands again. I launched a spell—lightning laced with fury—but it was off, wide, desperate. He batted it away with a flick of his wrist, and the deflected wave of force sent me crashing to the ground. My elbow cracked against the stone. My shoulder went numb. Blood filled my mouth.

He stepped forward.

"You were never meant to hold this legacy," he said. "You were only meant to deliver it. The legacy is meant for me."

I pushed myself up with one arm, trembling, teeth clenched. My magic pulsed violently...Killian's storm crashing against my skin, my own spellfire biting back, the Hollow's influence threading between the cracks. It was too much. It would tear me apart if I kept holding it.

And maybe...maybe that was the only way to end this.

I reached inside—past the pain, past the memory of Killian's death—and found the center. The place where our powers met. I didn't aim at him.

I turned it inward.

I opened every magical gate inside me and let Killian's power go.

It rushed out of me like a scream, crashing into the Hollow like a flood. Not toward the Seeker—but into the space between us, into the ancient foundation of the Hollow itself.

The backlash nearly killed me. My scream echoed through the cavern. My knees hit the ground. My spine arched. I couldn't breathe. Couldn't think. My veins burned—blinding white, then empty.

And just like that, the storm inside me was gone.

The Seeker staggered, his composure broken. The mist around him rippled like it had been slapped, faltering, fracturing. Cracks spread through the stone beneath his feet. Golden light surged upward, then turned black.

He lunged forward, claws of shadow ripping from his arms.

But all I had left was me.

My body was smoke. My thoughts a storm. But I raised my hands one last time, and with the last pulse of pure power still buried in my bones—just mine—I shoved.

The blast wasn't magic. It was force. Raw. Real.

The Seeker was thrown backward into the altar behind him. The stone shattered beneath him. The Hollow reeled like it had been struck across the face. Roots, vines and rocks reached up to grab onto him.

He rose, barely. Blood spilled from his mouth. Tugging to free himself. His form shimmered, warped. His voice cracked.

"You were nothing. A mistake. A child born of accidents and shame."

I staggered forward, my legs barely working. My chest felt hollow. My body ached with every heartbeat. But I looked him in the eye, and for the first time...he looked afraid.

"You were power without purpose," I said.

The ground shuddered violently beneath my feet, cracks spiderwebbing outward in every direction. The golden veins running through the walls turned black, bleeding shadows. Overhead, the mist peeled back in ribbons, exposing a ceiling fractured like brittle glass.

The Seeker staggered, mist leaking from his mouth, his body flickering.The roots and vines pulled at him.

I could barely stand. Every muscle screamed. My veins burned from the hollowed-out remnants of magic I'd forced away. But I stayed upright, my eyes locked on him.

And then—I heard them.

Boots pounding broken stone. Voices shouting through the mist.

Astrid was the first, blades flashing as she cut down a tendril of mist that tried to reach for me. Zephyr followed, his magic crackling, pushing the Hollow back with a blast of pure force. Caspian appeared next, blood streaking down the side of his face, but his eyes burning. He skidded to a halt beside me, planting his feet as the Seeker lunged one last time.

Astrid moved first, driving her dagger deep into the Seeker's side. Zephyr caught the next lashing tendril of mist with a barrier of sheer magic, throwing it back.

Caspian spotted a broken relic—a shard of blackened steel from the ruined altar—and seized it. With a grim shout, he drove the shard through the Seeker's chest, pinning him against the cracked stone.

The Seeker howled, mist pouring from the wound, body convulsing as the Hollow around him fractured. Still, the Seeker fought, twisting, snarling, the mist writhing like a wounded animal.

I forced my broken body forward, gathering the last thread of my own fragile and raw magic. With everything left in me, I hurled a final shove. It wasn't a spell, not lightning, not fire—just raw, battered force.

And it struck the Seeker squarely in the chest. Pushing the shard further in. The earth tearing him apart.

An awful, shuddering cry escaped him as the ground beneath him split open, golden veins turning black. The Hollow roared louder, the mist convulsing, and the altar crumbled into dust.

The Seeker fell into the fissure, dragged screaming into the Hollow's dying core.

And then—

silence.

The ground stilled. The mist thinned into nothingness. The air lifted, just slightly, as the Seeker's dominion crumbled to ash.

He was gone.

I turned, the ache in my body magnifying with every breath, and my knees gave out before I even realized it.

Caspian caught me mid-fall, lowering me to the shattered stone with terrifying gentleness. His hand pressed against my ribs, trying to anchor me somewhere solid, somewhere real.

"Lee," he breathed, voice rough and scared in a way I had never heard before.

I tried to answer, but my throat was raw, my limbs heavy and useless. Every nerve felt peeled open. The veins under my skin no longer glowed—they had faded to an ugly bruised black, the price of holding too much for too long.

Blood leaked from my palms, my arms, soaking Caspian's jacket as he tried to hold me together.

Astrid cursed sharply, her daggers clattered to the ground. Zephyr skidded to a halt at my other side, tearing off his jacket to press against my side, hands shaking.

"She's bleeding out," Astrid choked, her voice raw and furious.

Caspian shifted, one arm sliding under my shoulders, the other cradling my legs. His hands were strong, steady, but I could feel the way he trembled.

Zephyr whispered something—an incantation maybe, a broken prayer—but it barely registered past the roaring in my ears.

I tried to move, tried to reach Killian, but my body refused. Caspian pressed his forehead to mine, breathing like every breath he gave me might keep me tethered.

"You're not done," he whispered. "You hear me, Lee? You're not allowed to be done."

I wanted to believe him.

But the darkness was creeping in around the edges of my sight, heavier and heavier, and all I could do was hold onto the feeling of Caspian's hands anchoring me here.

His forehead pressed against mine, his voice rough and steady against the chaos.

"Stay with me," he kept repeating. "Stay, Lee. Please."

But the pain was too much.

The magic too broken.

The blood loss too heavy.

I blinked once, trying to focus on his face, and the world tilted sideways.

Astrid dropped to her knees beside Killian's still body, a choked cry ripping from her throat. She grabbed his jacket with both fists, shaking him, her tears carving raw tracks down her blood-streaked face.

"Don't you dare leave us," she rasped. "You stubborn, reckless idiot—you're supposed to be here. You promised."

Zephyr crouched low next to her, helpless, his hands hovering uselessly over Killian's chest as if willing him back to life. There was no spell for this. No magic that could undo it.

Caspian just sat there beside me, one hand still braced against my ribs, the other tightening around my hand. His jaw was clenched so hard I thought he might break something. His eyes were locked on me like if he looked away even for a second, I'd vanish.

"Come on," he said roughly. "Stay with me. Don't you dare leave too."

But I was slipping.

The stone beneath me was cold. The air was thin. The world was unraveling in slow spirals.

And then—

I fell forward into the dark.

There was no light.

No visions.

No last whispered words.

Just pain—and then nothing.

The Hollow crumbled around us, the last of the mist retreating like a wounded beast. Stone groaned and collapsed in heavy sheets, dust choking the broken air.

Somehow, we were still breathing.

But we were not whole.

Not anymore.

After The Storm | Selene

When I woke, the first thing I felt was pain.

It was heavy—anchored in my bones and stitched into every breath. My chest ached like something had been torn loose and hadn't been put back properly. My arms were numb, my throat raw. It took more effort than it should have to pry my eyes open.

The light stung.

I was lying on a bed—not stone, not rubble. A linen blanket was rough against my fingers. I could hear the wind outside, faint through the thick stone walls. Somewhere distant, voices echoed—low and tense, muffled by heavy doors.

Someone moved beside me.

Then a hand—gentle but firm—pressed against mine.

"Lee?" Caspian's voice was hoarse. He was seated beside the bed, his knees brushed the side of the mattress. His hair was a mess, his knuckles scraped raw. When I finally managed to turn my head, he looked like he hadn't slept in days.

"Hey," he whispered. His mouth quirked like he wanted to smile. "Took you long enough."

My lips moved, but no sound came out.

"It's okay," he said quickly, leaning in. "You don't have to talk. Just—just stay awake."

His hand tightened around mine. I could feel how hard he was working not to fall apart. Even now, even here.

I turned my head slightly, wincing at the motion, and realized where I was.

The castle.

Odreazah.

The usual warmth of magic humming through the stone was dim. The scent of healing herbs clung to the air, sharper than it should have been. A small lantern glowed in the corner. My mother's cloak hung across a nearby chair.

I shifted and felt pain surge again, sharper, wrapped around my middle like a blade.

Caspian stood up quickly, pressing his hand against my shoulder. "Don't move. You're not—" His voice cracked, and he swallowed hard. "You lost too much blood. They weren't sure you'd..."

He didn't finish the sentence.

I forced the words out. "Killian?" Caspian closed his eyes. It was enough of an answer.

I looked away, even though every muscle protested. I felt the hollow ache settle in my chest. Not magic. Not pain. Just... emptiness.

Caspian moved slowly back into the chair, running both hands down his face like he didn't know what to do with them.

"Astrid hasn't left the courtyard," Caspian said, voice low. "Where they laid him. She won't speak to anyone. Zephyr brings her food, tries to sit with her, but..."

He stopped. "She just stares at the stone like it might undo everything if she stares hard enough."

I blinked slowly. "Where...where are we?"

He nodded toward the door. "You're in Odreazah. The lower

wing. The Hollow's collapse opened a safe exit. Mother led the retrieval team. She's the one who found his body. She stayed behind when the rest of us were trying to stabilize you."

My throat tightened. "She stayed...with him?"

"Yeah. She wouldn't leave him until they brought him back inside. He's in the courtyard now. Astrid made them swear to bury him here. Said if anyone moved him, she'd bury them next."

A flicker of something—grief, sharp and staggering—rose and curled around my ribs.

"And...my parents?" I asked, bracing for the ache.

Caspian's jaw shifted. "They came. They stayed. But they couldn't do much. Their magic's still gone."

That hit harder than I expected. I'd forgotten. I'd been so far beyond myself I forgot they were hollow too.

"Then how...how am I alive?" I asked.

He hesitated. "Mother summoned a royal healer. High-level. She got here fast. They stabilized you, but barely."

He looked at me then, eyes dark. "You were gone, Selene. I mean it. Gone. And then your pulse came back like a wave. Like something gave way just long enough to let you stay."

I didn't answer. My hands curled weakly against the blanket, my fingers twitching. I closed my eyes and reached inward. Toward the part of me that used to hum with fire and spellcraft. Toward the storm Killian left behind.

Nothing.

Not just drained. Absent.

I reached again, deeper. Still nothing. No heat. No lightning. Not even a flicker of residual energy. I opened my eyes, panicking.

"It's gone," I whispered. "Caspian—my fire. My—my power.

It's..."

He didn't answer right away.

"You used it all," he said finally. "To stop him. To save us. I think...it burned out with him."

I looked down at my trembling hands. They didn't glow anymore.

"What's left?" I asked.

He was quiet for a moment.

"Maybe just you," he said gently. "And that's enough."

I looked down at my hands again, willing them to spark, to flare, to do anything. The silence was louder than any scream. For a long time, I just stared.

The door creaked open behind us.

Mom entered first, her steps quiet, eyes puffy from exhaustion. Dad followed, slower. They looked different somehow—more human. Smaller. I knew it wasn't physically possible. It was the loss. The weight they carried now without their magic to lift even a fraction of it.

Mom came to my side, her hand brushing gently against my hair. I expected her to say I looked stronger, that I'd pulled through, that she was proud. But instead, she looked at my hands the same way I had—searching.

"I can't feel anything," I whispered. "No fire. No Pulse. Nothing. "

She nodded slowly. "Your fire is gone and that's okay."

I didn't cry. I didn't have it in me.

But then she said, softly, "But you didn't lose everything."

Reaching behind her, she retrieved a small silver spoon from the bedside table—the kind used for tonics and herbal paste. She held it out, palm up.

"Try," she said.

I frowned. "Try what?"

"Move it."

I stared at her. Then at the spoon. Then back to her. The rational part of me—the exhausted, fractured part—wanted to say I couldn't. That I was too drained, that it was hopeless.

I exhaled and focused.

The spoon twitched.

It slid half an inch across her palm.

A smile lit her face, her fingers curling protectively around it. "You haven't lost everything," she said. "You still have that. Maybe not much else yet. But that spark is still yours."

I didn't realize I was crying until my dad stepped forward and gently wiped my cheek with a callused thumb.

"I need to see Astrid," I said, voice catching. "Please. I need her to know I'm okay. Or...not okay, but here."

Mom glanced at Caspian, who nodded immediately and pushed to his feet.

"You shouldn't be walking yet," he warned.

"I don't care," I said. "She lost him. And I—I didn't even get to say goodbye."

Leia sighed but nodded. "Ten minutes. No longer."

Caspian helped me up slowly, carefully, like he thought I might break apart in his hands. I probably would've if he hadn't been holding me. Every muscle ached. Every breath hurt. But none of it compared to the weight in my chest.

We moved slowly through the hall. The castle was quieter than I'd ever heard it, like it was grieving too. No guards. No scholars. Just silence and shadow and the faint scent of dried blood and sage.

When we reached the courtyard, the world shrank.

Astrid was kneeling beside the wrapped body, one hand flat on the shroud covering Killian's chest. She didn't look up. Didn't turn.

"Astrid," I rasped.

She froze.

Then she turned, and the moment she saw me, she stood so fast she nearly fell.

She rushed forward and wrapped her arms around me like she was trying to hold the world together with sheer will. I clung back just as hard, pain exploding through my ribs, but I didn't care. Her sob broke somewhere between her shoulder and mine, ragged and furious and full of grief neither of us had been able to voice.

"I thought I lost both of you," she said into my neck.

"You didn't," I choked out. "I'm here."

"I should've—" Her voice cracked. "I should've stopped him. Or gone back. Or—"

"You saved me," I said. "You were the one holding him when he came back for a second. He saw you. You were the last thing he saw."

She pulled back, wiping her eyes furiously with the back of her hand. "I hate this place," she muttered.

"Same."

Caspian hovered nearby, watching us both with glassy eyes. Zephyr was seated in the corner of the courtyard, head bowed, his usual fire dimmed to a flicker. When he saw me, he gave a weak wave and then covered his face with both hands.

We didn't speak. We just sat there together, broken and bound, near the boy we'd all loved in our own way.

And even though I had no storm left, no fire, no magic that could fix any of this—

I had them.

And they had me.

Magic? Never Heard of Her | Selene

The first time I walked back into class, I thought it would feel like things were normal again.

They weren't.

Technically, I was still on partial recovery. The royal healer had said I needed at least a week of rest. I'd made it four days before the silence in my dorm got too loud and the walls started pressing in. Astrid just handed me clean clothes and walked me to class.

Now we sat side by side again, her hair in a messy braid, her notebook filled with half-sketched dagger diagrams, tablet no where in sight. I caught her doodling a rune into the corner and raising her eyebrows when the lines glowed faintly. She still had all her powers. So did Zephyr. I didn't resent them for it.

Okay, maybe a little.

I still had my telekinesis. That part hadn't left. But the fire—the spell-energy that used to flare in my palms and pulse in my chest—was gone. I could still move things with my mind. Flip books open from across the room. Slam a locker if someone was annoying. But that was it.

I stared at the faded burn scar still curling around the inside of my wrist and didn't let myself miss it too much.

The Professor was halfway through a lecture about the

Odreazah-Rivenmark Accord when the door opened and Zephyr slipped in. He wore a navy hoodie over his uniform and carried that same energy like he knew everyone loved him, and if they didn't, that was their problem.

Odessa followed a beat later, sliding into the seat next to him easily. Her braid was slick, her eyeliner sharp, and her expression unreadable. She nodded at me once when our eyes met. It wasn't friendly. But it wasn't hostile either.

That was how we were now.

Not enemies. Definitely not friends. Somewhere in the uneasy middle. She hadn't fought beside us in the Hollow, but she'd seen the aftermath. She knew something bad had happened, even if she didn't know the details.

Zephyr looked between Astrid and me, his eyes flicking briefly to the bracelet on my wrist—one that Queen Grizél had given me after the Hollow collapse. A reminder that surviving was a kind of magic, too.

Astrid leaned closer and whispered, "Think we'll survive another hour of magical treaty talk without setting something on fire?"

I gave her a look.

She winced. "Too soon?"

I shrugged. "Yeah"

She didn't apologize. But she reached over and bumped her shoulder against mine.

"After this," she said, "we sneak off campus and visit Caspian. You need the fresh air, and I need something less irritating than this obsession with enchanted agriculture reforms."

I didn't argue. I'd gone back to see Caspian three times already since waking up in the castle's infirmary. The armoire portal still worked, and it wasn't like anyone at the Academy checked where we went after classes ended.

Astrid didn't visit as often. Seeing Killian's courtyard marker hurt too much. She never said it, but I could read it in her hesitation every time we stepped through the portal.

Sometimes grief feels like gravity. And hers pulled harder than mine.

Class ended, and we gathered our things. Zephyr caught up with us in the hallway.

"Odessa says the dining hall has lemon tarts today, which apparently overrides all emotional damage," he said, adjusting the strap on his bag. "Y'all coming?"

Astrid raised an eyebrow. "Is this her way of bribing us to socialize?"

"Obviously."

"I'm in," I said before Astrid could say no. "I could use sugar."

Zephyr grinned. "That's the spirit, Trueshadow."

The three of us walked down the corridor together, the sunlight slanting through the tall windows like it had no idea what we'd been through.

The world hadn't stopped for our grief.

But we had survived it.

And even though the fire was gone, and nothing about life felt easy or fair or right—I was still here. Still breathing. Still pushing doors open with my mind and refusing to fall apart in front of people who wanted a spectacle.

Maybe that was my power now.

Not the magic.

But the refusal to break.

Note To The Readers

Hey hey Yall!

Thank you for reading *The Manifested Lie* and for choosing to step into Selena's world. Her journey—shaped by secrets, power, and difficult choices, was one that stayed with me long after the final page was written. Writing this story meant exploring what happens when the truth is hidden for too long, when loyalty is tested, and when the line between who we are and who we're expected to be begins to blur.

Selena's story is about more than magic or mystery. It's about identity, courage, and the cost of living behind a lie. If any part of her journey resonated with you, challenged you, or made you feel seen, I'm incredibly grateful you took that journey with her.

Stories like this exist because of readers like you. Readers who believe in found family, in questioning the systems around us, and in the power of choosing ourselves even when it's hard. Your support allows me to keep telling stories about hidden worlds, dangerous truths, and characters finding their strength in the chaos.

If you'd like to continue exploring my stories, I hope you'll join me next for my upcoming middle grade novel, *The Midnight Library*, launching September 2026—a story about curiosity, courage, and the magic found in unexpected places.

Until then, thank you for reading, for supporting indie authors, and for carrying this story with you beyond the final page. Enjoy

the book club discussion questionson the following pages!
With gratitude,
Sheyanne Warren

Discussion Leader's Guide

This discussion guide is designed to support ongoing conversation throughout the reading experience, not just at the end of the book. The questions are intentionally arranged in chronological order, allowing your group to pause, reflect, and discuss as the story unfolds. Leaders should feel free to adapt the pace of discussion based on the group's energy, time, and comfort level.

You will find two types of questions throughout this guide:

- General discussion questions, which focus on character development, relationships, tension, emotions, and story choices
- Faith-based discussion questions, which invite reflection through a Christian lens, including themes of identity, calling, waiting, trust, and growth

Both sets are optional. Groups may use one, the other, or a combination of both depending on the purpose of the book club and the comfort of the readers.

How to Use This Guide

You do not need to answer every question. In fact, it is often more effective to choose a few questions per meeting and allow conversation to develop naturally. If a question sparks strong reactions, debate, or emotional responses, lean into it. Those moments often lead to the most meaningful discussions.

Some questions are intentionally open-ended and do not have clear answers. This is by design. Selene's journey is complicated, unfinished, and emotionally layered. Encourage participants to explore how characters feel, react, and change, rather than focusing only on plot outcomes.

Creating a Safe and Engaging Discussion Space

Book club leaders play an important role in setting the tone. Before discussions begin, consider establishing a few group agreements:

- Respect different interpretations and opinions
- Avoid spoiling future chapters for readers who are behind
- Speak from personal perspective rather than trying to "win" the discussion
- Allow space for disagreement without judgment

Encourage quieter members to share, but never force participation. Some readers may need time to process before speaking.

Leaning Into Relationships and Tension

Many of the questions focus on relationships, social dynamics, crushes, rivalry, and emotional tension. These elements are especially important for teen readers and should not be dismissed as "less serious" than plot or worldbuilding. Encourage discussion around:

- Conflicting feelings Selene experiences toward different characters
- Moments of jealousy, insecurity, or social pressure
- How friendships, authority figures, and romantic tension influence Selene's choices

Remind the group that discussing feelings and motivations does not require revealing future events. Focus on what characters know and feel at that point in the story.

Using the Faith-Based Questions

The faith-based questions are designed to invite reflection, not debate. Leaders should present these questions as an additional lens, not a requirement. Participants may answer from personal belief, observation of the story, or curiosity rather than certainty.

When using the faith-based questions:

- Allow space for honest questions, doubt, and uncertainty
- Avoid turning discussion into a lesson or sermon
- Encourage connections between Selene's journey and real-life experiences such as waiting, fear, purpose, and trust

It is perfectly acceptable for some meetings to focus entirely on general discussion and others to include faith-based reflection.

Managing Spoilers and Pacing

Because the guide is chronological, leaders should clearly state which chapter range will be discussed at each meeting. Remind participants not to reference events beyond that range. If someone accidentally shares a spoiler, gently redirect the conversation without embarrassment.

For groups reading at different speeds, consider summarizing where discussion will pause and resume so everyone stays aligned.

Final Discussions

The final discussion questions are designed to help the group reflect on Selene's journey as a whole. These questions encourage readers to consider growth, unresolved tension, emotional impact, and future curiosity rather than closure. Leaders should allow these conversations to breathe and avoid rushing toward conclusions.

Above all, remember that the purpose of this guide is not to reach agreement, but to create conversation, connection, and deeper engagement with the story.

General Questions To Discuss

Questions 1-5 | Chapters 1-5

1. Selene is introduced through danger, legacy, and survival. What do these opening chapters reveal about who she is beyond her parents' reputation?
2. How does Selene's arrival at the Academy shape her expectations of herself and her future?
3. In these chapters, where do you see Selene struggling most with belonging?
4. How does comparison to other students begin to influence Selene's confidence early on?
5. What themes or conflicts feel most prominent by the end of Chapter 5?
6. How does Selene react when other students recognize the Trueshadow name, and what does that reveal about her discomfort with attention?
7. Astrid immediately takes on a protective, outspoken role. How does Astrid's personality contrast with Selene's, and why do they work well together?
8. When Selene first notices Zephyr, how does that moment shift her emotional focus or self-awareness?
9. What does Selene's internal reaction to the Academy's social atmosphere suggest about her fears around being

judged or measured?
10. Which early interaction made you feel most nervous for Selene socially, and why?

Chapter 6-10

1. Selene encounters new realms, unfamiliar rules, and powerful figures. How does she respond to uncertainty and lack of control?
2. What do you think manifestation represents symbolically at this point in the story
3. Which relationships start to shape Selene's view of herself during these chapter?
4. How does Selene's fear impact her choices more than her actual abilities?
5. By the end of Chapter 10, what questions do you have about Selene's past or potential
6. Nyx enters Selene's life with authority and mystery. Do you trust Nyx right away, or does her secrecy make you suspicious? Why?
7. Caspian presents himself as calm and reassuring. How does his behavior toward Selene differ from how other authority figures treat her?
8. How does Selene's awareness of Zephyr change her confidence or self-consciousness in group settings?
9. Sunna brings curiosity and openness into Selene's circle. How does Sunna's personality shift the group dynamic compared to Astrid?
10. Which character in this section makes Selene feel the most seen, and which makes her feel the most insecure?

Chapter 11-15

1. As secrets about Selene's lineage and history begin to surface, how does her understanding of herself start to shift?
2. How does the idea of legacy become more complicated in this section of the book?
3. What moments show Selene beginning to mature emotionally or mentally?
4. How does Selene react when answers are delayed or withheld?
5. What do these chapters suggest about patience versus force?
6. King Victor and Queen Grizél clearly know more than they reveal. How does their withholding of information affect Selene's trust in them?
7. How does Caspian's connection to Selene's past complicate her emotions toward him
8. When Selene learns more about Leia and Kofi's history, does she feel closer to her parents or more burdened by them? Explain.
9. Astrid openly challenges authority when Selene hesitates. What does this say about how the two girls handle fear differently?
10. Which secret revealed in this section felt the most emotionally destabilizing for Selene?

Chapters 16-End

1. In the later chapters, how does Selene's definition of power change?
2. How do the challenges Selene faces prepare her for what comes next rather than offering resolution?
3. In what ways has Selene grown compared to who she was in the opening chapters?
4. What unresolved tensions or questions feel most intentional rather than frustrating?
5. What are you most eager to see explored in the next part of Selene's story?
6. Odessa's behavior toward Selene is consistently sharp and dismissive. What do you think motivates Odessa's attitude, and how does Selene choosing not to fully engage with her show growth?
7. Selene's interactions with Zephyr carry tension even when nothing is said outright. How does Selene's internal reaction to Zephyr reveal her emotional vulnerability?
8. Caspian and Zephyr represent very different energies in Selene's life. Without choosing sides, how do these two relationships challenge Selene in different ways?
9. Sunna often notices things Selene avoids acknowledging. How does Sunna's presence push Selene to confront feelings she would rather ignore?
10. By the end of the book, Selene is surrounded by unresolved emotions, unspoken conflicts, and complicated dynamics. How does she handle that emotional mess differently than she would have at the beginning?

Final Discussion Questions

1. Looking back at Selene's journey from the beginning to the end of the book, what moment best represents her growth?
2. How did your understanding of manifestation change as the story progressed, both as a magical concept and as a metaphor?
3. Which character challenged Selene the most, and why was that challenge necessary for her development?
4. How does the story explore the tension between destiny and choice? Do you believe Selene's path is predetermined, or shaped by her decisions?
5. In what ways does legacy act as both a gift and a burden in the story?
6. Discuss Selene's relationships. Which relationship felt the most meaningful or transformative, and what made it stand out?
7. How did the pacing and unfolding of secrets affect your reading experience? Did it build anticipation or frustration, or both?
8. What theme from the book resonated most strongly with you on a personal level?
9. The book ends without full resolution. How did that ending make you feel, and did it strengthen or weaken the story for you?
10. After finishing the book, what question would you most want to ask Selene if you could speak to her directly?

Faith-Based Questions To Discuss

Questions 1-10 | Chapters 1-5

1. Selene enters the Academy already carrying expectations tied to her parents' legacy. Read: Jeremiah 1:5 In this verse, Jeremiah is called before he feels ready or capable. How does this context help us understand Selene's pressure to prove herself before she even knows who she is yet?
2. Selene feels watched and evaluated almost immediately. Read: Psalm 139:13–14 David writes this knowing God sees him fully, not critically. How does that contrast with how Selene feels seen by others, and how might that difference matter for teens today?
3. Selene struggles with belonging even in a place she is supposed to fit. Read: Romans 8:1 How does freedom from condemnation speak into Selene's fear of not measuring up?
4. Selene compares herself to other students early on. Read: Galatians 6:4 Paul is warning against comparison within community. How does comparison damage Selene's confidence, and how does this verse challenge how teens compare themselves today?
5. Selene feels behind before she has even begun. Read: Ecclesiastes 3:1 This passage speaks about seasons, not

speed. How does understanding seasons change how we view Selene's lack of progress early on?
6. Selene's reaction when other students recognize the Trueshadow name shows discomfort rather than pride. Read: I Samuel 16:7 How does God's focus on the heart help explain why Selene resists being defined by reputation?
7. Selene quickly bonds with Astrid, who is bold where Selene is cautious. Read: Proverbs 27:17 How does Astrid's presence sharpen Selene rather than overshadow her?
8. Selene's first interactions with Zephyr trigger self-awareness and emotional distraction. Read: Song of Solomon 1:5 How does Scripture acknowledging attraction help normalize Selene's reaction without shaming it?
9. Selene's internal dialogue at the Academy reveals fear of judgment. Read: Isaiah 41:10 How does God's promise of presence connect to Selene moving forward despite fear?
10. By the end of Chapter 5, Selene is questioning whether she truly belongs. Read: Ephesians 2:10 How does this verse speak into Selene's worth before she proves anything?

Questions 11-20 | Chapters 6-10

1. Selene feels surrounded by students who appear more capable than she is. Read: 2 Corinthians 12:9 How does Paul's understanding of weakness help reframe Selene's insecurity?
2. Selene experiences attraction while feeling unsure of herself. Read: Song of Songs 1:5 Why is it important that Scripture does not deny emotional complexity?
3. Selene fears being exposed as unworthy. Read: Psalm 32:8 How does God's promise of guidance differ from Selene's

fear of judgment?
4. Selene struggles to fully trust authority figures. Read: Proverbs 3:5–6 How does trusting without full understanding mirror Selene's situation?
5. Selene feels blocked while others move forward. Read: Habakkuk 2:3 How does waiting challenge Selene's sense of fairness?
6. Nyx's secrecy makes Selene unsure who to trust. Read: Psalm 25:4–5 How does this verse reflect Selene's desire for direction without full answers?
7. Caspian treats Selene with patience rather than pressure. Read: Colossians 3:12 How does Caspian model compassion in a way Selene needs right now?
8. Zephyr's presence heightens Selene's self-consciousness in group settings. Read: James 3:16 How does jealousy or insecurity complicate Selene's emotions here
9. Sunna's curiosity draws Selene into conversation when she wants to withdraw. Read: Ecclesiastes 4:9–10 How does Sunna function as support during Selene's uncertainty?
10. By Chapter 10, Selene feels torn between confidence and fear. Read: Psalm 62:8 How does this verse invite Selene to bring emotional honesty instead of hiding it?

Questions 21-30 | Chapters 11-15

1. Selene learns that important truths about her past have been withheld, which shakes her trust in the adults around her. Read: Psalm 13:1–2. David openly questions God here without losing faith. How does this passage help

FAITH-BASED QUESTIONS TO DISCUSS

frame Selene's frustration as honest struggle rather than rebellion, and how might that resonate with teens who feel ignored or misled by authority figures?
2. Selene wants clarity but receives partial answers instead. Read: Isaiah 55:8–9. These verses explain that God's perspective is larger than human understanding. How does this context help explain why Selene is not given full explanations yet, and why faith sometimes requires trusting without knowing everything?
3. Selene wants truth even when it hurts. Read: John 8:32. Jesus connects truth with freedom, not comfort. Why does truth often feel painful before it feels freeing for Selene, and how does that reflect real-life situations where honesty changes everything?
4. Selene feels torn between who she is and who others expect her to be. Read: Romans 8:15. This verse speaks to identity rooted in belonging rather than fear. How does this passage challenge the pressure Selene feels to perform or conform in order to be accepted?
5. Selene's emotions feel messy and unresolved during this section. Read: Psalm 66:10. This psalm frames testing as refining rather than destroying. How do these chapters show Selene being shaped by difficulty instead of broken by it?
6. King Victor and Queen Grizél clearly know more than they reveal, which strains Selene's trust. Read: Proverbs 13:12. This verse speaks to hope delayed making the heart sick. How does delayed truth affect Selene emotionally, and why does waiting for answers often feel harder than bad news?
7. Learning more about Leia and Kofi complicates Selene's feelings about legacy and responsibility. Read: Hebrews

12:1. This verse talks about carrying what came before without being weighed down by it. How does this help Selene understand her parents' influence without being crushed by it?
8. Astrid challenges authority when Selene hesitates. Read: Acts 4:19. This verse highlights choosing conviction over fear. How does Astrid's boldness contrast with Selene's caution, and what does each approach reveal about handling pressure?
9. Selene begins redefining what power actually means. Read: Matthew 20:26. Jesus reframes power as service, not dominance. How does this idea align with Selene's growth in these chapters?
10. By the end of this section, Selene is learning that forcing outcomes does not work. Read: James 1:4. This verse connects patience to maturity. How does Selene's struggle with patience contribute to her emotional and spiritual growth?

Questions 31–40 | Chapters 16–End

1. Selene's journey remains unfinished by the end of the book. Read: Philippians 1:6. This verse reminds readers that growth is ongoing. How does this help normalize Selene not having everything figured out yet?
2. Selene holds unresolved emotions toward others as the story closes. Read: Proverbs 4:23. This passage emphasizes guarding the heart. How does Selene show greater emotional awareness rather than emotional shutdown by the end?
3. Selene moves forward without clear closure or answers.

Read: 2 Corinthians 5:7. This verse centers faith over certainty. How does Selene choosing to move forward anyway show growth compared to earlier in the story?

4. Selene feels stronger but still unsure of herself. Read: Isaiah 40:31. This verse describes strength as endurance rather than confidence. How does Selene's resilience reflect this type of strength?

5. Selene responds to conflict differently than she did at the beginning. Read: Colossians 3:12. This verse links maturity to response rather than reaction. How does Selene's behavior show emotional growth here?

6. Odessa's hostility toward Selene remains unresolved. Read: Romans 12:18. This verse focuses on choosing peace where possible. How does Selene's restraint reflect growth rather than weakness?

7. Selene's feelings toward Zephyr remain complicated and unresolved. Read: Proverbs 4:23. How does guarding the heart apply to Selene learning to acknowledge emotions without being ruled by them?

8. Caspian offers stability and patience without demanding answers from Selene. Read: I Corinthians 13:4. How does Caspian's patience reflect love without pressure, and why does that matter to Selene's growth?

9. Sunna consistently encourages Selene to acknowledge feelings she tries to ignore. Read: Ecclesiastes 4:12. This verse highlights the strength of support. How does Sunna function as emotional reinforcement in Selene's life?

10. By the end of the book, Selene handles emotional mess with more self-awareness than before. Read: Psalm 9:10. This verse shows trust growing through experience. How does Selene's journey reflect that kind of developing trust?

Final Discussion Questions

1. Selene finishes the book still growing, still unsure, and still figuring things out. How does her unfinished journey reflect what it feels like to be a teenager who does not have everything figured out yet, especially when it seems like everyone else does? (Optional Scripture: Philippians 1:6, about growth being ongoing rather than complete.)
2. Throughout the story, Selene carries pressure from expectations, relationships, and her own self-doubt. Where do you see that pressure affecting her choices, and how does it compare to the pressure teens feel in school, family, friendships, or future plans? (Optional Scripture: Matthew 11:28–30, about rest in the middle of burden.)
3. Selene struggles with comparison and feeling behind others. How does her journey challenge the idea that worth is tied to talent, popularity, or progress, and where do teens see that pressure most in real life? (Optional Scripture: Psalm 73:26, about strength beyond ability.)
4. Selene's relationships are emotional, confusing, and unresolved. How does she learn to acknowledge her feelings without letting them fully control her decisions, and what does that balance look like for teens navigating friendships and attraction? (Optional Scripture: Proverbs 4:23, about guarding the heart without shutting it down.)
5. Selene chooses to keep moving forward without clear answers or guaranteed outcomes. How does that choice reflect courage rather than certainty, and how does that apply to real-life decisions teens are facing right now? (Optional Scripture: Proverbs 16:9, about planning while trusting direction.)

About the Author

I'm Ashley Johnson or Sheyanne Warren. My whole name is Sheyanne Ashley Warren. Johnson is my families name. Originally from Syracuse, New York, I now call Charlotte, North Carolina, home.

I have a master's degree in forensic psychology (yes, I'm fascinated by the human mind!) and spend my days shaping young minds as a special education teacher.

But long before I stepped into a classroom, I was a book-loving kid who found magic in words. When I was three, my grandparents took the TV out of my room and replaced it with a bookshelf—best decision ever! From that moment on, stories became my escape, my passion, and ultimately, my calling.

Writing has always been second nature to me, but for the longest time, I didn't realize becoming an author was *actually* within reach. It felt like an unspoken dream—something I carried in my heart without fully acknowledging. But now? I'm here, doing the thing I love, and I write with purpose.

Representation matters. It's not just a phrase; it's a commitment. I want my readers—no matter who they are or where they come from—to see themselves in the pages of my books. Whether it's a fantasy world filled with adventure or a gripping mystery with unexpected twists, I write stories that reflect the diversity and richness of real life. Because everyone deserves to be the hero of their own story.

So, if you love books that blend heart-pounding suspense, intriguing mysteries, and unforgettable characters, you're in the right place. Let's embark on this literary journey together!

You can connect with me on:

🌐 https://foreversevenpress.com

Subscribe to my newsletter:

✉ https://foreversevenpress.com/subscribe

Also by Sheyanne Warren

I write young adult fantasy and speculative fiction that explores identity, power, and the cost of hidden truths. My stories center on teens navigating secret worlds, dangerous magic, and the choices that shape who they become.

Spied: A Deceptive High Novel
Dion and Lanelle are ready for a carefree summer before high school—until their parents reveal they're spies and enroll them in a secret boarding school for future agents. While Dion is intrigued, Lanelle is overwhelmed, especially when she discovers she has powers, new enemies, and a world of hidden dangers. Can the twins survive life at Deceptive High?

Sorcery and Suspicious Shenanigans
At Deceptive High, secrets are currency—and magic is real.

Lanelle wants swim team glory. Ayana just wants to survive the new school. But when a dark force threatens their world, these unlikely allies must uncover the truth behind The Garden before everything they know unravels.

Trust is hard. Time is running out. And magic? It's dying.